C000155931

FALTON RIDGE

MADELINE FLAGEL

Copyright © 2024 Madeline Flagel

All rights reserved. No part of this publication may be reproduced, distributed, or transmitted in any form by any means, including photocopying, recording, or other electronic methods without the prior written permission of the author, except in brief quotations embodied in reviews and certain other noncommercial uses permitted by copyright law. For permission requests, please contact the author at the email address below.

Madeline Flagel

madelineflagelauthor@gmail.com

Paperback: 979-8-9878295-5-4
EBook- 979-8-9878295-6-1

Cover Design by Rachel McEwan, Rachel McEwan Designs

Editing by Alexandra McLaughlin

Published May 2024

Published by Madeline Flagel

This is a work of fiction. Unless otherwise indicated, all the names, characters, businesses, places, events and incidents in this book are either the product of the author's imagination or used in a fictitious manner. Any resemblance to actual persons, living or dead, or actual events is purely coincidental.

Content Warning: this book contains scenes that may be troubling for some readers, including but not limited to mentions of cheating, mentions of murder/suicide, depictions of death and murder, and explicit sexual content.

To my readers—

It's okay to keep your heart guarded. Just make sure those walls you're putting up don't become the walls that imprison you from truly living.

Playlist

1. DIE FROM A BROKEN HEART - MADDIE & TAE
2. I HOPE - GABBY BARRETT
3. DRIVE YOU OUT OF MY MIND - KASSI ASHTON
4. YOUR HEART OR MINE - JON PARDI
5. THE CHAIN – FLEETWOOD MAC
6. SOMETHING IN THE ORANGE - ZACH BRYAN
7. YOU SHOULD PROBABLY LEAVE - CHRIS STAPLETON
8. FEEL LIKE THIS – INGRID ANDRESS
9. WAY DOWN WE GO - KALEO
10. WILD – CARTER FAITH

CHAPTER
ONE

MY FLIGHT ARRIVING an hour early has been a godsend. Not that I didn't have fun in Napa with my girls—I'm just ready to be home. It was definitely the relaxing weekend I needed, though. Spa sessions and endless brunches all overlooking the vineyards...celebrating *me* as a future bride. Until this weekend, I hadn't really come to terms with it, and Layla did a great job of making me forget. If she had it her way, I'd forget my way to the altar.

I glance down at her text. It's a long, spiraling mess about how I could do better and that I'm rushing into this, even though it's been years in the making. She says he's too controlling, too wrong for me, but she's always failed to see how right he is. How good we fit together. I send a generic eyeroll gif in response and tuck the phone away.

I twist my key into the door and hearing the unlatching sound of the lock warms my stomach. To know that I'm moments away from my bed and Rory eases my soul. God, I missed him. We haven't really been away from each other like this before. Since the first night we met, we've been joined at the hip. It's a running joke with our friend group at this point.

"Hello!" I call out as I enter. I wait and listen...but no signs of Rory. I hang my keys up by the door on the brown wooden key rack that Susan, Rory's mother, got us for Christmas one year. A rack that essentially holds all of our clustered, unopened mail. I take a deep breath and feel the pressure in my chest ease. I can't really describe what home feels like, but I do know the moment I step inside, no matter the chaos of the day, I feel grounded. Myself.

I tiptoe into our bedroom, pushing the door open slightly to see Rory still in bed, shirt off, arm hanging off the side, snoring as loudly as a chainsaw sawing logs. I press my lips into a grin. He must have had a good weekend if he's sleeping in this late. He said his bachelor party was pretty tame, but I know when he gets with his friends, it's almost impossible for him to say no to every drink they want to hand him.

I grab my softest shorts and an oversized T-shirt and make my way into the bathroom, remaining as quiet as possible. Not bothering to latch the door before I lift my shirt soiled with the morning of travel off my head, and I throw it into the laundry basket as my pants come off next. Getting out of these tight leggings feels amazing and the anticipation of my cold comforter wrapped around my bare legs has me practically jumping through my skin. I pull up my pajama shorts and grab my shirt as I bunch it around the neck. But as my head fits through, my eye catches something in the trash can. I squint and throw the T-shirt on fully as I walk closer and crouch down to observe. An opaque yellow object, semi-wrapped inside toilet paper is in my line of view. I reach my hand in, push the tissue paper away, and my stomach drops instantly, a solid rock forming at the pit of my belly. My throat swells with the thick air around me as I gasp. My eyes grow wide, and I feel the stinging tears building up behind them as my heart pounds, practically thumping through my chest.

A fucking condom.

We don't use condoms.

He's got an alert on his phone to update me on my own birth control *specifically* so he doesn't have to use them.

I hesitantly pick it up, my hands shaking relentlessly as I try to steady them. I'm gasping for air, gasping for breath. My heart sinks in my chest, a feeling I know so well from our fights—where it feels like it's falling, dropping violently—and I always swear one day it will cause me to have a heart attack. I stand up, trying to gain any composure I can as I storm out of the bathroom, slamming the door against the wall.

"Are you fucking kidding me?" I scream at the top of my lungs as I move around the bed to stand in front of him.

His eyes spring open as he jolts up, collecting the covers in a frantic state. He eyes what's in my hands, blinking about a thousand times before his pitiful excuse runs past his dry lips.

"That's— That's not mine!" he stutters.

"It's not?" I yell. "Then whose is it?"

"It's...well, it's..."

"You're a fucking asshole!" I shout, throwing the condom at his face, only giving me a second of satisfaction when it sticks on his eyebrow across his nose and lips.

I stomp out of the bedroom while he screams and chases after me. "She meant nothing, Kaiton, please! It was a mistake!"

"A mistake? What, did your penis accidentally slip into her vagina?" I throw my hands up and spin around to face him.

"It was mostly anal!" he says, as if that makes it any better.

I scoff, completely in disbelief at what is happening. I want this to be a dream. I want to be on the plane, half asleep, waking up from the nightmare in front of me. But it's real, right here, and suddenly, the sanctuary I couldn't wait to race back to feels like a prison.

Rory, the man I've loved for four years, *my fiancé*, who has only ever wanted to do quiet missionary with me *every once in a while* has brought some girl back to *my* house, in *my* bed, not only to fuck at first sight, but to fuck her in the ass?

"I'm fucking *done*, Rory. Done." I flail my hands around as my voice shakes and the tears stream down my cheeks at a pace so fast I can't catch up wiping them away with my hands.

"No, you're fucking not." He grabs my wrist tight, squeezing so hard my hand feels like it will go numb in a matter of seconds. At first, I think I'm hallucinating it. Rory gets angry often, has said things he's regretted, but he's never hurt me. Not like this.

"You're not leaving me, Kaiton. We can work this out. Listen, I'm sorry. It meant nothing. It won't happen again, but you're not leaving me." His tone is growing more loud, more aggressive as each word slips through his lips. "Do you hear me?" he screams in my face. "You're not leaving me. You're mine, Kait. You can't even eat without telling me what you're having, you think you're just going to leave? Where are you going to go? I'm your life."

The most painful part isn't even his words, or how he's saying them. It's that he's right. I have Layla, my parents, my job, but my life is built around him...and it's all shattering around me quicker than I can process.

"Get your fucking hands off of me!" I shout, pulling my wrist from his grip before he snatches it once more.

"Think about this, Kaiton. Long and hard. Where are you going to go without me? Your parents' place? This house we built is ours, this life we built is ours. You're not going anywhere. You have nothing without me. You *are* nothing without me."

The anger inside of me rises while his words spew, and his grip tightens. "Let me go, Rory!"

He grabs my shoulders in an instant and leans his face into me, his nose practically touching me as he snarls his lip. "If you leave me, Kaiton, so help me God, I'll kill you, then kill myself," he growls behind gritted teeth.

I pause, my shuddering breath the only sound in the room. I don't know if I heard him right, if the words he said with ease actually came out of his mouth. The switch from a man I love to a man I now fear has happened so violently that I feel my knees weaken.

"Do you hear me!" he yells so loudly my ears sting and shakes me so roughly my teeth clatter against one another. I nod, the only thing my brain registers my body to do. He has never yelled at me like this...*ever*. Sure, we've had fights...and it's not the first time he's threatened suicide if I left him. This is, however, the first time he's said he would take me along with him. My fight or flight senses have flown out the window as I stand practically limp, emotionless, as he breathes heavily through his nose. His lips are pressed tightly and his teeth are clenched so hard together I can see the definition in his cheeks become more prominent. My heart beats so fast I don't know what else to do as I slowly step away from him.

His body relaxes as he straightens up and clears his throat. "I'm sorry, Kaiton," he says one last time with a curt nod. "Let me make you some breakfast."

"Thanks, Mom. I'll see you in a bit. I'll let you know where I'm at, I promise." My throat dries as I hang up the call. I haven't ever really been away from my parents for very long either. I've always lived in Illinois, right near them. Even on vacations, I was never gone for more than four of five days. I swallow hard as I close my eyes to try to stop more tears from falling, when I hear footsteps leading up to my front door. The loud knock makes my heart skip a beat, but Rory wouldn't be knocking. He'd barge right in. I rush over and unlock it and fall into my dad's arms to sob like a child.

He holds me firmly for a good moment before taking me by the shoulders to pull me back and look into my eyes. "Are you packed?"

"Almost," I say hesitantly, still not certain I have everything I need or at least unwilling to accept my entire life can be packed into a single suitcase and a duffle.

"You have a plan?"

"Drive...somewhere, anywhere."

"You're not good with new places, sweetie. You get nervous." The anxiety in his tone is so present and real. "Will you be okay? You can come home. I want you to come home."

"And if he comes there? Threatens you two?"

"I'm not afraid of him. I'm not afraid of much."

"But I'm afraid."

He swallows and takes a moment to look around the place before looking back at me again. "I need you to tell me something, and be honest with me."

"Okay."

"Has he hurt you before, and you didn't feel like you could tell us?" His voice breaks.

"No, Dad," I assure him.

God, do I hate lying, especially to him. But if he knew about last night, even though it was the first time...it would be Rory on the run instead of me. Because my dad would fucking kill him.

"You'll call or text every night?"

"Yes."

"I'll do my part here. I have a friend, an attorney. I'm going to find a way to get him out of your life for good."

We pack up my car and then continue hunting down anything I'll need inside. I'm too rattled at the thought of Rory returning early so I send my dad along with the promise I'll be following behind him shortly, with a new plan to meet my mom at a local coffee shop.

I stand in the middle of the living room and look around, mourning the loss of my home. My safe place. The walls that never let me down when I needed to escape the world. But more so, I mourn the loss of the memories they hold with Rory.

Maybe I never knew him, not really, but I can't just forget everything.

I walk into the kitchen to find my favorite coffee mug and peek out the window, only to see Rory's car pulling into the driveway.

I gasp loudly and take a step back when the door handle jiggles and without a second to think, I race to the slider against the back wall, darting outside and around the house. The tops of my feet get wet from the freshly rained-on grass, touching the skin exposed from my sandals. Once I hear the front door shut, I rush to my car. My fingers fumble with the keys as I open the driver's side door and I throw my body inside, closing and locking it almost simultaneously. I fumble again, trying to get the key into the ignition before the front door flies open.

"Fuck!" I scream as the key finally aligns and I start up my car, throwing it into reverse, not even bothering to look behind me. I speed out of my driveway, my tires making black marks on the concrete, but I don't care. I keep an eye on Rory from the rearview mirror. He runs back inside the house, and I breathe a sense of relief as he fades out of my sight. I glance around to find my phone, knowing I threw it over toward the passenger seat in my panic. I look around and bend forward to find it lying on the floor. My foot on the accelerator, I reach my arm down and pat my hand around, trying to locate it while I keep my eyes on the road. I grip it tight once I find it and bring it into my line of sight to call my mom.

"Meet me at Sparky's. Rory came home early," I say frantically the second she picks up.

"Are you okay?"

"I'm fine, Mom. Just meet me there. I'm about to pull in."

I hang the phone up and flip my left blinker on, waiting for the traffic to pass before I turn in quickly, finding a parking spot right on the side. My foot taps wildly, desperate almost, while I look around to try and spot her silver Malibu. It seems as if hours pass before she pulls in, though the reality is she was merely forty seconds behind me. I jump out of my car, practically leaping toward hers as she squeals in, rolling her window down as she hands me a wrapped iPhone box.

"I love you, Kait, please...let us know where you are," she says quickly.

I lean in, kissing her on the cheek. "I love you too, Mom, thank you."

I run back to my car, quickly glancing over my shoulder at the main road that leads back to my house.

No sign of Rory's SUV.

My mom hurries off and I'm right behind, turning opposite of her at the light. I take a breath once I'm back on the road, speeding as much as I can with the traffic flow, trying to get to the highway even a nanosecond faster. I glance in the rearview, traffic backed up fully behind me. My sweaty palms grip the steering wheel with force as my eyes shift quickly between the mirror and the road before me. As I glance at the mirror again, my stomach knots when I see Rory's black Jeep weaving between cars, switching lane to lane, trying to catch up.

"Fuck." My breath is shaky as I mutter to myself. "Fuck!" I scream as I slap my hand on the steering wheel.

I flip on my blinker, finding a sliver of space between cars in the right lane, and step on the pedal as I push my little Nissan into the gap. I glance back up, finding Rory only four or five cars behind me. I flip my blinker once again, trying to weave as quickly as I can to speed and gain some length against him. Tears fall again as I sob, scared and driving erratically. I pick up my phone to try and find

Susan's number, pressing it immediately once I see it, now going eighty in a fifty-five as I gain some headway ahead of the cars.

"Susan?" I plead as she answers. "Please call Rory! Tell him there's an emergency, please!"

"Kaiton, what's going on? What am I supposed to say?"

"I don't know, tell him Don fell or something and you need help. Anything, please Susan, he's going to fucking kill me!" I scream at her.

She knows her son. She knows what he's capable of. On the outside, Rory is a tall, lean model of a man—perfect bone structure, manicured eyebrows, blond hair styled flawlessly at all times and bangs that naturally swoop over to the side. But on the inside, Rory Keppner is a fucking monster. Maybe I always knew this but refused to let myself believe it. I was in love with him and I made excuses for him because of that love. I excused the mental abuse, the narcissism, his need for control. He hadn't even wanted me to go on the trip with Layla because he was certain she was poisoning my thoughts. He made me call every day, text every hour.

He was controlling, needy, and he frightened me, but I was his. He was mine. I thought that was enough. At first he swept me off my feet. So charming I was convinced we were soulmates after the first week we had spent together. We had our fair share of fights, what couple doesn't? But somewhere, lost between the years, the line of a healthy and unhealthy relationship blurred together. His words usually hurt the worst, but I learned to never react back...just take it, and things would be all better by morning. He would practically forget our fights, act like nothing had happened. So that's how it went—he would tell me horrific things, ruin my self-confidence with nasty remarks on my appearance, make me feel worthless for not wanting to go out and do something he wanted to—but if I just took it all on the chin, we would move past it quicker.

He never fucking cared about me. And I wasted years on this prick, for what? To get threatened with murder for trying to do the right thing for myself?

"Kait, honey, I can try," she says finally as I continue to sob.

Susan has always been in my corner, thankfully. With the knowledge that her son can be controlling, she's always tried to help me out. I think she viewed me as the daughter she never had. But I need her, I need her help right now. More than ever.

"Please, Susan!" I scream. "I have to go. Please...do this for me," I beg once more before I hang up.

I continue driving as Rory stays behind me, only a couple of cars between us now. He honks, one long horn sound after another. Cars slow down and stop left and right, clearing his path to me as we continue on this chase.

"Please, Susan," I pray to myself, looking back, waiting for a miracle. I need her to call him, I need him to turn around.

As the highway approaches, I cut in front of a car to get on first, getting honked at by the black Range Rover behind me in the process. I speed onto the ramp as Rory still follows. My foot pushes hard on the pedal, going as fast as my little car can take it. I keep going, not slowing down in the least, and then...the fucking miracle happens. Rory slows as he approaches the first exit, getting off to turn around...and go right back to his mom.

I cry.

A weary smile stretches across my lips as my tears flow and my snot runs with it. I let my foot ease up on the gas, slowing down to a more appropriate speed to not cause anyone, including myself, any more danger than I already have. I breathe a sigh of relief as I lean back in my seat, relaxing my body as I push forward at a more leisurely pace. I glance at my tank—three hundred miles left until empty. I continue to calm my breathing, glancing to my right as I see my phone in the cup holder. I roll down my window and toss it out.

Good luck tracking me now, Rory.

CHAPTER THREE

MY GAS LIGHT DINGS and I look for the nearest exit that has a station close to the highway. I reached the Nebraska state line a while back, but I've just kept going—sometimes getting over to the left, sometimes getting over to the right as the signs direct me to keep moving west. The yellow glow from the tall Shell sign beams to my right and I wait for the exit signs before I signal. I swing into an empty pump and grab the handle before shoving it into my fuel tank. The gasoline hisses as it runs, and I wipe my hands on my jeans, the smell of fuel still lingering on my fingertips. I reach into my car as my tank fills and open up the iPhone box my mom gave me. Pressing the side to turn it on, I wait for the white logo to appear. It's fully charged, and the background is already set to my childhood dog, Coco, who lives with my parents. I smile slightly, seeing her white fluffy face on my screen, knowing that my mother set it. My phone buzzes as the texts come through.

MOM: Hi Honey, let us know when

"Oh lordy, okay I'll be awake for you then. I'll see you in a while, Kaitlyn."

"It's Kai— Okay, thank you," I start to correct her but see no point.

A motel shouldn't be that expensive, so I didn't bother asking for the price, nor did I bother asking why I shouldn't stay there a month. I've never stayed in a motel before, but I guess from this day forward, my life deserves some new experiences.

A fresh start.

And one hell of a *new beginning*.

CHAPTER
FOUR

MY EYES ARE NEARLY glossed over in a haze of dryness. Sixteen hours on the road with only one candy bar that I could stomach doesn't mix well with what very little sleep I'm running on, but I'm driven by fear. The very thing keeping me awake is the hourly check in the rear-view mirror to see that he hasn't tracked me down, that he isn't speeding after me.

The night is so dark, but the sky is filled with stars, illuminating my way as I exit off the highway. The trees line either side of the road with not another car in sight—just me, the forest, and the stars. The road winds and twists and my headlights shine on a large sign, tucked away between the pines so well, I almost miss it in the shadows. "Welcome to Falton Ridge," it reads. I smile, only slightly due to my severe exhaustion, as I've finally reached my destination.

"Turn left, then turn right," my GPS voices through my speakers. I signal out of habit and turn right into the parking lot of Boot's Inn. The glow of the clock on my display screen reads 1:21 A.M and I park my car, taking a deep breath before moving another muscle. I grab my bags, throwing the duffle over my shoulder before I push through the front door. The tiny bells above chime and clang together as I open it, and the woman who was nearly asleep at the front desk jolts awake when she hears it.

"Oh, you must be Kaitlyn! I was waiting for you. So glad you're here." She smiles at me with her tired eyes and crevices, and a certain amount of guilt tugs at my chest.

"Thank you for waiting for me."

She looks inviting and warm, like she just might very well give the best hugs. Certainly a grandmother to some, and I already feel at ease looking at her. "You can call me Kait." I grin while walking up to the counter, getting a closer look at the dark blonde strands in her hair that mix with mostly gray.

"Kait, darlin', I've got you set up in room number four. Now, I wouldn't recommend you staying here a month—hell, I wouldn't recommend you staying here more than a night if you don't have to. Lord, Waylon would kill me if he knew I said that." She laughs. "But you're wanting to stay in town for a month, correct?"

"Yes, that's the goal," I reply, my hands clasped lightly together as I lean on the counter.

"You traveling for business or something?" she asks curiously as one brow raises.

"I just...need a break from my life," I let out with a heavy sigh. I can't think of a better lie at a time like this, running on an inadequate amount of sleep and hardly any food laced with feelings of desperation and resentment toward a man who took my heart and shoved it in a fucking blender, pulsating it at the highest speed to make sure not a shrivel of it was left.

She clicks her tongue against her teeth as she nods. "I get it...sometimes we all need a little break. My daughter-in-law is a Realtor here in The Ridge. How about I have her come by tomorrow and take you around, see if she can't find you somewhere nicer to stay for your trip? You're just in time, too. Our Falton Lake Blues Festival starts in just three days." Her smile is warmhearted, and I hope for a moment that everyone in this town is *exactly* like her. She slides the pine-colored key against the wooden desk, the number "4" dead center in a bold white font, with "Boot's Inn" scribbled underneath it in a delicate cursive. The key itself is worn down, leaving the edges with some chipped color. I slide it off the desk, clutching it in my closed fist.

"Thank you." I grin. "How much do I owe you?"

"How about you get some rest, and we'll talk tomorrow."

"You don't—"

"Hush now, let's both get some sleep. I'll have a pot of coffee on at seven in the morning if you want some."

"Thank you so much," I say, almost turning to leave before I ask one more question. "I'm sorry, I didn't catch your name."

"It's Hattie, dear. Hattie Boone. My husband Waylon and I own this motel. Been in the family sixty-two years," she continues while we walk out together. Her steps move side to side as she nearly waddles, pushing from her cane to take weight off one leg. Now I feel even worse keeping her up this late to wait for me.

"Well, thank you, Hattie," I say gently before we part ways and I follow the dim lighting from the overhang until I reach the same green pine-colored door with a silver "4" attached above the peephole. I fit the key in, twisting until I'm able to turn the handle. The bed is in the middle of the room with a gray knitted blanket resting on top, and a large colored photo hanging above. A rodeo cowboy on a beautiful brown horse takes up most of the wall space and my eyes trace over every detail, starting with his jean jacket and ending with the white on the chest and belly of the horse. I take a few steps in, closing the door behind me before I walk to the bed and throw my bag down, laying my suitcase flat on the floor next to it. I kick off my sandals and walk to the TV console, grabbing the remote and turning it on as I look above it. More artwork—a smaller portrait, hand drawn with what looks like pen, made to look like the motel, only with large mountains in the back. I flip through the channels as my eyes focus back to the TV. I land on a cooking show and turning the volume down nearly all the way. I grab my phone and send a group text out—a much more efficient approach considering the fight to keep my eyes open.

ME: Made it to Montana!

Love you all, I'll call in

the morning

MOM: So happy. Love you

LAYLA ARLO: Yay! Night K

DAD: Send pics, I'm so jealous.

Happy you're safe. Love you, kiddo

I set my alarm for seven in the morning, unsure if Hattie's mention of coffee was an invitation, but already, I would hate to let the woman down. I lay my phone against the light wooden bedside table before I get some clothes from my duffle bag to sleep in. I yawn loudly, grab an old T-shirt, then rifle through some more, not able to find a pair of shorts, but not caring enough to keep looking.

"Fuck it," I mumble, pushing my duffle bag off the bed. It falls to the floor with a thud as one shoe falls out. Kicking it slightly with my foot, I move it away from my walking space before I undress. My arms fit through the shirt, riddled with tiny holes, and I shut the light off before crawling under the sheets, the woven comforter resting on top. Another yawn escapes my lips, and I can't keep my eyes open any longer—which I'm grateful for. When I close them, I don't think about the awful events that led me here, Rory's dark eyes haunting me, the threat of him always looming around. I'm just too beat, my mind ready to bury it all. I don't shed an ounce of sadness for the egocentric, manipulative, narcissistic man I once cared for.

Who, right now, *I couldn't give two fucks about.*

I just sleep.

CHAPTER
FIVE

MY ALARM BLASTS next to my head that hangs slightly off the bed. I reach up, hitting it from left to right as my eyes stay shut and the rest of my body remains still. I finally slap my phone, sending it into a jolting spin as it falls to the floor.

"Fuck," I mumble, my eyes slowly peeling open. I reach down to grab it and hit snooze on accident. I rub my eyes, waking myself from the five hours of sleep I'm running on.

Stretching my arms up wide, I sit up in bed, taking in my surroundings as the morning light pours through the only window in here. I take a moment to myself, breathing in through my nose as a dull pain in my head starts to form at my temples.

Need coffee. *Stat.*

I throw my legs over the side of the bed and dig in my duffle to grab my toothbrush and toothpaste before I head to the bathroom. The decor is simple in here, light. Muted colors with only a touch of Western photography. The shower curtain is pure white with a pattern that reminds me of a crochet doily. Turning the faucet on, I run my toothbrush under the water, looking up at my reflection after I squeeze out a glob of toothpaste. My hair is feral, like I wrestled with a bear in bed, and the bear won. A frizzy collection of golden, pale yellow, and bleached pieces stick up across my head. My middle part is cowlicked on both sides. I pull at the bags under my eyes, then groan as I wipe away traces of sleepiness from the corners. My toothbrush still hangs from my lips and, in this moment, I feel it may have been this exact sight that made Rory unattracted to me. I riffle between my suitcase and duffle, searching for the comfiest clothes I can find. Lucky for me, they're mostly pajamas. So hopefully I don't get invited to any masquerade balls or black-tie events while I'm here. I pull up my white crew socks over my black leggings and shove my feet into my light brown hiking boots. I throw on a quarter zip pullover and brush my hair, sticking my black hat on top.

Glancing quickly at the time, I grab a small crossbody bag that I'm almost positive is a fanny pack and snatch the room key from the dresser table before I head out the door in hopes that Hattie makes the best coffee in town.

The breeze outside picks up as I walk, and a light haze falls over the motel and the road in front of me. The smell of smoke and pine whirls with the wind and I look up—enormous mountains paint the landscape far off into the view. It's the most beautiful sight I've ever seen. Snow-tipped and dark gray, they almost blend with the fog. Everything is vast, timeless, and still. I finally understand why my dad wants to visit. I take out my phone and snap a picture for him.

Near the end of my sight, a line of small buildings on both sides of the road fit in with the trees in row with them. *That must be the rest of town.*

I push open the main office door, the familiar bells ringing above as Hattie's smiling face stands behind the counter.

"Good morning, sunshine," she calls as I approach her. How does she have this much energy on so little sleep? I envy her. "Coffee's hot." She points to the back wall, and I turn my head to follow her finger.

"Thank you so much." I smile, walking to the tall, skinny table that holds a pot of coffee and a bowl of mixed creamers and sugar. I grab a white porcelain cup and pour the hot caffeine directly in, only grabbing one sugar packet to add to it. I hold it in my hands, warming my palms from the chill of the short walk outside, taking a small sip as I walk closer to Hattie. The front door bells chime once more and my sight falls on a lean woman, probably in her forties. Her hair is a rich chestnut color, loose curls that fall just to the tips of her shoulders.

"Ellie!" Hattie calls and the woman smiles, walking toward us.

"Well, good morning to you," she says as she beams widely. "Hi, I'm Ellie Boone." She extends her hand toward me.

I take it firmly. "Kaiton Riggs, really nice to meet you."

"Kait, honey, Ellie is my son's wife. She's the best Realtor around and I told her to find you something a little more comfortable than Boot's for your longer stay," Hattie explains.

"I've got a couple houses I'd like to show you with short-term rental options available," Ellie interjects right after.

"I'd like that a lot." I beam at them both.

Is everyone like this? So welcoming and kind, jumping at opportunities to help others? I don't know why I feel at home already, so at ease with my choice.

"Well, whenever you're ready, we can get goin'. I'll drive us both," Ellie says, her hand running against the slightly sheer button-down that fits against her thin frame.

I take a sip of coffee, the nutty bitterness coating the inside of my mouth. "I'm ready now, let me just..." I take another large gulp, the coffee still nearly scorching as it slides down my throat. "Where should I leave this?" I hold the cup up to Hattie.

"I'll take it, go on...get going, enjoy The Ridge," she says, waving her hands toward her for me to set my cup down. I take one last sip, nearly drinking all of what was in the small diner cup and set it on the counter.

"Thank you," I whisper to Hattie as my gaze catches hers. She nods with a pressed smile, and I follow Ellie out to her dark green Subaru.

Following suit, I open the passenger door as she opens hers, clicking in my seatbelt once I'm situated.

"Hattie said you're lookin' to stay here for a month or so? What brings you to The Ridge?" She turns her head, looking behind as she backs the car out of the parking space.

If I close my eyes now, I'd feel it all over again—his hands on me, the chilling look in his eyes. I'd drift to a place I don't want to be. Not now. Not ever again. I shrug off the thoughts and blink myself back to reality. "I just needed to get away, I guess."

There is a pause, during which I imagine she's wondering why on earth I chose this place of all places to get away. "Where are you from?"

"Illinois. I've lived there all my life."

"Have you ever been out west before?"

"Never. But the drive here was beautiful. And this...is stunning." We drive, the light fog nearly lifted from the trees as we make our way into the town, where the sun casts down on the weathered buildings with a golden glow.

"It is. Never gets old, I'll tell ya that. We like it here in Falton. Our town is small, maybe three, four thousand people at best. It seems like everyone knows everyone too. Falton Ridge expands just beyond this town up ahead and the lake off to the side. But everything you need is right here. No sense in goin' any further. Just forests and scattered houses outside this area, really," she explains as we come into town. A strip of businesses line each side and she navigates the tight-knit community of charming storefronts.

A cafe, movie theatre, hardware store, bakery, bar, grocery...everything you need all standing proudly next to one another. Some buildings are made of brick, while others look like log cabins.

"So, there's two houses that are available for rent just outside of town near the lake. Hattie said you wanted to stay for a month but neither of us recommend stayin' at Boot's." She laughs loudly. Her smile is infections, beaming bright and wide. Her laugh causes me to grin unexpectedly.

"Why not?" I keep my smile.

"We get a lot of passersby here. Not many tourists, just people passing through. Some get rowdy, messy, like their mama's never taught them any manners or something. Also, there's no kitchen. We've got two restaurants to choose from. A month's time would drain your wallet and hurt that stomach of yours if you kept eating Neddy's fried fish every day."

I laugh with her. She does have a point. And I like to cook, so a kitchen would be nice.

I face ahead, looking out through the windows as the large mountains grow closer and closer. We make our way through the stoplight, past the businesses, and to open road. We travel for at least three more miles, weathered houses and trees lining our path, until she slows the car down near a small log cabin. We pull into the long driveway, creeping up until we get to the garage.

"Here's the first one," she says, putting her car in park. "Now, there isn't much to look at around here, but it's got what ya need. Two bedrooms, one bathroom, and not a house on either side of you."

I walk with her out of the vehicle and up the three steps onto the porch. Waiting behind as she opens the door with her key, I follow as she pushes through the threshold. It's all log inside as well, with a large wood-burning stove in the corner.

"You've got your kitchen and living area, then your bathroom and a bedroom on this left side here...with another bedroom to your right." We move through the small house. "Rent here would be nine fifty a month but unfortunately, they will not do anything less than a six-month lease. You could possibly sublease it, I could help you find another renter, but on the off chance we can't find anyone, you'd be stuck in that."

I suck in air through my teeth, parting my lips slightly. "Oh man," I say, my fingertips brushing against the chipped laminate countertop in the kitchen.

"What about the other one? Would they do a smaller lease?"

"I'll call them on the way, maybe I can work somethin' out for you. The other house needs some work but damn, it's got incredible views of the lake."

My cheeks warm as I hear her talk about the second one. Almost a thousand dollars is expensive for something I might have to pay for, for six months straight. Granted, I don't have an apartment anymore...but I didn't plan on staying here that long either.

"Can we see the next one?" I ask.

"Absolutely. I'll try to give them a call and see what I can do as we drive over."

I follow her out as she locks up, getting into the car and buckled before she backs out and brings her phone to her ear.

"Hi, this is Ellie Boone with Falton Realty, I'm bringing my client over to the house now but I'm wondering—would you be opposed to offering a smaller term lease at all...?"

Her voice has a slight twang to it when she speaks. Like maybe she grew up in the South, and I find myself in a trance with her words. Ellie's beautiful, sharp bone structure and flawless skin have aged so wonderfully, she reminds me of my own mother.

I didn't know in the last couple of days that I would be in Montana, looking for a place to rent, not knowing a single soul...well, besides Hattie and Ellie now. But I'm thankful for it, thankful for them. They just...automatically go into help mode. A random stranger shows up at the motel and all they think to do is "how can we assist?" They aren't like this in Illinois, and it's refreshing. Being here, with the greenery, the scenery, the fresh air...this will be good for me. Good for my soul, good for my *healing*.

CHAPTER
SIX

"WELL, WHAT DO YOU think?" Ellie says as we stand in the backyard, a higher elevation than the lake as we look below to the wooden dock.

"It's...surreal," I say, unable to find the right words to describe the view. The wind blows ever so slightly, hardly enough to make the pines move, but enough to make the dark blue water ripple.

Ellie turns to face me. "So I talked them down to a three-month lease. Rent is seven hundred and fifty dollars but they said if you paid in advance, they'd knock off two fifty for you. Might not be a bad deal if you only want to stay a month. Or, if you're not partial to The Ridge, Helena's only about a twenty-minute drive from here. You could stay in any name brand hotel," she says as her tone grows softer.

I know this house needs work, but cheaper rent...*with this view?* My breath is lodged in my throat, unable to escape as I stand in the tall grass. It may be my nerves, it may be my heartbreak, but whatever it is...it's pushing me to stay.

"I'll take it," I whisper, only...it was loud enough to hear over the quiet sounds of nature.

"Yeah?" she questions with a grin.

"I'll pay in advance only if they can help me cut the grass...I don't know how to do that." A soft giggle escapes my lips.

This house is a fixer upper—mostly some paint and minor repairs but using a lawn mower was never something I was taught and where I lived, our landlord took care of it.

She laughs. "I'll have Rodney do it for ya." She grabs my shoulder while we walk back to the house.

I climb up the couple steps to the back porch, looking behind one last time on what will be considered *my* backyard. I've only seen this view in paintings. Pine trees line the lake, staggered together for what seems like miles, placed right in front of mountains ranging in peak height.

"I think I'm going to stay the full three months," I decide, turning back around to walk into the house after Ellie and stepping into the small kitchen from the sliding glass door.

"You don't have views like that in Illinois, do ya?" She grins so wide, the corners of her mouth form small dimples.

"Definitely not."

"I'll step out and let the landlord know. I've got keys on me so I can get you back to the motel and get you right back here for immediate occupancy." She flashes a grin, phone in hand as she walks back out to the weathered wooden porch and closes the slider behind her.

I take a couple of steps into the kitchen, resting my hands on the wooden countertop. The entire home is rustic, with not a single functioning light. Ellie said it was probably just the light bulbs that needed to be replaced, as the owner stated everything should be working properly. The light wood floors creak as I move to the long dining table, a chandelier of candles hanging above it. It needs some love, but with the view, it's hard to say no to this place. I want to stay. Something inside of me is yearning for the peace being here brings me. I'm not scared of Rory here. There's no way he could find me. And the longer I stay, the more time he has to move on, and so help the next fool who falls for him.

I take my phone out of my purse, searching for signal as I pace around the tiny cottage. The floor crackles beneath my boots from the kitchen to the living room. One bar finally pops up and I try to call my mom, needing to hear her voice.

"Hi, sweetie," her delicate tone sounds from the other end.

"Hi, Mom. So I found a place to stay here."

"You did? How is it? How's Montana? You know, your father is very envious."

"It's amazing. The views, the people, I can't explain—but everything about this place is just so serene. I found a house to rent, but the lowest they will do is a three-month lease…" I wait for her to respond, a silent pause sitting between us before I give in. "So, I've decided to stay the three months."

"Really?" Her voice grows softer. "What about your job, hun?"

"They can easily find a replacement. It's just a call center, Mom. I'll find something here part time, and I still have some money in my savings left over, even after I pay the rent."

"Okay..." She hesitates. "Three months is a long time..."

My eyes well with tears but I try to hold them back. "I know. I'll see you soon, though. I need this, Mom. I can't explain how I feel here. I'm...I'm not afraid...I mean, of course I'm devastated." The tears escape as I continue. "The love of my life fucking ruined me. I haven't even had time to process it. I'm in shock, in disbelief...I don't— He threatened to kill me. I can't go back home, not for a while. I need this, I..."

"I know, honey. We just...will miss you, that's all." I can hear her voice as it shakes, crumbling while she speaks, holding back the same tears I've already let flow.

"I love you, Mom," I manage to say, choking back my quiet sobs.

"I love you more. Call us often, okay?" She lets out a small laugh, masking the tears.

"Of course. Bye, Ma."

"Bye, baby."

I hang up, more tears streaming as I sniffle. I wipe my face with my sweater sleeves as Ellie returns inside.

"Oh, Kait, are you okay?" Her expression drops once her eyes fall on me.

I just nod, pressing my lips tightly as I try to hold everything in. Not able to keep another sob at bay, I throw my hands up, laughing and crying simultaneously as I touch my fingertips to my face, wiping away the tears now falling heavily. "I'm sorry." I laugh, still crying all the same.

"Oh honey," she says, walking toward me, wrapping me up in her arms for a warm embrace. The feel of her hug reminds me of my mom's—one hug I didn't manage to get before I left town. One hug that was robbed from me as I fled from a psychotic excuse of a man. I sob in her arms, unleashing every emotion that was stuck in my bones. She rubs my back, squeezing me only tighter as I cry. She smells of faint vanilla and citrus, not overbearing, as I nuzzle my face into her. I don't know this woman, just met her a little over an hour ago. She must think I'm nuts.

I slowly lift my head from her chest, sniffing again so I don't ruin her shirt further.

"I am *so* sorry." I laugh, gasping for air slightly as I continue to wipe my face.

"Don't ever apologize for showing your emotions. It's healthy to let it all out every now and then." Her palms rub down my arms, warming me with her touch. "Anything you need to talk about?"

"Maybe another time." I give the best grin I can.

"I'll be here if you ever need. How about some breakfast before I bring you back to the motel? We can swing over to the landlord and pay your rent—knock out everything at once?"

"I'd like that." I nod. I'm sure my face is bright red from crying, so hopefully my hat hides my puffy eyes well. One person in this town may already think I'm crazy, but I can save face for the rest of them.

CHAPTER
SEVEN

THEIR BIG SKY PIE after breakfast was the very last thing I needed, but Ma's Cafe was simply *too good* to say no. Only, the way I immediately need to take my pants off is making me regret every bite of the warm apple pie laced with cinnamon and nutmeg. It was some of the best food I've had in a while, and I didn't think my morning could get any better until Hattie refused to let me pay for my stay. I ended up buying a Boot's Inn sweatshirt and keychain because of it, figuring she should take my money one way or another.

As I pull into the cottage, I sit in my car for a moment, just absorbing what's mine for the next couple of months. The white siding is worn, nicked, and cracked in some places, while the door looks worse off. Light brown and bland, its paint is chipping worse than the gray shutters. Tall trees surround the cottage, only making the lake slightly visible from the front. It's secluded, with a long driveway leading up to the hill it sits so proudly on. I don't get scared easily, but the thought of being alone here at night sends a slight chill down my arms, raising goosebumps. I shake it off, warming my hands against the skin on my arms, and push myself to think of different things.

I should paint the door is what my mind immediately springs to, not giving another thought to the fact that I haven't really been on my own in years, and here I am...a thousand miles away in another state, living in a secluded cabin, in a town I know nothing about, with strangers all around me.

What else should I do?

My mind runs through a list of things I can do to make this feel more like home. The landlord said whatever adjustments I wanted to make were fine by him—painting or redecorating, just so long as I didn't tear down any walls, he was fine with it. Lucky for him, I'm not handy in the least. But I do know how to use a paintbrush. *Sort of.*

I shut my car off, walking up the steps into the cottage, making my priority the lightbulbs. Not a single light works in here, and I'm hoping Ellie was right about it just needing replacement bulbs, and not anything electrical. I walk to the side table, next to a battered leather couch, and reach my hand up the lamp, skimming against the cold ceramic before I unscrew the bulb. I walk toward another light. This one, a tall floor lamp, stands in the corner of the living room. I retrieve the bulb in the same fashion as I look to the kitchen, unsure of how to replace the recessed lighting in the ceiling. Making one last stop into the bedroom I'll be sleeping in, I take the lightbulbs from both lamps, observing the four in my hands as I look for any markings or indications on what brand or wattage I need.

Back in my car, I try to fidget with my GPS, limited service not aiding as I search for the hardware store I saw in town. I give up after a feeble attempt at locating any signal, and back out of my driveway, heading in the same direction I came from. I think it was right, left, right that brings me into town, so I cross my fingers and make a wish that I'm right. While this area is beyond beautiful, getting lost between the trees and mountains would be nothing short of a horror film.

I crack my window slightly, letting the soft June air fill my car while I drive on the winding road, coming to my first right...*I think*. The radio plays a local country station, and as I look beyond at the mountains, I'm quickly reminded of one minor detail I forgot about.

My job.

I haven't notified anyone to let them know I'm not coming in next week...not that they would care, anyway. I'm just one in five hundred that sit in a cubicle, answering questions about washing machines and blenders. It's a thankless job, as everyone only calls when they have problems. Most days, I'm getting yelled at on the other end of the line, like it's *my* fault they don't know how to turn on their new washer.

I could just not even call.

I could just not show up. Let them figure it out on their own.

But I can't. My guilty conscious would soon kick in, and that feeling of letting someone down would rip at my soul so much, it'd eat me alive.

I pick up my phone, glancing between it and the road as I make another turn. I hold it up higher, hoping that the closer I am to the sky, the more service I'll get.

It doesn't work.

And *this* is why I would not want to get lost here. I wouldn't even be able to call for help. Although, I am thankful that at least Ellie and I swapped numbers before we parted.

One bar shows up in the tiny corner to the right of my screen and I search for my supervisor's cell number, clicking on it the instant I find it.

It rings, and rings, and in the pit of my belly, I'm hoping to hear her voicemail. I grin as my dreams come true and the sound of the beep prompts me into my speech. "Hi Anne, this is Kaiton Riggs. I wanted to let you know that I will not be coming into work next week or the week after. I, well, I'm no longer in the area, so... I'm really sorry, but I can no longer work for your company. Um, thanks again for the opportunity and sorry I couldn't give an earlier notice." I try to sound as cheerful as possible, knowing that could have gone a lot smoother. But I hang up in hopes the message is received clear enough I don't get a call back.

I make my last turn, praying I remembered correctly, and I'll see the town just up ahead. This car is running on nothing but wishes and gasoline and so help me God if I'm wrong, I'm going to cry. My stomach drops as a breath I was about to take stays wedged in my throat, and I exhale loudly when I see the buildings in sight.

"Thank God." I sigh, relieved at my incredible memory for direction today, which is otherwise terrible.

I slow down, looking both ways as I try to read the business names. A small floral shop called Bitterroot Blooms stands next to The Wright Tools and my cheeks warm as I find a parking space right in front of both.

I stare at the flower shop, taking in the wooden crates stacked outside used as vases that hold the most beautiful purple and pink petals. Hanging under the silver awning are two large green plants, with vines that fall halfway to the ground, framing the front door. My curious mind wanders into Bitterroot Blooms first, my eyes meeting with the woman behind the counter as soon as I step in. She has glossy red hair cut right to her shoulders, just like Layla's, and the warmest smile that reminds me of summers back home.

Her muted yellow apron fits faultlessly with her crisp white button-down shirt and matching yellow dangle earrings.

"Welcome to Bitterroot Blooms! Anything specific I can help you find?" she says between glancing at me and using her shears to cut the stems off the tulips scattered below her.

I hum, thinking for a split second, contemplating on what I even need flowers for. "I'm just looking around." I smile, moving through the store. Pre-made bouquets sit on a rustic table in the center of the room, vases ranging from bronze tins to large coffee mugs and small wicker baskets. My fingers touch the soft petals of a rose, already in place with baby's breath and tulips. As I get closer, the floral scent of each flower piled together tickles my nose and I grin at how comforting it is. A bouquet in the center of the table draws me in with a light pink flower I haven't seen before. I glance back at the woman, trying to meet her eyes once more to ask her the questions surging through my mind. She tilts her chin up and I catch her gaze. "What kind of flower is this?" I ask, my fingertips touching the skinny petals.

"Gerbera." Her smile stretches across her lips. "It's a type of daisy."

"Would I be able to create my own bouquet?"

"Of course!" Her tone is riddled with excitement. "One sec," she says as she wipes her hands on her apron and marches toward me. "Do you want to start with some of these light pink Gerberas?"

"Yes, please." I grin. Then, I follow her around while she brings us to the section of her store with metal pails full of loose flowers.

"What else would you like to add?" She turns to me, my Gerberas in her hand. I glance between them and the assortment.

"How about those orange and pink roses?"

"Great choice," she says as she pulls them from their buckets, some more bloomed than others. "Do you want to add any of these fillers, like baby's breath or wax flowers?"

"Could we do both?" I stare at the simplicity of them together, enamored with their beauty and vague similarity.

I've never bought myself flowers, and certainly never received any from Rory, but the excitement of making my own bouquet has me ready to get back to the house and stick them right in the center of the dining table.

"Do you like this?" she asks as she arranges them neatly before bundling them up between her fist, showing me the assortment.

"Perfect." I nod and smile.

"Great, did you want anything else today?"

"That's it, I think." I chuckle lightly and follow her back to the front counter, weaving around compact tables filled with small local handmade items. Jams and jellies fill a shelf near the front door, and a small table next to it holds an assortment of clay earrings, just like the yellow ones she has on.

"Are you new in town?" she asks as I continue to follow behind her.

"Yeah, just got in yesterday. I'll be here for a couple months." I can't help containing my grin before it falls in an instant, remembering I'm now unemployed and two thousand dollars down. "You guys wouldn't be hiring by any chance, would you?"

She turns to look at me, her eyebrows raised and faintly pinched while her mouth hangs open, only the ends curled up slightly as she sighs. "I wish, I would love to have you, even for a couple months. But business is so slow here there wouldn't be any need. You'd be bored to tears and we're only open three days a week. This week is an exception because of the blues festival in a couple of days. You might have better luck at Neddy's though, if you don't mind waitressing."

"That's okay," I assure her.

A small thought flashes in my mind of me actually waitressing, walking away from a table completely forgetting what they ordered a second before, or maybe toppling a tray full of beers down the front of a patron's body. I was safe at my desk job, with four walls to keep me from making any silly, clumsy mistakes. Everything had order there—answer the calls, log everything into the computer, clock out at six. The food industry is chaos, pressure—a hustle I know I'm not cut out for. The thought rushes out just as fast as it came in, and I decide that I would probably be the worst waitress to ever live.

"Do you need a vase to put these in, hun?" she asks as she walks behind the counter, entering my total into the antique cash register.

"Oh. Yes, please."

"They're right over there." She points to my right, and my sight shifts to the tall shelving displaying them all.

I walk over, staring at each individual piece, landing on a soft green pot, the same green that matches the dated stove in my new kitchen. I reach for it and bring it to the counter, setting it next to the flowers.

"I really like your earrings," I say as I gaze at the peculiar shape of them both.

"Thank you so much! There's a local gal here that makes these. Aren't they just the cutest? And of course, it's my favorite color."

"I do love the yellow."

"Isn't it great?" she asks, picking up the vase, peeking at the bottom to enter in the amount. "Yellow is such a happy color. It signifies positivity and optimism. A brighter future ahead. It brings confidence and warmth, like the sun. That's why it's my favorite." I just smile, listening to her speak. "That will be thirty dollars and twenty cents."

I hand her two twenties out of my purse. "You can keep the change."

"Are you sure?"

"Absolutely," I say before I head for the front door, my flowers and vase in hand.

"Thank you!" she calls from behind and I flash her one last smile before I leave.

I set the flowers in my car, laying them neatly in the back seat before I snap a photo on my phone of all four lightbulbs and their markings, then walk into the entire purpose of me coming to town, The Wright Tools. I push through the door, slamming straight into a hard wall of nothing but muscle and sweat. Before I have the chance to form any words, he speaks, low and gruff, while he holds onto my arm with a firm but gentle touch. A touch that sends a string of pain straight to my chest at the memory of Rory's grip.

"Excuse me, Miss."

"I'm— I'm—" the words tumble out of my mouth like a kid learning how to do summersaults for the first time. I'm half tempted to apologize for accidently body slamming him in the doorway. But the other part of me wants to scream and yell at him for blocking the entrance.

But that's not the reason I'm stuttering.

I ran into *him*. I'm just mad at him for grabbing me.

Another man grabbing me.

My hand peels away from his arm that feels like a pack of bricks lying under smooth, tanned skin, but nothing else comes out of my throat. No words, no sounds. Just a gawking stare that I'm sure will haunt me later the more I think about it. He smiles at me, and under the scruff of his beard are dimples that could easily be missed at first glance. He moves out of the way, pushing past me with ease, and my body stays still, frozen in time. I turn around to say something, *anything*, but he's gone. I knit my brows while I question the pace of my pulse that I feel through my chest and hear in my ears, but it all comes to a halt when an employee shouts at me.

"Good afternoon!" she calls and I shuffle inside, throwing her a quick "hello" before I spot the paint samples ahead.

My mind reels back to earth and my focus shifts as I remember what I came here to do. I glance from left to right as I admire the assortment of ranging colors. A large amount of different blues, plenty of different grays. My mind crowds with so many ideas, so many—

"Could I help you with some paint today?" The woman appears next to me suddenly and it takes everything in my soul not to yelp in surprise. I do, however, gasp as I jump back from the startle. I laugh in embarrassment and she giggles too. "I'm so sorry, I did not mean to scare you."

"It's fine, I'm sorry. I was…lost in the colors." I wave my hands over the selection. My smile grows wider with hers. "I would like to get some paint today, but I'm not sure what color."

"Okay, no worries. What are you painting?"

"My front door," I reply, facing the colors again, skimming over each one.

"Really?" she questions. "Have you thought about painting the door for a while now?"

"I just moved in today." I shrug my shoulders with a cocked grin. "It needs some loving, that's for sure."

"What about this gray," she says as she plucks a card from its holder, bringing it closer for me to look.

"Mmm..." I hum. "I was thinking..." I bite the inside of my cheek as I skim one last time. "What about yellow?"

"Yellow?" Her eyebrow raises.

"Yeah, yellow." I nod, more secure in my decision the second time I say it. "A brighter future..." I finish quietly.

"Like this?" she says, pulling the brightest banana yellow I have ever seen.

"No." I giggle. "Maybe something like this?" I pull up the card of a soft yellow, nearly resembling a lemon starburst, only more muted.

"Oh," she says, surprised. "Oh!" The excitement grows in her eyes as whatever thoughts she's coming up with swarm her mind. "I like it, a lot. Okay, exterior door. Want to do a semi-gloss finish?"

"Sure," I agree with her, not understanding a sliver of a difference between paint finishes.

"Just doing one door?" she asks, taking the swatch out of my hand and walking near the paint shaker. I nod and follow her. "Let's do one quart, and if you like the color and want to paint more, you can always come back."

"Deal." I nod.

"What brand of paint do you want to go with?"

My eyes widen as she asks. I don't know. What's the difference between brands? I just want the normal kind.

"Any is fine." My grin becomes more of a grimace as I try to mask my ignorance.

"Okay. Do you have anything to paint with already?"

"I have nothing." I shake my head with a sheepish expression.

She laughs with me. "Don't worry. I got you," she says as she grabs a paint bucket from the shelf next to her, looks around for a cart, then pushes it over to me. She grabs a couple more items from the shelving unit behind her, and soon enough, the small cart is nearly full. "We've got primer, sandpaper, brushes, rollers, a pan, and some extra stirring sticks. Do you need anything else while I mix your color?" she asks, finishing off her list as she puts her hands on her hips.

"Light bulbs," I say with one curt nod before I pull my phone out from my crossbody bag.

I locate the photos I took and pass the phone over to her. Her doe eyes stare at the screen as she purses her lips, the lines forming deep crevices as she puckers.

"Follow me," she says with a wave, bringing us to an aisle halfway into the store. Shelving stacked full of bulbs—yellow, blue, and white boxes—stand side by side, fitting tightly together. She skims each shelf, pulling two boxes with the word *LED* in bold letters. "These should be it. Do you live close? I can exchange them if you don't like the color. These are soft white, but you may decide you want daylight or bright white instead."

My face twists in uncertainty. "I'm sure these will be fine, but if I have any problems, I'll come right back here," I state.

"Perfect. Need anything else?"

"I think that's it...for now."

"Okay." She hands me the boxes. "Put these in the cart and bring it to the front. I'll be there in a second with your paint." Her smile is soft, mixing with the lines on her face and her suntanned skin. She's pleasant, and so helpful. Just like everyone else in this town.

"You, uh, wouldn't happen to be hiring, would you?" The words gush out like lava as she walks away. I don't know anything about *anything* in this damn store, but I feel I could do a better job at learning this than trying to figure out how to carry a tray full of shots to a table successfully without spilling.

"Well, actually, I would love to have a couple days off."

"I'm only in town for a couple months," I interject. "But I would love to help out in the meantime if needed. I, *obviously*, don't have a lot of knowledge in household hardware, but I'm a quick learner."

She pauses for a moment in thought. "Let me get you an application." Her smile is bright as ever.

I grab the cart, pushing it to the front as she sweeps behind and pulls a piece of paper from below the counter, grabbing me a pen from the cup next to the register. "Here you are." Her fingertips slide the paper toward me. "I'll be right back."

I look down, grabbing the pen in hand and filling out as much as I can before having to look through my phone, glancing at the one text from Ellie that has my new address on it. I pencil it in between the boxes and continue on, filling out my most recent job, with a small description on the reason for leaving. "Moved to Falton Ridge" is all I jot down, figuring that will be as good of an excuse as any. I toss the pen back into the cup and slide the application over to the other side of the counter, waiting for her to return. My sight travels around the shop—crates, shelves, and drawers fill the walls and the aisles. Even though it's a smaller store, it's nearly filled with every kind of tool one could imagine. The soft lighting is easy on the eyes against the wooden accents and I get the feeling they usually aren't very busy in here. The shelves below the counter are filled with candy bars, gum, and mints. Some look like they've been here for a while. It's cozy, for its size. It probably wouldn't take me long to figure out where every tool goes. It's just what they are *used for* is where my lack of knowledge shines through.

"Here you are," she says as she comes up from behind me, setting the paint can on the counter. She lifts my application, skimming through it as she peeks over at me before setting it back down. "Kaiton, it's nice to meet you. My name is Laura." She smiles with her hand extended, waiting for me to shake it.

"Nice to meet you, Laura." I beam, taking her hand in mine.

"I'll give this to the boss when he comes back in. I don't know how he's going to feel about hiring an employee only for a couple of months but let me tell you...I'm gonna beg." She laughs. "I've been wanting some days off to spend time with my new grandbaby...this would be perfect." She rings up my items, scanning each bar code with her handheld device. "It's going to be seventy-seven dollars and thirty-eight cents."

She bags my items after I pay, handing everything to me at once as I try to carry it all. The weight of the cans pinches my fingers, and I stifle out a "thank you" under the pain.

"Hopefully I'll see you soon, Kaiton!" She waves as I leave, hobbling to my car, my arms already tired. I fumble with the keys, regretting locking the doors as my fingers become numb.

I wouldn't mind working here, and I certainly wouldn't mind working with Laura. She seems knowledgeable enough to run this place herself, and I could definitely learn a thing or two from her.

I just hope the boss feels the same.

CHAPTER
EIGHT

I TAKE A STEP BACK, wiping the sweat from my brow to admire my masterpiece. The soft tone of yellow brightens the front of my house, and I can't do anything but smile. I stand in my leggings and sports bra with my hands on my hips and my eyes glued to the door. The scraping and sanding was all worthwhile, I realize, as I gaze at the finished product.

I pack up my painting supplies, throwing everything into the silver pan before I bring it inside. The dim lights from the living room glow just enough as the sun sets behind the mountaintops. Luckily for me, there are enough windows in here to not need light for most of the day. Not so lucky for me, I didn't bother to grab curtains while I was in town today, so I'll just remain cooped up in the bedroom the second darkness falls. *Every single night.* I did, however, grab the most beautiful flowers, and they are currently resting in the center of the dining table in *my* new little cottage.

I walk to the sink, washing my hands of leftover paint, when my phone buzzes on the wooden table. My neck jerks to the side quickly, then back down at my wet hands before I wipe them on my leggings and jog over. I pick my phone up in a panic, mildly out of breath only from that small exertion.

"Hello?" I pant, only *slightly* contemplating if I need to get a gym membership while I'm here because I should not be this out of breath from a simple jog.

"Hi, is this Kaiton?" a man's voice rings on the other end. My heart only skips one beat before I realize it *isn't* Rory. This voice is deeper, richer, like a delectable velvety chocolate.

"It is." I sigh, my heart still pumping hard from the excitement.

"This is Dutton Beck, I own The Wright Tools. Laura gave me your application today, so I just wanted to ask you a couple of questions, if that's okay."

"Yeah, anything," I say eagerly, still trying to determine how I'm even going to pretend to know what I'm doing at a hardware store, but ready to learn.

"She said you're only going to be in town a couple of months. You're just living here temporarily?"

I clear my throat. "That's correct."

"Okay, well, I wouldn't usually hire someone if they were leaving so soon, but Laura's been the only one in this town willing to work, and uh...she needs a break." His laugh makes me grin. "Do you know much about power tools?"

"Not really," I say with a soft tone. "But I'm willing to learn."

"Do you know much about home improvement?"

"I, um...I painted my front door today."

He laughs again. God, it sounds so smooth. He doesn't sound very old, either, for a store owner. I shake it off quicky. What good was a smooth voice or rich laughter? Rory had the same and did nothing but ruin me.

"Well, that's a start. Would you be able to come in tomorrow and train some with Laura? I'd be happy to hire you for a couple days a week until you leave. It'd give both Laura and I the break we need. I'll have to pay you in cash, though. Too much work to get you on the books for just the temporary hire."

"I can absolutely come in tomorrow. What time would work best? And that's fine, cash is good. I don't mind." My grin stretches ear to ear, partially because I don't have to go back out and apply anywhere else. This job will get me at least a couple hundred bucks a week that I can skim for living expenses. Granted, it's not a career by any means, but who gets a job when they're on vacation, I mean really?

"Can you come in right when we open? Nine o'clock?"

"I'll be there!" I'm finding it hard to contain the excitement in my voice.

"Great, thanks again, Kaiton. We'll see ya tomorrow," he says before we say goodbye.

I hang up, my mind bursting with exhilaration. I look outside, only a small sliver of daylight left. Phone in hand, I walk through the back sliding door to sit down by the lake. Stepping through the tall grass, I make my way to the Adirondack chairs by the dock, kicking my shoes off once I take a seat. I lift my phone up, checking for service before I FaceTime Layla. It only rings twice before she answers.

"Oh my *God*, I miss you!" she shouts.

"I miss you more. It's been like, three days since I saw you."

"Three days too long. How is your new house?"

"Hold on," I say, flipping the camera, showing her my view of the lake. Pines wrap around the water's edge as the mountains stand proud and tall behind them. I've been here long enough to get used to it already, and yet, every time I look at the view, it feels like the first time.

"Holy *fuck*, K." Her mouth hangs open, eyes growing wider and wider while I slowly show her the entire landscape.

"I know, right?" I say as I turn the phone back to face me.

"That's so beautiful, I'm insanely jealous. How are *you*?"

"I'm good."

"Yeah?" she says, almost in a whisper.

"I mean..." My mind suddenly races and the looming thoughts creep back. I try to come up with the words, but my eyes well with the tears I didn't even know were close to the surface. "Layla..." My voice cracks as one falls. "What do I do with my wedding dress?"

"Burn it," she snaps. Not a second of thinking, not a shred of a doubt.

I let out a cackle right away. Layla's fire-red hair matches her fiery personality and I love her for it.

"Has anyone heard from him?" I ask, wiping the tears away with my fingers.

"No. Not at all. He's been MIA since you left."

I don't know if it's relief I'm feeling, or more nerves. I'm in the wind and now he is, too?

I swallow hard, not wanting to talk about this piece of shit, but somehow my brain can't disconnect the man I thought was the love of my life and the man who threatened to kill me. I'm torn. My head is fighting a battle with my heart. He couldn't have loved me. No man that loves someone deeply enough would say those things, *do* those things. But *I* loved him, it was just...he didn't love me back. Or maybe he just loved me in some severely fucked up way that I accepted for far too long.

I groan. "I'm sorry, I shouldn't be sad. He's really a dumb fuck."

"Oh, so stupid, Kaiton. So fucking stupid. This is not a moment where I am going to tell you I told you so. I would never, ever put you down like that. But K... I—"

"Told me so." I let out a chuckle. "I know."

"I didn't say it, *you* said it." Her smirk brings me comfort.

I take a deep breath. "I painted my front door yellow today," I say, changing the subject abruptly, my face still slightly red from the tears.

"Okay, girl," she squeals. "Can I ask why?" Her smile twists as her eyebrows dip.

"It's a happy color. You know, like the sun. It's supposed to mean a bright future, I guess...I just thought—"

"I love it," she interjects. "Send me a pic of it tomorrow. It looks like it's getting dark there."

I look around, forgetting my surroundings as the stars appear in the sky. A branch snaps in the distance and while back home that might mean a deer, here in the mountains, I'm very well aware it could be numerous other things.

"Stay on the phone with me," I say in a hushed tone, bolting out of my chair. I speed walk to my back porch and slamming the door shut as I enter. I lock the slider, my phone clutched in my palm with Layla probably only getting distorted views of the ground.

"You okay?" she asks after I hastily bring the phone back to my face.

"I'm fucking scared already." My tone is still and quiet as she laughs loudly.

"You'll be fine, K. You're a big girl. Remember when you beat up Marshall in seventh grade?"

"I didn't beat him up, Layla. I accidentally closelined him in dodgeball."

"Same thing. Just do that again if there's an intruder."

"Thanks for the tip," I scoff.

Layla starts to talk again but soon enough, the picture of her freezes. With no sound for a minute, the call finally drops. Fucking service in the mountains. I huff, dropping my arm and walking to the front door to triple-check it's locked before I turn the lamps off in the living room and head to bed. Getting in my comfy shorts and extra-large T-shirt before I crawl under the blanket decorated with brown bears and fish, I close my eyes in hopes of falling asleep quickly. But it's never that easy, especially *now*. The house creaks with the wind and I try to shift my focus on something else, only landing on Rory and the constant state of a dull ache my heart remains in because of him. I grab my chest, feeling the pain once more and nuzzle my head into the pillow. The tears cascade again, warm and wet down my cheeks, and I sigh, hoping that this is the last time I'll ever cry for that bastard.

CHAPTER
NINE

THE BELLS CHIME against the door frame as I enter the store, my stomach a pit of anxiousness as I walk toward Laura. She has the biggest grin swept across her features.

"Good morning! I tell ya, I was so excited when Dutton called last night." She beams.

"Me too." I give her a little laugh hoping to ease my nerves.

"Okay, come here," she says as she waves me over behind the counter.

I stand next to her as she bends down, grabbing a cloth from the shelf below. She unfolds the apron and holds it up to me, gauging the size. "Put this one on and let's see if it works," she says as she hands it to me. I bring the strings of the tan apron around my waist and secure them over my jeans. "Perfect," she says before she looks around the desk, grabbing a couple pens, a boxcutter, and a measuring tape. "Put all this in. It'll make your life easier if you always have them on you." She laughs once more. I smile and nod, taking everything in her palms as I shove them in the pockets of the apron. "Have you ever worked a POS system before?" she asks. My face twists in confusion. I've had a P.O.S ex-fiancé, but I've never heard of a system.

"I don't think so," I reply.

She moves to the side, making room for me to stand in front of the cash register. "This is the POS system we have," she says. I stare at her, wondering why she keeps calling it a piece of shit. "Point of sale," she says after my mindless blank staring has gone on long enough.

"Oh!" I say as it finally clicks.

"It's pretty simple to use. Here is the barcode scanner, it's as simple as a click. Our weight scale is right here, and every time you press this button, the drawer opens for you," she says at the same time the cash drawer springs open. "Say you've got a customer, and you're ready to ring them up. Just type in your number. You're going to be number three, okay? Dutton is one, I'm two, you're three. Remember that. So, you're going to press three, and then you can scan away. Press this button here to total 'em out. It'll add your taxes, and that's it," she finishes.

My mind is going at a glacial pace as I try to keep up. It sounds simple, but the way she was pressing keys frantically made it look like she's Ray Charles on the piano. Talented, of course, but too quick for me to learn.

"Now, follow me. Let's give you a crash course in hardware." Her smile rings excitement, while my clenched grin screams panic.

I follow her through the shop most of the day, trailing behind her like a lost puppy while she shows me the ins and outs of the layout. While the store itself is small, adding the backroom and break room to the mix has me slightly overwhelmed.

"Make sure to not shut this all the way if you're in here alone," she says as she holds onto the door of the stockroom. "Slide this chair over to catch it because when it latches, it gets stuck from the inside. You can only open it from out there." She points back into the main store area.

"Okay, got it," I repeat. "Don't lock myself in the stockroom. Check."

I spend the next couple of hours learning the difference between certain treated woods, nails and screws, and of course, light bulbs.

During lunch, she walks down to Neddy's and grabs us a couple of sandwiches while I man the front desk, crossing my fingers that no one actually comes into the store. We've only had three customers today and they were fairly easy. She let me handle every transaction, while she stands over my shoulder, of course. But as luck would have it, I get the most complicated customer with the most confusing questions when she's gone. The bells chime above the door and I swear my stomach drops into my ass until I see Laura pushing through, her back against the door with a bag and a drink carrier in her hands. I quietly sigh in relief as she nods past me, indicating to follow her into the break room.

"Today is stock day. Twice a week a truck comes by with everything we ordered to replenish our inventory, it's usually not much, so don't worry if you're here by yourself later on. It's comin' at a good time though, because our store helps with the supplies for setting up the blues festival in a couple of days," she says as we divvy up our food. "Are you going?"

"To the festival?" I ask as I take my wrapped sandwich from her hand.

"Yeah, are you goin? Should be a good time, always is. Live band, beer tent, some carnies come in too if you like elephant ears."

"It sounds fun." I flash her a smile.

"I'll give you my number before your shift ends. If you end up goin', you can text me. My daughter taught me how to text from this iPhone thing last week. I'm gettin' pretty good at it." Laura laughs as she proudly holds up her phone. The home screen displays a photo of what seems to be her daughter, holding her newborn baby.

I grin, sharing in her pride. It reminds me of the time I had to help my dad close a tab on his new laptop. "Press the red X, Dad," I told him. He thought I was a genius. But he was happy, proud that he now knew how to work modern technology. I can see that in Laura, when she tucks her gray hair behind her ear and focuses on typing out a message. Her chocolate brown eyes home in on her screen and I can tell from here the text size is set twice as big as mine.

We finish our lunch and get back to work just before the truck arrives. We unload piping and fittings, bringing everything to the back, until Laura has me check inventory. The rest of work goes by without a hitch, except for me almost locking myself in the stockroom. But I handled my first customer completely by myself, directing them to where the PVC pipes were before they had me ring them up. Laura, of course, high-fived me once they left and I truly felt like I could easily get the hang of this gig.

My phone buzzes through my back jean pocket and I pull it out quickly while Laura and I go through the store, shutting everything down.

ELLIE BOONE: Rodney will be over at your house tomorrow to mow your lawn. Want to go boot shopping for the festival? You are going, right???

ME: Boot shopping? Yeah, I think so! I don't really know where it's at but I'd like to go

ELLIE BOONE: Tag along with Rodney and I, we're meeting Hattie down there. It's right in the center of town. They block off the roads and really transform the place. With a center stage and all.

ELLIE BOONE: And I need new boots. I like to get a new pair for every occasion. Don't tell Rodney ;-)

ELLIE BOONE: Wanna get some too? You can't go to a Ridge event without some boots now.

Her texts flood in one after another, and I shove my phone back in my pocket as Laura comes out of the break room.

"Go ahead and click off the neon 'open' sign and turn the one on the door. Last thing to do is for me to clock out and you to write your hours down before we lock this joint up," she says as she takes out a small notepad from the shelving below the counter. "Write your name on top and today's date. You worked eight hours today so put that there." She points to the pad. I jot down what she tells me then slide it back to her. "You did great today, Kaiton. Think you can handle the store on your own tomorrow? Dutton has you down for four hours in the morning. Did you see the schedule in the break room?"

"I did. I got a photo of it, too. I think I'll be okay. If I have any questions, should I call you or him?"

"Call me. I'll be just down the road at my daughter's house, but I think you got this." She nudges my arm with her elbow as she makes her way closer to me, flashing me a wink and her tender smile. "There's no alarm here so just use the key I gave you to unlock the door, flip and turn on the signs and lights, and start that register. You'll be good to go."

"I think I got it." I nod, fairly confident I can turn on a couple things here and there.

We both walk out of the door, and I watch Laura lock it up behind me.

"I'll be in at noon tomorrow to relieve you. Great job today, Kaiton. Happy to have you here in Falton." Her hand brushes my arm with the gentlest touch.

We part our separate ways and once I'm in my car, I text Ellie back, letting her know I'm always down to shop. Right after my first solo shift, of course.

CHAPTER
TEN

THE GRAVEL CRUNCHES beneath my tires as I pull into the long driveway. Pines and Western Larches intermingle on both sides until I arrive at the open area where the house rests on top of the hill. Not just any house, *my* house. A burly man on a lawnmower comes around from the back as I park next to a large silver truck with a trailer attached behind. I see Ellie in the passenger seat and who I'm assuming is her husband, Rodney, mowing the tall grass. I stayed a little longer past my shift today to finish with the customer I was working with before Laura took over. I'd say it was a success for the four hours I was there. I mixed two cans of paint all by myself after calling her *only* once to ask about the instructions she left. She's a wonderful woman, but God, her penmanship is terrible.

"Sorry to keep you waiting!" I call to Ellie as we both step out of our vehicles at the same time.

"No worries. We just got here, and I was doin' a little online shopping in the meantime."

Ellie loves to shop, noted.

"You want to get going? I can drive since you've got the trailer hooked up," I say.

"Perfect." She smiles, walking to my car to open the passenger door. "I'll tell you where to go. Service is shit here."

"Yeah, I've noticed." I give a little laugh before I start my car again, throwing it in reverse immediately.

"Go right out of your driveway," she says while she points simultaneously. "You'll be on this for another three miles." I nod my head. "I think I want some white boots. I have this really pretty celadon colored dress I think would go great with some kick ass white boots." She beams from ear to ear.

"What color is that?"

"Celadon? Well, I guess...I guess it's like a mint green. Really pastel. Gorgeous against my tan." She winks as her elbow nudges the side of my arm. I smile back. "What color are you gonna get?

"I don't really know what I'm wearing yet, but I feel like brown would go with anything?"

"You're damn right it does." Her smile remains as she turns her gaze back to the road, laying her head against the headrest.

I continue to drive, checking my speed regularly to keep it right at the limit. I don't know why, but Ellie reminds me of my mom, and being with her is like being with the unofficial speed police, otherwise known as Jill Riggs.

"How are you liking your house so far? Love the door, by the way," she says after some time, springing back up to look straight at me, her eyes wide with excitement.

"I like it!" My tone pitches higher than normal. "And thank you. It took me a while but I'm really happy with it."

"You should be. Such a warm color, like the sun," she says with another point of the finger. "Take a left at this next road."

We drive and drive as I twist and turn on winding roads, slowing down in a town I haven't seen before, then picking up speed back on the open pavement.

"So, what does your family think of your long vacation to The Ridge? Or is that who you needed a break from?" Ellie says, holding a pause only slightly before she blurts out, "Sorry if that's too personal, don't answer that if it makes you uncomfortable. I'm just nosey. Don't pay me no mind."

I giggle at her erratic mind, her ability to think of multiple things at once and spit them out equally as fast. "They are glad I made it safely," I say. "My dad's pretty jealous I'm here. But I think they miss me, a lot. Even though it's only been a couple of days. Just the way I left was so abrupt. We didn't get a chance for a proper goodbye."

"Sorry to hear that. Sounds like you've got a good relationship with them though, nothing stronger than that type of love, I'll tell you."

"We are really close, always have been. I think it's the only child syndrome."

"No brothers or sisters for you?"

"None. But it's okay, I never felt lonely growing up."

"Good, that's really good." Her soft smile rests on her lips.

"Do you and Rodney have any kids?" I ask, almost putting my foot in my mouth instantly. I don't like asking strangers personal questions, especially when it comes to their choice of having or wanting children. I guess Ellie isn't much of a stranger now, so hopefully the question doesn't come off the wrong way.

"We do." Her smile still sits, and a weight lifts off my chest. "Just one, she's about your age. What are you, twenty-one, twenty-two?" she asks.

"I'll be twenty-five next week."

"Well, happy early birthday, Kaiton. We will have to go out and celebrate of course." She beams. "Belle is twenty-two. She's off to Oregon, living there full time. She doesn't call much but I miss her constantly." Her smile faintly dissipates as the realization hits, and my heart aches at the sight of it.

"I think when I was twenty-two, I didn't call my mom much. Now, I probably annoy her with the constant communication." I interject in her pause, giggling slightly to try and lighten her mood.

Ellie continues, "She might come to visit next month. She usually comes back home once a year in the summer. I hope it's when you're here. You two would fit like a glove."

"I hope so, too."

Only five more miles go by of talking about our families before I'm slowing down in another town and whipping into a parking space right in front of Woody's Boot and Saddle, a cedar shake roof crowning the small store on the corner by the stoplight.

The shop is vividly lit with yellow-tinted fluorescents hanging above. The smell of leather pervades my nose the moment we enter and rows upon rows stacked full with cowboy boots line the walls and the center shelves. Only a small section to the left houses multicolored saddles, headstalls, and reins. The clerk greats us and I follow Ellie to the right, going down the first aisle of boots—some with rhinestones, some with threaded patterns, others brown with turquoise accents. I've only worn these kinds of boots once for a country concert at Tinley Park and they were Layla's size six's that I had to shove my size sevens into. Did not make for a great experience and left my toenails bruised for weeks.

"You own a pair yet?" she asks as she picks a white boot from the shelf, looking at the back of it.

"I do not," I reply as I tuck my arms into my sides, fitting through the narrow aisle.

"Good, today's your lucky day. It's on me," she says with a wink and a smile.

I shake my head at her, telling her she's *not* going to spend the money on me. But after thirty minutes of searching, I find a beautiful pair of brown square-toed boots with an embroidered stitch pattern of a cow skull and feathers. Two hundred and twenty dollar boots that Ellie insisted she buy for me. I tried, I really did. I even offered to find a cheaper pair if she wouldn't let me get my own. She refused, and stated these were her favorite brand, a good quality that would last me, and whenever I got back home, they'd be a reminder of my time here in Falton. That's how I ultimately lost the battle and caved in, only thanking her a million and one times from the store back to the car.

CHAPTER
ELEVEN

"JUST UP HERE TO THE LEFT," Ellie directs, and I flip on my signal, turning onto dirt and rocks. The open view of her farm placed directly in front of mountains makes my jaw unlock, dropping slightly as I suck in a breath loud enough for *her* to hear. Dark wooden fences on both sides of the drive hold large cows on the right and horses on the left. An oversized apple red barn trimmed out in white sits behind the large brown home, and I drive slowly as the dust kicks up, eventually parking in front of the three-car garage.

"Looks like Rodney's already finished at your place. Want to come in for a bit? You haven't eaten lunch, have you?"

"I have not." I grin and shake my head no.

"Neither have I. Let me fix us up something quick. How does that sound?"

"Sounds good." I nod in agreement before we get out of the car.

I follow her to the front steps of her house. Cherry wood columns connect to the dormer above and each peak in the roof has gable end windows, which I can assume bring a plethora of natural light inside. The moment Ellie opens the front door, I'm greeted with the glorious mix of knotty pine and a cathedral ceiling, tying the spacious floor plan together.

"Rod, I'm home!" Ellie shouts. Her voice echoes throughout.

She sets her purse on the center island counter and opens her refrigerator. I move around to the black stools with wicker seats, sliding one out to sit.

"Do you like BLT's?" she asks, her back still facing me.

"I love them."

"Really?" Her surprised grin flashes at me as she turns her neck around. "They are Belle's favorite. I would make one for her every day after school." Her voice softens when she turns back to the fridge, grabbing the bacon from a crisper drawer and a head of lettuce from another. She stuffs them in the crook of her arm as she grabs the rest of the ingredients, shutting the refrigerator door with her elbow once she's done. Turning her entire body around, she plops everything onto the marbled countertop.

"Your home is really beautiful," I say, my eyes continuing to travel around the open space, taking in the subtle decor. Brown leathers, deep red rugs, and scattered European mounts fill the home, but don't clutter the space. Three black and white portraits hang near the dining area. The furthest one to left is a photo of a younger Ellie with an open-mouthed smile on her face as if she was mid-laugh, hiking up a wedding dress to show off her cowboy boots with a younger looking Rodney standing proudly next to her in a black tuxedo with a beer in his hand. The middle is a toddler, lying in the grass with light colored hair splayed on the ground around her, that same smile as Ellie on her face. And the last one, the one closest to me, displays all three of them years older as Rodney squeezes the pre-teen's cheeks and Ellie kisses the side of her head. All three of them wear Mickey Mouse ears with the Epcot Ball behind them.

"Thank you," Ellie says sweetly. "It's our little slice of paradise."

Just the open space we're in is three times the size of my apartment in Illinois, not to mention the addition I saw from the outside that's not visible from these three rooms.

The front door opens swiftly as the burly man I've decided is Rodney steps in.

"Hey, babe," Ellie calls, fishing for a pan in a bottom cabinet.

"Hey, darlin'. Oh, you must be Kaiton. I'm Rodney." He extends his hand for me to shake.

I was right.

"Thank you so much for mowing my lawn. How much do I owe you for it?"

"Don't be silly. Just let Ellie know the next time you need me out there. I'm happy to help," he says before his eyes travel over to his wife. "You gonna make me one of those?" He points with a smirk.

"Yeah, yeah. You bought us boots today, anyway. It's the least I can do." She laughs.

"Oh, did I now?" He walks over to her, sweeping his arm around her waist as he pulls her in to kiss the top of her head. "I'm gonna go clean up. Bunny and Poppy are already fed but Bunny's been moping around still. She might need some extra lovin' today," he says and she nods, placing a small peck on his lips before he walks away.

"Nice to officially meet you, Kaiton," he says with a curt nod to me before he disappears through the rest of the house.

"Bunny and Poppy are our two horses out there," she says, waving the knife she's using to cut the package of bacon open toward the front door. "Bunny's bestie Jelly Bean just passed away a couple weeks ago. She goes in spurts. Some days she's ready to run the trails, some she's low-spirited. Sometimes I'll go out there and read her a story or two. Maybe after lunch we can give her some treats before you leave?"

"I'd like that." I nod.

The bacon sizzles and sears as Ellie places it in the pan, grabbing a toaster out of another cupboard once all the strips are cooking. She grabs a plump tomato from the counter and places it on a cutting board, carving away carefully. The blade of the knife glides right through, creating perfectly thin slices. She wipes her hands on the checkered towel hanging from the stove and chops up the lettuce next.

I know Ellie is a Realtor, but both of them being home on a Wednesday makes me wonder what Rodney does for a living. It's very possible this gorgeous home on however many endless acres came from Ellie's income alone, but still... It makes me wonder, nonetheless.

"So, what does Rodney do for work?" My curiosity gets the best of me before my brain has time to stop the words flowing out.

"He owns a plumbing business." She turns her head around quickly with a smile. "But he's essentially retired. Just does payroll and all the bookwork...things like that."

"Wow, well that's neat. He seems young to be retired."

"Rod had a heart attack about three years ago. Figured it'd be less stress on him if he just stepped back from the business. So he retired...or, his version of retired." She laughs.

"Oh my, everything is...fine now?" I ask.

"Everything is fine now." She nods, smiling faintly. "Are you in school or anything? Have another job back home?" she asks, her back turned to me as she flips the bacon pieces over. Grease pops left and right, but she doesn't budge.

"Neither..." I say, rather slowly.

I hate talking aloud about my non-existent career. Or my hypothetical dreams and aspirations. The truth is, I have no idea what the hell I want to do with my life. I've tried. I've tried to think of something, *anything*, I might like to do for a career. The truth is, I met Rory when I was nineteen, and my plan—*our* plan—was to get married, start a family, and just stay home with the kid, or kids. It's what *he* wanted. Said it was the *traditional* way. So, I agreed. But of course, all of my friends have great jobs and careers. Layla is a surgical tech, my other friend Heidi is an accountant, and the list could go on. Then there's me, who worked in a call center. Making just above minimum wage, holding out until I became that picture perfect wife and mother. *Look where that got me.*

"Nothing wrong with that," she says. "I didn't go to college. Rod and I got married young, had a baby young, did all the things backward with zero direction in life." She chuckles. "But man, I wouldn't trade it for the world. Everything happened as it should. I've only been a Realtor for five years. Up until then, I just had odd jobs and even now, my career is inconsistent. There's no right or wrong way to do life. Not everyone needs some fancy goal to achieve. Some of us just want to live," she says, assembling each sandwich on separate plates. "Just enjoy your time here in Falton while you can. Then when you go back home, to reality, you can figure out the next step of your life. Or don't. The beauty of your life is exactly that: it's *yours*. You do what *you* want, and don't let no one tell you any different." Her words flow out like a lullaby, soft and sweet, gentle and kind, as she places a plate in front of me, sliding the other to my right.

As she takes a seat next to me, I glance at her. "Thank you," I say with a smile. "For everything today."

"Of course." She tilts her chin down. Only a small moment of stillness remains between us before we both dig in. As I take the first bite, my soul fills with tiny glimpses of happiness. Being around Ellie, her presence, her words, her gestures—it feels like being with my mom. I miss her terribly, but being with Ellie helps fill that void, if only a little. And for that, I'm thankful—that out of all the places I could have ended up, I ended up here. Right in the heart of Falton Ridge.

CHAPTER
TWELVE

THE PAST TWO DAYS off I've spent deep cleaning the house and grocery shopping at the local market. I even bought myself a couple cooking magazines for recipes since my internet hardly functions out here. I did take a drive too, to the next town over, and even though it's still the same gorgeous Montana, it doesn't have quite the charm Falton does. But all my exploring and sightseeing has me running late as I scramble to get ready.

I slide on my new boots, taking one last look in my small bedroom mirror as my finger glides over the light pieces of hair framing my face, trying to fix the strays that have wandered. I tilt my head, staring back at my reflection to analyze the face before me. I feel like I hardly recognize it. My fingers run against the faint crow's feet already forming and I raise my eyebrows, looking at the indents and lines that appear in a row. I look more tired, if anything. More defeated. I never used to analyze myself in this manner. I've always tried not to think negatively of myself. But for some reason, I can't get away from it now.

My phone buzzes on my dresser as the FaceTime tone chirps on and I swipe to answer it, propping it up against the lamp as I step back, getting as much of myself in the frame for Layla to see.

"Okay, little miss cowgirl you." Her eyes widen.

"You like?" I giggle, kicking my foot up, showcasing the entirety of my boot.

"Love the fit. What does your sweatshirt say?"

I glance down, pulling at the threads so I can refresh my memory. "It says Boot's Inn. I got it from the motel I stayed in the first night I got here."

"I want one!" she exclaims, shoving popcorn into her mouth. "Where are you going anyway, all dressed up?"

"All dressed up? Layla, I'm in a sweatshirt and jean shorts."

"Yeah, but you got cute new boots on. You know I'm going to want to borrow those, right?"

"Yeah, yeah, how do I look?" I ask as I spin my body halfway, showcasing my lightly curled strands and the back of my Wrangler shorts.

"You look fucking fantastic. You tryin' to pick up a hot date or something?"

"Jesus, Layla," I say, grabbing my phone to walk out to the kitchen, searching for more natural light. "No, I'm not looking for a hot date. Just want to make a good impression. I'm new here. And know like, three people," I say, slightly irritated she would even ask that since only a week ago we were on my bachelorette trip together. The thought of him crosses my mind and I know I shouldn't ask, but that doesn't stop my mouth from running at the speed of light before I have a chance to form another thought. "Has anyone heard from—" I don't even have to say his name aloud before Layla cuts me off.

"Still MIA. I think your dad is handling some things with the police, but I guess there isn't much they can really do with such little evidence of his behavior."

"Maybe he will just drop off the face of the earth forever and I'll eventually forget he even existed."

"Kait, I wish the same. I can't imagine what you're going through, or the feelings you're having. All I can say is that everything happens for a reason. You know I'm a firm believer in that."

"I know." I resist the urge to roll my eyes—Layla and her words of fate and wisdom and how the stars tell stories. She's my dreamer friend, and I wouldn't change her for the world, but sometimes leaving things up to fate gets you racing to Montana to disappear.

Like she can read my mind, she interrupts with, "Well, you're where you're supposed to be right now. So, enjoy it. Live it up. And if you see any hotties wherever you're

going, make sure to send me pics." She laughs. "Where *are* you going, by the way?"

"Um, it's a Blues Festival downtown I guess."

"Sounds very small town. Love that for you," she says with her mouth full of popcorn. "I'm staying in this lovely Friday night, missing my best friend, watching comedy movies all by my lonesome."

"I miss you too, Layla." I tuck my arm around my midriff, hugging my body as I help prop up my other arm with the phone.

"Have fun tonight, K. I'm serious about those hottie pics."

"Literally everyone I have met so far is old enough to be my parents or my grandparents." I giggle, not bothering to mention my literal run-in with the completely jacked asshole who looked my age. Yes, *I* ran into *him*, but I'm still peeved at the manhandling grab he used on me. Or am I just peeved he's a *man*? Probably both.

"Well, if you see a silver fox, send it over. I'm lonely and bored on a Friday night. It's honestly the least you could do for me."

I laugh so deep the pit of my belly stings. "Love you. I have to go now," I finally let out.

"Love you more," she says before she hangs up the call.

I glance at my phone before it shuts off, noticing a text from Ellie.

ELLIE BOONE: We're almost
to your place. See you soon.

I click my phone off, shoving it in my back pocket as I grab some cash, my ID, and a credit card out of my purse, pushing it down in the other pocket. I think quickly if I have everything—money, ID, pants...what the fuck am I missing? I glance around the kitchen, spotting my keys on the counter. I walk to them, swiping them from their resting place and twirl them around my finger as I head out the front door, locking it behind me. Only a minute or two passes before I hear the tires on the gravel and see the truck peek over the hill.

"Oh, you look so cute, Kaiton!" Ellie exclaims as I walk up to her side of the truck once it's parked, her window rolled down halfway.

"So do you!" I tell her back. She was right—the color of her dress goes extremely well with her suntanned skin and I'm kind of jealous I don't have that outfit in my own closet.

I hop in the back seat, greeting Rodney while he backs out of the drive. We cruise downtown, listening to the country music station on radio as we go. My mom thinks it's a little odd everyone I've met seems so nice. She's only mentioned it once during our calls, but I admit—I guess it is a little strange I was in some random person's house a day or two after coming here. But the feeling I get is just indescribable, even to my mother. Never once have I felt out of place in a town I've never been to. Not once have I felt unsafe or taken advantage of. I've always been a trusting person, a *forgiving* person. I know it's a flaw about me that hasn't worked out so well in most recent events. But there's no other way to describe it. I feel *secure* here.

Rodney and Ellie discuss where to park as we come into town. The street is blocked off by orange and white barricades as a swarm of people fill every inch of the town I've been driving through. We find a spot in a semi-open field already crowded with vehicles, and the second I step out, the sounds of live music in the distance fill my ears along with the rich smell of corn dogs, fried Oreos, and funnel cakes.

"You ready?" Ellie says with a grin as she links my arm with hers. We walk in front of Rodney as I let her lead the way. She greets most people as we weave through the crowd, stopping to chat with some, only for small seconds. "Hattie said she was by the beer tent."

The music grows louder the closer we get to the center stage. People dance in front of it, some stepping side to side, while others swing their arms around their partners, all with smiles and grins as the guitars play.

"Ellie!" Hattie shouts from a distance, waving her arm up as high as it goes. Both of our eyes lock on her and I can't help but smile remembering how short her stature actually is.

"Hi, Mama," Ellie says, letting go of my arm to give Hattie a hug.

"Oh, Kaitlyn, I'm so happy to see you here!" She reaches for a hug from me.

"Hattie, it's 'Kaiton' like *Kait*-un," Ellie says into her ear, tsking her "T" loudly.

"It's fine, really," I say in a hushed tone.

"I'm sorry sweetie, you'll have to forgive this old bag. This here is Waylon," Hattie says as she slaps his arm.

He's tall and burly, just like Rodney. I can see the resemblance—their dark eyes and dark hair, although Waylon's is more dusted with gray than Rod's.

"Nice to meet you." I smile and raise my hand in a very still wave.

"Kaiton!" I hear my name from a distance. My head snaps behind me and I see Laura, hurrying toward me. "You came!"

Shit, I forgot to text her to let her know.

"I did!"

"You've got to try one of these," she says, holding up a small container filled with mushrooms, potatoes, and what looks and smells to be chopped steak.

"Hey, Laura," Ellie says, hugging her at the waist. They talk briefly before Laura is pulled away by a couple of locals.

"Let's go get some beer tokens and dance, shall we?" Ellie says as her gaze shifts to mine.

"Okay," I say, rather unsure about every word that just came out of her mouth.

"Mama, want some tokens?" she says as we walk past Hattie.

"No, I got some already, doll."

We enter the large white tent floating a few feet off the ground and tethered with ropes. String lights hang slightly from the tall peak in the ceiling all the way to the end of it. We stop at a long table. Several people are behind it with cash drawers, wristbands, tokens, and T-shirts as Ellie greets the first man we see.

"Can I get five tokens..." she says, looking to me next. "How many beers you think you want?"

"Oh, I don't really drink."

"You don't? Okay, no worries, hun."

"Thank you, though," I add in before she starts back up with the volunteer.

"Just five tokens is all."

She hands him the cash, exchanging it for round casino-looking chips, stamped with the Falton Lake Blues Festival logo I've seen everywhere down here.

"Come on," she says with a tilt of her head as we make our way deeper into the tent.

The band switches to play the next song and a slow guitar solo starts as I look to the crowd, some of them dissipating, and some of them getting up from the picnic tables in the center and walking to the stage area. Women throw their arms over their partner's necks as they start to sway with the music, slowly moving from side to side as the drums kick in, still keeping with that smooth, slow flow of a beat.

"I'm going to bring this to Rod, I'll be right back," Ellie says, holding the beer up high in her hand.

I continue standing, watching everyone dance. My eyes graze over the inside of the tent. People sit, stand, and dance around the long picnic tables. Cheers and laughter ring throughout.

"Hey!" a group of guys shout to my right and my head turns to look at them.

They all hug on a tall dark-haired man, bringing him in for handshakes and hellos. Every one of them looks my age too. I'm sure this is what Layla would want to see, so as swift as I can, I pull out my phone, nonchalantly snapping the blurriest photo of five men in a circle.

ME: Attachment 1 Image:
ME: Here. You happy?

LAYLA ARLO: Fucking
ecstatic! Plz give Mr. Tall
Dark and Handsome in the
white long sleeve my number.

I grin, beaming at the screen as I shake my head before sliding my phone into my back pocket. My head turns to the stage as the dark-skinned lead singer rips on the microphone. The soul from his voice, filling and vibrating every inch of my bones as he pours his heart through the speakers. The sweat glistens on his skin as he backs up, strumming on his white guitar. His fingers look like they're floating, gliding along each chord. His eyes squint as his shoulders raise, his whole body in tune with the music. I haven't witnessed live music like this before—full of emotion, intensity, and artistry. It's mostly been drunk karaoke at the local bar back home, whenever Layla would force me for a night out...and Rory approved.

"Kaiton!" I hear Ellie call as I turn my body toward the sound of her voice. "You haven't met Dutton yet!" she exclaims as I come face to face with her...and that familiar ripped asshole who I body slammed. Also *now* known as Layla's Mr. Tall, Dark, and Handsome.

My eyes widen when I realize I just snapped an unsolicited picture of my new boss from afar like a fucking creep.

"It's nice to finally meet you, Kaiton," he says, extending his hand.

I swallow hard, thankful that in my time of anger the other day I didn't snap at him. Only just gawked like a fucking idiot.

"Nice to meet you!" My voice unwillingly raises an octave, almost coming out in a shriek as I dart my hand to his, completely missing and smashing into the plastic, full cup of beer in his other hand. Golden liquid sloshes out, spilling down his white long-sleeve that clings to his body, turning the material nearly sheer. "Oh my God, I am so sorry," I say as my hands cover my mouth, wishing they were covering my entire face to hide the pure embarrassment running across my features.

He laughs, grinning from ear to ear with his straight, pearly white teeth. Behind his short, trimmed beard are laugh lines and those dimples I noticed before. "It's okay, this beer was warm anyway. I've been babysitting it all night." His voice is deep and rich, soothing and comforting all in one.

I still cover my mouth, wishing in this moment I could just go back home and crawl into bed. "Can I get you another?" I ask, as my hands finally fall.

"Don't worry about it, I've got like forty tokens from last year I never used. These things don't expire." He laughs again, and it sounds like a symphony playing as his Adam's apple moves with it.

"I'm really sorry." I sigh, smiling slightly in hopes he can't see the warmth I feel in my cheeks.

"It's fine, I promise," he says, his hand reaching up to my shoulder, grabbing me slightly before pulling away. "So, how's Laura treating you? She said you're learning pretty quick."

"Everything is great, yeah, really great. She's so nice, and a great teacher," I say, feeling like I'm a rambling lunatic as my hands move when I talk.

"Well, we're happy to have you, that's for sure."

The song changes to an upbeat tune as Ellie grabs my arm. "Let's go dance!" she says excitedly.

I smile at her, then at Dutton. "It was nice to meet you. You'll be here tomorrow, right?" he says as I'm getting pulled away by a very eager Ellie.

"I'm not sure!" I raise my voice, the distance between us growing larger.

"It's a battle of the businesses! I'm gonna need you on my team!" he shouts back before the sea of people on the dance floor crowd my vision of him.

Ellie twirls me around, grabbing my hand and raising it above my head. "Don't be nervous. Dutton is like a big puppy dog," she says.

"You can tell I was nervous?"

"Girl, everyone over in Helena could tell you were nervous. Your face is redder than a stop sign." She laughs, twisting me once more.

"Oh my God," I groan.

"Don't worry. That's why I got you out. He's a sweetheart, but I have a feeling you didn't come here to find love."

"Oh God, from him? No! Oh my God, did it seem like I was flirting? He's my boss! I— No way, he's just tall. I spilled his—"

"Hush now," she soothes while we lock hands, my feet following her lead. "It's all good, he didn't notice a thing. And you weren't flirting. It's getting a little hot in the tent. I'm sure that's why your face was heating up."

I can't tell if she's being serious or only saying it to calm me, but it's working. I'm not here to find love. I'm here to find myself, or whatever is left of me after Rory.

"Oh, okay." I breathe, releasing my tension with a sigh and spin her around this time.

"There ya go," she says after I twirl her. "You're getting the hang of it."

I laugh as we dance around and, in this moment, I don't have a care in the world. Sure, the stickiness and humidity are slowly rising inside of this sweatshirt and I can feel the sweat as it beads. But I'm having fun, and I don't want it to end just yet.

As we hold out for two more songs, we both agree the temperature in here is getting significantly hotter. The packed crowd and the limited space don't mix well with the late summer heat.

"Want to get some food?" she shouts, leaning toward my ear since we've danced our way to the stage. I nod my head, grinning as she smiles back and leads us out of the trenches.

Getting out from the tent feels twenty degrees cooler as the swift breeze caresses my skin and blows through my hair, chilling the sweat on the nape of my neck.

"We've got some really great options," Ellie says as we walk toward the row of carnival food in their respective trucks.

"Steak and potatoes," she says as she extends her hand out, showcasing them all. "Sausage and peppers, or about five different barbecue places. I wouldn't recommend the chicken fingers. You'll get a better bang for your buck at Neddy's."

I hum, thinking about which sounds the best. "Steak?" I say, more so in a question form because truthfully, I'd get whatever she got.

"Perfect. Me too." She smiles as I follow her to the truck, getting in line behind the twenty people already standing.

"So, there's another night of this?" I ask.

"Yes, and Sunday. Sunday is the last day, though. Tomorrow, they have a lot of activities going on. Animal showings, rodeo, more music, and a battle of the businesses where the winner gets an expensive bottle of whiskey. Thrilling, really." Ellie laughs, although the last bit seems a little more sarcastic.

"Is Hattie in that, too?"

"The battle? Hell no, she's too grown, too tired to do all that shit."

I smirk, excited to have something to do, plans for the weekend. Maybe I can meet a few new friends too, fill my time here at The Ridge. I look up at the sky, wide dashes of peach and lavender perfectly blended like a priceless painting. That's how I know the nighttime is getting ready to fall—the sky paints a pretty picture to let you know it'll be gone for a while. Gives you one last look on the day that you had. Dusk seeps all over downtown as I faintly hear the band from afar. The air is clean, crisp. I breathe it through my nose. I'm happy, content with all who surround me. I can feel the shift in my body, the pressure leaving me. My only stress in life at the moment is what I'm going to wear down here tomorrow, and

I love it. And that is a celebration that calls for steak, especially the one smothered in garlic butter that's getting handed to me right now.

CHAPTER
THIRTEEN

"LET'S GO!" Ellie screams at the top of her lungs as she holds on to the top of her cowboy hat.

The announcer calls out the next man's name as a whistle blows and the gates open. The horse bucks and leaps, trying to fling the man off as the crowd yips and hollers. His hat goes flying and his body nearly snaps in half like a dead tree branch in a storm while his arm stays up in the air, trying to keep his balance on the horse.

"Hang on!" the announcer shouts into the microphone, and another whistle blows as the horse starts to calm, the rider's body becoming less whiplashed by the second.

"He nearly took a dive." Ellie laughs.

The sun beams on my skin, sizzling my bare arms as the last rider prepares in his cage, his horse already trying to throw him off. The whistle blows and *this* rider is more composed. His tan cowboy hat stays firm on his head as he bucks his hips with the horse's rhythm. The whistle blows as we all rise on our feet, cheering as loud as we can as the pickup man helps to dismount the rider from his still-bucking horse. The crowd roars, throwing their hands up, waving their hats in the air. The energy is surreal, even with the expected smell of cattle stalls, hogs, and lamb from the small petting area. This is my first rodeo, and it certainly won't be my last. I cheer loudly, clapping my hands as they show the top three riders. Ellie sits at my side with Rodney, Hattie, and Waylon down the line next to her. We didn't get home until midnight last night because Rodney entered a pit spitting contest—spitting the pit from a cherry and seeing how far it could go. Ellie and I cheered for him but he unfortunately lost to Laura. I did high-five her though, and we laughed for an hour, dogging on Rod that a big burly man like him lost to a girl. I didn't see Dutton anymore last night—thank God, because I'm not sure how much more embarrassment I could have withstood had he seen me with a barbecue stain down the center of my Boot's Inn sweatshirt. I wanted to make a good impression on my new boss, and it didn't even take me a whole five minutes before I fucked it up.

"Wanna get some food?" Ellie asks, leaning into me.

I groan, running the flat of my hand against my stomach. "I ate two dinners last night, Ellie...*two*." I laugh.

"Well, you had to try the barbecue. I wasn't leaving until you did. But today's a new day, girlfriend."

"I'll have a lemonade for now. I'm still full from breakfast."

What I don't tell her is my breakfast was around noon, shortly after I was forced to wake up by my blasting alarm.

As we shuffle out of the bleachers, moving with the crowd, I take Hattie's hand to help her step off, making sure her little legs and walking cane don't fail her.

"Thanks, dear," she says as she brings my hand to her lips, gently kissing my knuckles before she lets me go.

"Rod, we're gonna look for some food. Take your mother by the tent, we'll meet you over there," she says loudly as she grabs my arm and starts to whisk us away.

"Jesus, Ellie, we just ate!"

"Rod, you better shut it. You know I go feral at these things."

A deep laugh escapes Rod's lips as he smiles widely at his wife. I can't help but grin at the two of them.

"Now that I think about it, I ain't even that hungry. I just really want an elephant ear," she giggles as she whispers to me.

We walk to the stand and she orders her cinnamon and sugar-coated fried bread and I get the largest lemonade they have, pumped full of lemons, copious amounts of *more* sugar, and water. My phone buzzes in the back of my jeans and I pull it out to see a text from Laura.

LAURA WRIGHT TOOLS: Battle of the businesses is starting in 10. We need you this year!!!! Meet by beer tent.

ME: On my way!

"Ellie?"

"Yeah, doll?"

"I've got to go over for the battle thing, by the beer tent. Which way was that?"

"Oh shit, that's startin' now?" she says with a mouthful of elephant ear. "Follow me." She takes off, darting past the endless trucks, stands, and tents from local vendors. We weave through people near the arena where we watched the rodeo and go around toward the back when I see the familiar white tent. The sweat is already pooling between my breasts when we finally get there. My heart races and I feel out of breath from the fast pace I maintained to keep up with Ellie, but she looks unfazed. Smiling once she sees her family, her grin spreads across her tanned cheeks, the lines creasing near her eyes and mouth. Her jeans and T-shirt fit her thin frame like paint and the sight of her standing next to Rodney is the funniest of all sights. She's so small and he's so...not.

"Kaiton!" I hear Laura call and I look over. In the distance, she's coming toward me from a large open field with multiple tents, tables, and folding lawn chairs.

"I'll be back," I say to the Boone family.

"We'll be there in a bit to watch, good luck!" Ellie says.

I have no idea what I'm about to be doing, nor why I need such luck. But I'm assuming I'll soon find out.

I shove my hands in my back pockets as I walk up to Laura.

"Alright, I'm gonna explain some things really quick," she says as I walk with her toward the field. "This is a battle of the businesses. Almost all local businesses here in Falton Ridge participate. The Wright Tools has only won once before, and that was six years ago. Each business gets to designate four constants. But I heard Ma's Cafe only has three this year, so that might be a huge advantage for us."

"Who's our fourth?" I interrupt accidentally.

"Dutton's friend, Colby. He's our delivery driver. Even though he only works twice a week." She laughs. "Anyway, there's usually three big events. You go head-to-head with another business, single elimination style. The winner gets a six-hundred-dollar bottle of whiskey this year, plus bragging rights. And trust me, would we brag." Her laugh continues, infectious enough for me to start giggling too.

"Alright, let's do this, then," I say, determined to make a better impression on the boss this time.

I follow Laura and we find Dutton standing next to a man of similar height who I recognize as one of the friends from the photo I sent to Layla. A photo that I may or may not have analyzed in bed last night until my eyes felt heavy.

"Kaiton!" Dutton cheers when he sees me, his eyes lighting up as he throws his hands in the air. "This is Colby, he's our truck driver."

"Nice to meet you." I shake his hand. Thankfully, he's not holding a beer I could spill.

"Battle of the Businesses will start in five minutes!" an announcer says, his voice nearly muffled from being so close to the microphone.

The crowd starts to gather, sitting in their folding chairs, some underneath tents with coolers.

"Alright, listen," Dutton says as he wraps his arms around his employees' necks, fitting us in the crooks of his elbows. We form a small huddle, fitting Colby in as we tuck our heads in together. "We've got to win this year. If I have to hear one more person from Neddy's talk about how they're reigning champs, I'm going to lose it. Also, I want the whiskey."

"You're sharing that, right?" Colby chimes in.

"Yeah, sure, Colby," Dutton replies with a mischievous grin.

"Wright Tools on three," Dutton says as he places his hand in the middle. Laura lays her hand on top of his, Colby next, and finally, mine on top. I've had two shifts at this place, but it does feel nice to be included.

"One, two, three," Dutton counts as we all chime in together.

"Wright Tools!" we shout as our hands raise.

"Let's kick some ass!" Laura adds and I laugh to myself. Everything I thought I knew about Laura—the sweet, innocent grandma—has been a complete facade as I've seen her chug more beers than most men here at the festival. Not to mention her grand win as "Pit Spittin' Champ" last night. And now, her "let's kick some ass"attitude. Laura's ready to win. And I'm all here for it.

Four men dressed in referee costumes emerge from a tent. One has a whistle wrapped around his neck, another with a cowboy hat on, all four of them already visibly drunk. The announcer stands beside them and we join the rest of the groups while the crowd envelops us on all sides. I wave to the woman resembling Layla who works at the flower shop and she waves back before the announcer starts once again, his lips brushing the microphone as he mumbles into it.

"Welcome to our fifty-seventh annual Battle of the Businesses! Our first game requires a set of special skills—speed, precision, and teamwork, just to name a few. The name of the first game is flip cup," he finishes like he's announcing a WWE match and the crowd roars and cheers. "Bitterroot Blooms"—he pauses—"and The Wright Tools, you're our first contenders." The cheers grow louder as I look to my right, noticing Ellie and Rodney sitting in the grass. Hattie and Waylon are in folding chairs beside them. They wave to me and I flash a smile, trying to mask the nervousness forming at the bottom of my stomach.

"Please take your marks," the announcer says as he waves his hands, pointing us toward the long white tables with perfectly spaced red Solo cups.

My stomach twists and turns and I'm feeling less and less confident about my good impression I wanted to make.

"We got this," Dutton assures us as we walk over.

Laura stands at the end while I take the spot next to her. Dutton fits in to my right, and Colby next to him. As I look down, I see my cup is already filled with beer. My heart pounds and I can feel my palms start to sweat. I heat up like I'm being blasted in direct sunlight as Dutton bounces up and down next to me, pumping himself up. He smiles and laughs as he jumps and I tilt my chin to look up at him, a distraught look cast upon my face.

"Dutton," I loud-whisper.

"Yeah?" He flashes me a smile, still bouncing.

"I don't drink."

"You what?" he says, not able to hear my low tone. He still bounces, taking audible breaths as he gets hyped.

"I don't really drink," I say again, only this time a little louder.

He looks at me with that wide grin, then looks ahead, doing a double-take back at me as his eyes widen and his smile fades to shock.

"Uh." He pauses. "Okay, this is what we're gonna do," he says as he places both hands on my shoulders, his palms nearly covering the entirety of them with their size. He leans down, looking at me eye to eye, his face close to mine. "I'm going to drink yours too, but the second I slam it down, you have to flip it. Have you played flip cup before?"

My heart pounds. "Once, in like eleventh grade."

"Just bring the cup to the edge, let it hang off a bit, and flip it lightly, okay? Just be really gentle. Take your time, ease into it. You've got this."

"Okay." I nod.

The smile returns to his face while he keeps his hands on me, and it doesn't go unnoticed that this time, his touch isn't sending firing signals of displeasure against my skin. His dark green eyes stay focused on mine as he straightens up and flips his baseball cap backward. The ends of his wavy dark hair curl up underneath from the length.

"Everyone in position?" the announcer asks, standing near the head of the table, a referee on either side, getting ready to watch our every move. Dutton whispers to the ref with the cowboy hat behind us. I can't hear much, but I think he's letting him know he'll be drinking my cup too. From the corner of my eye, I see him give the okay and feel slightly better about the possible cheating we're about to do. "The rules of the game are simple," the announcer says, looking from left to right at the crowd on either side. The whole setup reminds me of a really large backyard party and the excitement rises inside of me as the announcer continues. "Starting at this end"—he points to Laura and the woman across from her—"contestants will drink the entirety of the cups in front of them, once empty, the cups need to be flipped top-side down on the table. Then, the next contestant on the team can go. First team to finish wins the round. Remember, folks, this battle is single elimination. Are we ready?" We all cheer and clap. Then he starts the countdown and my stomach knots. Dutton elbows me and I look up at him.

"You ready?" he whispers as he leans in. I flash him a weary smile and in a second, the whistle blows.

Laura gulps her drink, chugging as fast as she can before she slams the solo cup down, bringing it to the edge of the white table as she crouches slightly, trying to get a good angle on the cup as she flicks at it. It falls repeatedly on its side, but her contender still isn't finished with her drink yet.

"Come on, Laura!" I cheer for her while Dutton and Colby do the same.

Everyone yells, clapping and shouting for their favorite team to win. I hear the Boones chanting "Wright Tools" over and over again and then...Laura's cup flips upside down. She looks at me quickly, shouting in excitement as she does it. Without hesitation, Dutton grabs my cup, bringing it to his lips for merely five seconds before it's slammed down in front of me. I bring it to the edge and try to flip it right side up with my fingers.

"Hey! That's cheating!" the guy in front of me shouts, but it doesn't matter. I keep trying to land the flip.

The slurring referee behind me explains that I don't drink, and all is forgiven as the guy across from me starts to chug. My hands shake—he's catching up.

"Just take your time, you got this," Dutton murmurs at the side of my face, his breath nearly touching my cheek as he crouches down to my level, placing his hands on his knees.

I take a deep breath, moving the cup slightly over the edge as I push it up from the bottom. It flips...and sticks.

"Yes!" Laura shouts.

And it doesn't take Dutton any time before his own cup is to his lips. Some beer runs down the side of his mouth, dripping from his chiseled jaw as he takes each gulp. It only takes him two or three tries before his cup is fully flipped and now it all lies with Colby.

"Come on, Colby!" I shout.

Laura, watching from behind me, nearly punctures my eardrums with her shrieks. We've only got a small lead on the flower shop but my God, I hope we win. I clap so hard my hands start to sting and I know by the end of tonight, my voice is going to be gone. Colby and his opponent go head-to-head, trying to flip their cups at the same time. The game lies solely on them and all it takes is one misstep from Layla before her cup is on the ground, giving Colby an advantage. He flips once more and lands it.

"Let's go!" Dutton shouts, grabbing Colby and hoisting him inches off the ground.

I glance at Laura and we scream, hugging each other before we're turned back around to give Dutton high fives. The energy is unmatched, and in this moment, I couldn't care less about the losing team's feelings as they sulk off under a tent.

"The Wright Tools wins!" the announcer exclaims into the mic and the crowd roars.

We go take a seat in the grass as he announces the next two teams to go, and we chat while they get set up, relishing in our win. All of us watch as they start, taking note of the convenience store's competition and Neddy's contestants, sizing them up.

"Those fuckers," Laura says under her breath as Neddy's takes a clear win, miles ahead of the convenience store.

Only two more teams to go before we move on to the next round, and we sit and wait patiently as they get set up. Dutton is to my right, arms resting on his tall, scrunched legs, and Laura to my left, sitting criss-cross in the grass like me. Dutton and Colby chat, while I continually glance over at him, hoping to catch his eye. Eventually, I do.

"Thank you, by the way, for drinking my beer." I smile and tilt my head up to his. Even sitting, he's taller in stature than I am.

"It's really no problem at all. I'm sorry, I should have asked before forcing you into this. I hope you're not uncomfortable. The rest of the games are drinking-related so honestly, if you need to, you can bow out right now. I don't want to put you into any situation you're not comfortable with." His tone grows softer, sweeter, as he speaks.

"I'm not uncomfortable at all, I promise. I just don't really like alcohol. And I haven't drank in so long I have no idea what it would even do to me. Honestly, I'd probably just be really sick." I laugh. "But I promise, it's nothing that I can't be around, I just wasn't really allowed to, so it hasn't been something I've been interested in for a while."

"Not allowed to?" he asks before the crowd's cheers and screams become prominent enough that both our attentions shoot to the table where the post office has just been eliminated.

"The Wright Tools, Neddy's, and Ma's Cafe are our top three finalists. If you could please meet me in the middle here, we can begin our next elimination round," the announcer states through the microphone as he moves away from the folding table covered with red Solo cups. We all rise and I extend my hand to Laura to help her up from the ground before we make our way to the middle of the open area. Three baseball bats are lined up, lying flat in the grass as we approach. "This game is called "The Spins." Our volunteers are filling your cups right now," he says as he points to the left. My gaze follows his finger, where two people are filling Solo cups from a keg under a tent. "Each contestant per team will empty the contents of their cup, race down here to these bats, crouch down, rest their forehead on the handle, and spin ten consecutive times. First two teams to have every member complete their turn wins. Since Ma's Cafe only has three contestants, we ask the two remaining teams to please eliminate one person from this activity. I'll give you a few minutes to decide," he continues.

We form another circle, huddling up close as I offer myself first. "I can sit out this one since I don't drink."

"Deal," Colby says.

"Sounds good," Laura chimes in while Dutton nods.

"Let's break on three again so the other teams know we came here to win," Dutton says seriously.

We all laugh and throw our hands in the center. "Wright Tools!" we shout as we raise them up high to the sky.

"You know I would have drunk yours again," Dutton says as he walks backward to face me.

"I know. I thought I'd give you a little break."

"Well, I like beer. So, I don't mind." He shrugs. His smile is infectious, just like everyone else's, and he lets me see it for a while until he turns back around, heading to his post.

I go sit at the end with the bats, claiming my spot with the additional Neddy's employee. Everyone takes their place, and the referees get a quick drink in before they join, ready to count the spins. The announcer hops back on the microphone and the whistle blows. Dutton grabs the first cup, chugging for what only seems like seconds before he's running down toward me, smiling before he grabs the bat. He crouches low, bringing the end of the handle to his forehead, and spins. The two others catch up, spinning at the same time, and it's officially a race. Dutton darts back, dizzy and nearly slipping on the grass before he gets back to the start. Laura's next, drinking as fast as she can before she's headed to me. My stomach tightens at the thought of her slipping and falling but she handles her way back gracefully. Swaying from side to side, sure, but never misstepping for a fall. Colby is last, running like a bat out of hell after he slams the cup to the ground. We're one solid player ahead of Ma's so I know we're going to make it to the next round. That is, until Colby slips and falls on his way back.

"Ooh!" the crowd hollers.

We all laugh at the sight. Colby trying to stand after going down is like watching a baby giraffe learning how to walk and I swear both of his legs shoot straight up while his back is flat on the grass, but he's quick on his feet. He's back behind the starting line before anyone else. I scream with joy and clap my hands as the three of them hug at the start. Neddy's comes in second, and Ma's is officially eliminated.

"I need a break from chugging." Laura breathes, making her way over to me. Her shirt is riddled with wet specks from dripping beer, but a broad, toothy grin is stuck on her face.

"Our championship round will begin right now, with our infamous game of beer pong," the announcer says into the microphone, announcing like he's in front of a live audience on a game show. Only, this live audience has been drinking since nine in the morning and they've been stuck in the heat. Half of the men aren't wearing shirts, and half of the ladies are lying on blankets in the shade. "This championship round will consist of two players, but we do have one rule—one player *must* be the owner of the business they are representing. The other may be designated by the rest of the team. Once you have chosen, take your place at the table," he states.

"I'm still fuckin' dizzy." Colby laughs as we form our huddle once more, though this time, it's slightly less circular and more spaced as Laura tries not to get sick and Colby still wobbles.

"I can do it," I offer. "If you don't mind—"

"I'll drink yours. Let's do this." Dutton smiles.

Our "one, two, three" break is slightly less enthusiastic than the first two, but it gets the job done before Dutton and I take our places at the long folding table. Cups are already set up in a pyramid, filled halfway with that familiar golden liquid.

"Here are the house rules you need to know," the announcer starts as Neddy's finishes taking their place across from us. "No pulling cups until the turn is over. If a ball lands in your cup, you drink it. Bouncing is two cups. If a ball rolls back to you, the trick shot is behind the back. Any questions during, our refs will help you sort it. Are you ready?" We all cheer. "Heads or tails, Wright Tools?" he asks.

I look at Dutton.

"You pick," he says as he tilts his chin down to look at me.

"Tails," I say quietly.

"Tails!" he shouts, and the announcer flips the coin high in the air, slamming in down on his fist once it lands.

"It's tails," he drags out, lips pressed directly to the microphone as the crowd around us hollers.

"Good pick," Dutton mumbles and elbows me. The ref hands us two orange balls and the whistle blows. "You want to go first or want me to?"

"You," I demand.

I am in no way athletic. My hand-eye coordination leaves a lot to be desired. I would hate to royally fuck this up, so I'm going to do everything I can to relax and focus. Or at least just try and make it into *one* cup.

Back and forth we throw, Dutton making the first couple shots. We laugh, they drink, and Dutton and I surprise them by bouncing both of our balls at the same time, a tactic I suggested. I make the cup, my first out of the million it seems Dutton has. But a bounce counts for two. Dutton cheers as his face lights up, and I feel I finally contributed to this round. We have one Solo cup left while they still have four on our side. Dutton holds out the orange ball, extending his arm to me as it rests in his fingertips.

"Blow on it." He grins.

"For what?" I ask as the side of my lip curls up, my eyebrows twisted in confusion.

"It's good luck," he states.

I look at him through my lashes before leaning slightly over, puckering my lips before I gently blow on the ball. His grin never fades, and he brings it to his lips, blowing on it after me. He focuses, his eyes darting right to the prize as he takes an audible breath before releasing the ball from his grasp. It flies, almost in slow motion, before it sinks right in the center of the cup.

"Yes!" I shout as the crowd cheers.

I line up my shot. If I magically make this, the game is over. We win. *No pressure, Kaiton.* I close my eyes for a moment, trying to pretend I'm focusing even though I don't know what I'm doing and if I do make it, it will be because of luck alone. Once my eyes dart open, I hold the ball up, pinching it between my fingers, bend my knees, and release the ball as I spring up. It hits the rim of the Solo cup, plopping right into the beer.

"Fuck yeah!" Dutton shouts as he grabs me by the side, lifting me up slightly from the ground. His hand on me briefly does something to my mind again. I shudder at the reminder of Rory gripping my wrist so tightly that my skin turned purple. I can hear him in my head right now, the threats he made. How his eyes changed when he did it. No, no. I can't let him take this from me. I won't.

I shake it off.

I made it.

I really just fucking made that.

"We won?" I ask as I look back at Dutton.

"We fucking won!" he cheers.

The crowd goes wild, the Boone family cheering louder than anyone as we shake all of the contestants' hands. The bottle of whiskey is brought out, and Dutton holds it up like the Stanley Cup. We gather around, taking every photo needed for the town paper.

This is certainly a better impression than last night, and now I get to celebrate a much-deserved win with my new coworkers, friends, and town.

CHAPTER
FOURTEEN

I NEVER MINDED Monday mornings at work, but this past weekend was the fullest my social life has ever been. Especially since I didn't have someone telling me what I *could* and *could not* do. I did, however, stay home all day yesterday, recharging that social battery by sitting on my dock most of the day, admiring the cool blue shades of the water.

Today is my first time closing by myself, although I think someone is going to come in to help with the shipment we have coming. Most of the customers today have only needed piping and paint, two things I feel well versed in. So, it's been a very simple four hours. It's not really busy here, which doesn't help pass the time, especially with limited service and the only thing in my view being rows of shelving full of tools and hardware. The front door bells chime and I turn to look.

"How's it goin'?" Dutton asks while walking in.

"Good, kind of slow today."

"Everyone's probably recovering from the weekend," he jokes. "Colby should be here any minute. I came to help haul it in. Fertilizer can get pretty heavy after the tenth bag you bring to the stockroom."

"Thanks, I appreciate that."

Dutton walks to the counter, setting his phone down as Colby pulls up. I move from behind the front desk, following him out while we head to the back of the truck.

"I've got twenty-two bags here. Concrete's coming Wednesday," Colby says, handing Dutton the receipt. His eyes glaze over the sheet of paper, following the lines of black ink that show his purchases.

"Alright, let's get it in," Dutton says and folds it up, shoving it in the back pocket of his dark blue jeans.

Colby returns to the driver's seat, door open, leg hanging out as he analyzes his clipboard, checking off boxes while Dutton grabs the first fifty-pound bag. The muscles in his sun-kissed arm flex tightly, showing their true size. His short sleeve hugs against his biceps, snug as he throws the bag over his shoulder. He flashes me a quick grin before walking into the store. I pull on a bag, dragging it to the end of the truck, feeling the weight of what I'm about to carry. I fist both sides in my hands, lifting it to my chest, and push it up a little higher with the top of my knee. I grunt, hugging tightly onto the bag as I bring it inside.

"Just set them here, we can bring them into the stockroom after," Dutton instructs, pointing to the back wall.

I grunt again as the fertilizer starts to slip, and I shuffle my feet faster, plopping it on the ground next to the one Dutton brought in. I repeat this daunting task five times, but thankfully, Dutton brings in the most. My arms redden from the pinching of my skin on the slipping bags. Dutton shuts the back of the truck, banging on it twice before Colby pulls off. The bells chime as he walks in, and now we have to move everything to the stockroom. Luckily, I can just drag these the short distance they need to go. Dutton opens the stockroom door, placing the folding chair against it as a door stopper. I drag the first bag in and he hauls two at a time, setting them on the bottom black shelving unit we have back here. I drag the bags of fertilizer, one after the other, until I'm the only one moving them, while he stacks them on higher shelves, lifting with his legs as he hikes them up. The sweat beads at my hairline as I walk back out, groaning at the five bags I have left. I grab onto one, yanking it backward as it drags in front of me. My back aches as I keep pulling, hunched over in the same position I've been in for the last half hour or so. I tug at it harder as I get into the stockroom, but one last pull sends the fertilizer to the right, nicking the side of the chair and pushing it out of the way. The stockroom door closes before my brain can register that I should stop it. And now, in this moment, I realize we're locked in here.

"Shit!" I mutter.

"Shit." Dutton follows, running to the door, pulling and tugging on it to open.

His hand nearly slaps his forehead as he huffs.

"We're stuck. Do you have your phone?" he says quickly.

My hands fly to my back pockets, patting around until I feel the bulky end of it. I grab it, taking it out quickly before I hand it to him. He holds it up, moving it around for service.

"Fuck," he drags out.

"I'm sorry," I say quietly.

"It's not your fault," he says, not making eye contact with anything other than the phone he's trying to get signal on. "I should have gotten this door fixed a long time ago."

I stand slumped on my back leg and cross my arms against my chest. He paces back and forth, moving the phone around at all angles.

"Nothing." He sighs as he hands the phone back to me.

"Do you have yours?"

"My phone's out there." He points to the closed door.

Panic starts to set in. Being back here for even a short while is miserable. No air flow, no air conditioning, no windows—every time I open the door to come back here, a thick wall of humid heat hits me in the face. I can't imagine what it's going to feel like being stuck in here for a long period of time. Dutton paces a bit, his hands to his head as he tries to think. My mind is blank, forming no thoughts other than my impending doom of death by dehydration and heat stroke. He stomps back to the door, pounding on it repeatedly, shouting "hello," trying to make any noise for someone who might be on the other side. But we're the only ones here right now. I glance at the phone in my hand, checking the time. One hour until close—one hour for a miraculous angel to walk in the store and save us.

"Don't overexert yourself." My tone remains quiet as I try to stop Dutton from getting out of breath pounding on the door. "Maybe we can listen for the bells, and hope a customer comes through to let us out."

Dutton finally slows on the hits, and just for the sake of it, I try to dial Laura's number. "Call failed" immediately pops up on my screen and I try, and try again, repeatedly getting the same message.

"Goddamn it." Dutton sighs, sliding down the door, sitting at the foot of it. "It's already fucking hot in here."

"I know," I say, my hands waving at my face, trying to accumulate any sort of breeze to help keep my platinum strands from sticking to my forehead with sweat.

I sit across from him, leaning my back against the long built-in shelves. We remain silent for a moment, listening for any signs of life outside this faulty door. The heat rises under my shirt. My sweat is making the cotton material stick to my armpits. I'm uncomfortable, and the sweat stains are becoming visible through my shirt at nearly every crevice. I still fiddle with my phone, trying to call Laura, even dialing the emergency line multiple times, to no avail. I was under the impression a call to the police would go through, even with no signal. Apparently, my phone did not get that memo.

"So, uh, Laura told me you're from Illinois. How do you like it there?" Dutton says after a while. I guess sitting in silence isn't really his thing.

"Um, it's fine," I say, still messing with my phone.

"How come you moved here?"

"I, uh," I stutter as I look at him, my hand falling to my side as I set the phone down. "I needed to get away. Just...not a good situation."

"I'm sorry to hear that."

"Don't be, it's not your fault."

"I know that, but still—I'm sorry you went through something where you felt leaving your home was the only option."

"Yeah, I—" his words hit me like a truck full of bricks slamming the breaks to a dead stop. I come head-to-head with the blatant realization all over again. I can feel the prick of the tears stinging behind my eyes, but I refuse to let them fall any more over this. I swallow hard, trying to contain myself from another meltdown I feel is on the way. I clear my throat. "It's a long story."

"Well," he says softly. "We've got the time if you want to talk about it."

The temperature in my body only rises, and the sticky sweat clinging my shirt to my skin only gets worse. I take a deep breath, deciding now is as good of time as any to face the music.

The question isn't if I *want* to talk about it, though. It's *can* I? I've been running from it long enough and that's worked for me. Why not just keep running?

"It's complicated."

"That's life, isn't it? Come on now, what happened?" His eyes do something then, as if he's somehow known from the start—my short lease, my two-month job plans, skirting around all the *why* questions.

"I was going to get married this fall," I say as I tuck my lips in, stopping the grimace that wants to form on my features. "I am *no longer* getting married this fall."

Dutton tilts his chin and his mouth opens slightly, presumably understanding the urge to leave. He gives a casual shrug. "Fall weddings are overrated. Mind if I ask what happened?"

"He, uh...well, I guess he cheated on me."

"You guess?"

"I found evidence, he admitted to it, and I...left."

"You didn't want to stay in Illinois?"

"He didn't really give me a choice," I say as I swallow down the lump lodged in my throat. "He sort of threatened me..."

"Sort of?" His body shifts, his eyes widening while his gaze sinks into me. It slipped out. I hadn't meant to say it. He doesn't need to know everything.

"Yeah." I breathe. "Just not a good situation."

"Does he know you're here?" he asks somewhat timidly.

"No," I answer flatly.

He nods, taking my words in. "When we were talking on Saturday, you said you weren't really *allowed* to drink...Was he the one who wouldn't allow you?"

I only nod, no words slipping from my lips this time.

"That fucking douchebag," he mumbles to himself, barely loud enough for me to hear him. He exhales loudly, blowing out all the air in his lungs. "It's really fucking hot in here," he says, trying to change the subject. He lifts his shirt up slightly, unsticking it from his body. I shift my eyes away, not wanting to get caught staring at my boss's deep V that has just presented itself. He's chiseled right at his hip, but it's cut entirely too deep. I don't even know what exercises one must do to get that sort of look.

I pinch my shirt between my fingers, holding it away from my body to get some airflow underneath. I pulse it back and forth, creating a whirlwind of air through the neck and bottom hem of the shirt.

"So, how long have you lived here?" I ask, trying to strike up a conversation directed more toward *his* life rather than mine.

"All my life," he replies. "Born and raised here."

"You like it?" I ask and raise my brows.

"Love it, wouldn't trade it for the world. The views, the people, the lake..."

"The lake is really nice." I grin.

"You've been?"

"I live on it," I say. His eyes widen as his smile beams under rose-colored, heat-filled cheeks. "I'm renting the house at the top of the hill on Bear Run Drive."

"The small white one?" he asks curiously.

"That's the one." I nod my head.

"I built that back deck years ago, shit...I had to be...twenty-two. Probably looks like ass now. I had no idea what I was doing back then." He laughs.

"It's still holding up. God, I would kill to be in that lake right now," I say, fanning myself again to try and move the humid heat around.

"You and me both," he says, slouching down further as his T-shirt drags up, exposing more of his built frame underneath. "Damn it." He sighs as he lifts the hem up, wiping the pellets of sweat beaded on his face.

"It's like a fucking sauna," I add, trying to shift my body, lying flat on the concrete floor. "Oh, this is nice," I say as the cool touch of the concrete caresses my exposed skin. I turn my head, watching as he follows, lying flat on the ground next to me.

"You're so smart," he says before we both recline in silence, staring up at the ceiling. I only smile slightly, not responding, before I hear a faint sound of the bells.

We both shoot up. Dutton is first on his feet, pounding on the door as he yells.

"In here!" he shouts as his fist bangs on the brown metal door.

I move in next to him, pounding both of mine flat on the cold surface. "Hello!" I call, and only a few more seconds pass before the door opens and an elderly man stands before us.

The rush of the cool air conditioning hits my face and I'm filled with relief as I take a deep breath.

"Robert!" Dutton cheers as he grabs the man's shoulders lightly. "You saved our lives." He laughs.

"What the hell you doin' in there?" The old man chuckles as he and Dutton walk away from the stockroom. I hear Dutton mumble to him, but it feels like all my blood is rushing to my head. My body is cooling down at lightning speed and I just relish in the cold. I watch as Dutton helps the man pick out a garden hose and brings him to the counter, checking him out when I suddenly realize *I'm* the one on the clock here. *I* should be doing this. I turn around, remembering there's still fertilizer to be brought back. I open the cursed stockroom door and place the chair in front as a door stopper once more, this time being overly cautious to not even get near it. I drag a bag back, leaning it up against the shelving and continue to the next bag before Dutton calls after me.

"Kaiton! You go home, I'll do this. I'll lock it up."

"You sure?" I take a deep breath as I drop the fertilizer bag out of my grasp, wiping the sweat dripping from my forehead.

"I'm sure. Go jump in that lake." He grins.

I huff once more, out of breath and overly exerted. I'm not going to say no to the boss, that's for sure.

"Alright, well, you're more than welcome to jump in too when you're done. You know where I live," I say as I head for the front door.

"You serious?"

"Why not?" I lean against the door, pushing it open while my gaze is still fastened on his. His dopey smile rests on his lips while each strand of his wavy hair is laced with sweat, and I leave the store before he can reply.

My heart palpitations nearly burst through my chest, hopefully from the extreme heat conditions I was just in and not the invitation I just extended that could have come across as anything more than what it was.

A simple invite.

And not at all flirting.

CHAPTER
FIFTEEN

WHILE I'D BEEN scrambling to grab my belongings back home, a bathing suit had not been on the forefront of my mind, although I wish it had been. I flip through the dresser drawer, finding a couple sports bras that I could swim in. I hold them up, debating on a black, deep V-neck, or a baby blue square neck. I stop mid-thought as I realize—why the fuck does it matter which one I wear? I'm not trying to impress anyone. And Dutton probably isn't going to come here anyway. It's already been a half an hour since I've been home. If he was coming, he should have been here by now. I scoff as I throw the baby blue bra back into my drawer, tossing on a pair of spandex shorts before heading outside through my sliding glass door. The blades of grass tickle between my toes until I get to the rocks just before the dock. I carefully step over, putting light pressure on each foot as the jagged and uneven stone crunches underneath me. I step onto the wooden dock, and it doesn't take a second thought before I start to sprint, jumping right off the end into the deep blue water. The rush of the cold swarms over my body, sending me in somewhat of a shock. I spring up out of the water, gasping for a breath before I involuntarily laugh, a full-on belly laugh. I haven't felt this free since...ever. I haven't felt this fucking alive.

And what a time to be alive, it is.

"You laughing by yourself back here?" Dutton calls as he walks down the hill, grabbing his shirt at the hem before lifting up over his head.

"Yep!" I shout back, the water spraying from my lips as it drips down from my slicked back hair.

"You got room for one more?" he asks as he gets closer, stepping over the rocks before he hits the dock.

"Yep!" I say again, smiling, and wave my arms under the water while kicking my legs back and forth to stay afloat.

He makes it to the end of the dock, his bare chest completely exposed as he gets ready to jump. His frame is wide, his stomach muscles on full display as they tense up. He's carved, completely sculpted like an ancient Greek warrior statue on display at the museum back home. He backs up slightly, getting ready to run right off the dock before I call after him.

"Wait!" I shout.

"What?"

"You can't swim in jeans!"

"Why not?"

"Are you a serial killer? Only serial killers would swim with jeans on." I laugh, as does he.

"Kaiton, I didn't wear my swim trunks to work today, unfortunately."

"Suit yourself," I say. "Serial killer," I mumble.

He scoffs for a moment, rolling his eyes jokingly. "Turn around," he says as he waves his index finger in a circle.

I turn my body in the water, shouting to him from behind me, "I didn't mean to jump in naked!"

"I'm not! These boxers are a little small, okay? I'm self-conscious!" He laughs again, only kidding, I hope.

That man should not feel one ounce of shame for the way he looks. I roll my eyes and grin, even though he can't see me, and before I know it, I'm splashed. The biggest wave emanates from his cannonball when he plunges in right next to me. His head pops up out of the water, and he slicks his hair back like mine. Water droplets run down his face, off his long black eyelashes to the bottom of his full lips. His trimmed beard glistens with the water as he stretches his mouth open, curling it up into a wide smile.

"It's fucking cold." His voice almost shivers.

"It feels good after a minute," I say.

"It's fine. We nearly died today from heat stroke, why not shock our bodies some more?" he says as he lays his body flat in the water, trying to float on his back.

"We were in there for *maybe* half an hour."

"Yeah, nearly died, Kaiton," he banters back in a playful tone.

I can't do anything but laugh as I let my head fall back, touching the cool water once more.

"You should really get that door fixed," I say, tilting my chin back down to look at him.

He swims closer to me, out of the floating position he was in. "I'll have you know, I already called a locksmith, thank you very much."

We stay close together, kicking our feet beneath the dark blue water, waving our hands at our sides to stay afloat. Eyes locked, swimming merely inches away. I swallow hard, my mouth suddenly dryer than sandpaper. "Well, that's good," I whisper, mostly to myself, but he's so close, I know he can hear. The only sound between us is our breath, mixed with the rustling of trees and the birds inside of them. My heart thumps hard through my chest and I don't know why I'm suddenly that same ball of nerves I was back at the beer tent.

"I'm getting cold," I lie.

"Me too, it'll get dark soon anyway." He looks up at the sky.

"Fuck," I mumble, starting to swim closer to shore.

"What?" he calls behind me.

"I didn't bring a towel out." I push myself out of the water and he follows suit next to me. "Hurry, run!" I look at him and smile before I take off. Sprinting on the grass, I run up the steps to my back porch he supposedly built, and through the slider door. He's right behind me, tailing me as we laugh together. It's *cold*. Colder than the first shock of the water. The wind on my wet skin causes tiny goosebumps to form all across it. We stand in my kitchen dripping wet. "Wait here," I say before I tiptoe to the bathroom, my arms nearly frozen at my sides as I waddle and grab two towels for us.

"Why's it so dark in here?" he calls out to me.

I wrap a towel around my body before answering. "I don't know how to change those." My voice carries through the house as I walk out of the bathroom and point to the recessed lighting above.

I toss him a towel, bringing my own to my face to wipe off the remaining beads of water.

"I can change those if you want." He bends down, wiping his legs clear of water, bringing the towel to his chest next. I keep my eyes fixated on his, not looking any place I shouldn't.

"That'd be great. Whenever you have the time. No rush or anything."

"I'm sure I've got the bulbs in my truck. I can change them now."

"In your truck?"

"Yes." He laughs. "I've got a mini version of Wright Tools in there."

"I mean, if you don't mind—"

"I don't mind at all," he interjects as he rakes his hands through his hair, tousling his wet tresses so they don't lay flat on his head. He grabs his shirt from the counter where he set it, pulling it over him before he wraps the towel around his waist. "I'll be right back," he says as he walks past me to the front door. Even after the lake, the faint smell of his woody cologne still lingers.

The screen door slams and I quickly glance around, running to the counter to throw away my empty takeout boxes. I scoot over to the dining table, clearing the dirty plate I had left out from last night, and throw it in the sink, careful not to break the porcelain. I run to the living room, picking up the blanket that fell to the floor earlier, and throw it into my bedroom like a Hail Mary pass in the playoffs. The second it lands on my bed, my front door swings open again. I stand up straight, just about out of breath as he walks back in. Not noticing a thing, he grabs a dining chair and places it underneath the lights, opening one box before he climbs on it. He stretches upward, twisting the bulb, and his shirt raises, showing that strip of skin I tried hard to avoid minutes ago. He moves the chair to the next light, twisting the bulb out of that one in the same fashion.

"Shit," he mumbles as the towel slips from his waist. He grabs it in time before it falls completely but the loud slap of my hand covering my eyes directed enough attention to me.

He laughs deeply when he speaks. "Kaiton, it's okay. I still have my boxers on."

"It's good. You're good. Don't worry," I say, my hand still covering my eyes, squeezing down so hard I'm seeing stars behind my lids.

"You can look now."

I move my fingers slightly, peeking through the sliver of space as my vision becomes clearer. His towel is firmly back in place around his waist. He replaces the last bulb, getting off the chair one last time before he moves it back to the dining table and flicks on the light.

"So much better," I say as the light fills my tiny kitchen.

He moves slowly, picking up the empty boxes, and discards them in the trash can next to my kitchen counter. I watch as his focus shifts back to me and notice how his eyes trail down the length of my body. His tongue barely pushes through his lips as he wets them, pulling in his bottom one delicately with his teeth before his gaze returns to my eyes. The silence falls so thick between us that I can practically feel it on my skin.

"Well, I should get going," he says, his expression falling slightly. "Thanks for the invitation." He points to the lake.

"Anytime," I say, pressing my lips in a tight smile. "Thanks for"—I point to the ceiling—"that."

"Anytime," he mimics my response with a curt nod. "I'll uh…see you at work." He gives me a half-ass smile and a swallow so deep I can see his Adam's apple rise and fall.

I follow behind when he walks out the door, making it to his truck before I call after him.

"Have a good night!" I yell with a wave.

He sticks his hand in the air with a wave back, then gets into his blacked-out Chevy, and I'm left standing on my porch listening to his tires spin against the gravel, wondering why in the world that got so awkward, so fast.

CHAPTER
SIXTEEN

"LET ME GET THIS STRAIGHT," Layla says on the other end of the line as I watch her eyebrows pinch together, puzzled with what I'm telling her over FaceTime. "You get locked in a hot sauna of a room for almost an hour with *my* Mr. Tall, Dark, and Handsome, who just so happens to be your new boss. Then you invite him to swim in the lake with you and he does, stripping down to his boxers and all..."

"Yes?" I say with a pitch to my tone. When she puts it like that, it sounds much worse than it was.

"And then what?" she says after a long pause, ready for the rest.

"Then nothing. I mean, he helped me change the lightbulbs in here. Didn't you notice it's all nice and bright for us right now?" I laugh.

"And then?"

"And then he left."

"You didn't like, invite him to stay?"

"Why the fuck would I do that, Layla?" I scoff, still with a smile on my face but shaking my head at her words.

What is she expecting me to do here? This man is my boss, not forgetting the fact that just ten fucking days ago I was engaged. The entire thing is still confusing for me, and I haven't even begun to process the emotions that come with it.

"Kaiton, let's be real here."

"I am—"

"You are not." She cuts me off. "You are in an entirely different state, starting a new chapter of your life. You have spent too many wasted years on a relationship that did nothing but tear you down. Live a fucking little, would ya? You got a hot-ass man in your house and—"

"My boss, Layla." I cut her off this time. "He's my boss. And I am not a person who just goes out and...fucks people, okay?"

"Exactly," she snaps. "You're the girl who lives in the same apartment her whole life and works at a job where she's safe with all the same people every day—"

"Layla!"

"Everything has this...*order* for you. Everything needs to be predictable. I had to convince you to go on your own honeymoon!"

"Okay, I get it! I've been with two people, Layla, *two*. You know this. Now please, just drop it. It was nothing, it was friendly, he's my boss, and I work for him. End of fucking story. I'm done with this," I say, my tone growing more and more demanding as I finish.

"Okay, okay, I'm done. Won't mention it again." Her voice borders on defensive, and I know I need to apologize. Because she's right, she's so right. I've spent years living in such a controlled environment with a controlling fiancé that nothing about this situation is normal for me.

"Listen, I'm sorry. I'm just not here to find love, or...whatever you want me to do, okay? I'm here to hide out, you know, wait for Rory to calm down so I can come back home in peace."

"I know."

I take a deep sigh to chop up the wall of silence. "Miss me yet?" I say.

She smirks. "Only, like, every second." She playfully rolls her eyes.

"You lie." I stretch on the couch, arching my back off the crisp leather as my body sinks in. I'm ready to crash and burn for the night.

"Yeah, I'm kidding. It's not like every, *every* second. How could I not miss you telling me I'm wrong when I'm right?"

We both giggle, and I lie on my side, snuggling into the tattered couch as the cool material chills my skin. I stretch my arm out from under me, keeping Layla in my view as she tucks herself into bed.

"Are you—" I start to say before I hear a thump.

I shoot up, listening closer to the sound again.

"Kaiton?" Layla asks on the other end.

My door handle jiggles, and I snap my neck to look at it. It's pitch black outside, with no outdoor lights, leaving me zero help to see any further beyond the jiggling of the doorknob.

I run to my room, tucking myself next to my dresser. The panic seeps into my body, threatening to leave me immobile. "Layla," I whisper as the tears start to well behind my eyes. "Someone's at my door." I keep my voice hushed, strained from holding back the sob that wants to escape.

"What?" she whispers back.

The handle jiggles again.

"Layla, I'm scared." I cry, the warm tears slowly running down my face.

"Kaiton, it's okay. No one knows you're there. What if...what if it's a bear? I see it all the time, bears try to get in. Some of them even sleep in people's cars!"

"Fuck," I drag out, the tears still flowing. "I have to go, I'm going to see if Rodney can come check it out."

"Who's Rod—"

"I have to go, Layla," I whisper and hang up, immediately dialing Ellie.

"Pick up, pick up," I murmur as the line rings and rings.

"Thank you for calling Ellie—" I hang up, getting her voicemail.

The handle jiggles again.

"Oh my God." I continue to cry.

Looking at my phone, I wonder who else could come. I can't call Laura—she always has her granddaughter. I've exhausted all my options except... fuck. *Fuck.* I don't want to call him. The handle jiggles again and I bounce my foot up and down, shaking my leg over and over, nervously trying to think of something else.

"Fuck." I sigh and dial Dutton's number.

"Hello?" he mumbles, drowsiness coating his throat as he answers.

"Dutton? I'm so sorry to be calling, but I don't have anyone else to call. I think there's something at my door," I whisper, trying not to cry. "I think it's a bear, or—"

"Hello?" a man's voice groans from outside. The door handle jiggles again, only this time, more vigorously.

"Oh my God! Someone's trying to get in, oh my God! What if it's him? I have to call the police!" I sob, my voice still hushed but uneven. Broken.

"What?" I hear Dutton mutter before pulling the phone away from my ear, hanging up and dialing 911 as fast as my fingers can type.

"Hello!" the man outside demands, his voice muffled by the thick walls of the cottage.

"911, what's your emergency?"

"Hello! Someone is trying to get in my house."

"Ma'am, what's your name?" she says calmly.

"Kaiton, my...my name is Kaiton Riggs. I'm at 8031 Bear Run Drive. Please, you have to come. Someone is trying to break into my house!"

Banging ensues from the door and it sounds like my handle is on the brink of falling off with how much it's moving.

The woman speaks, but I'm too concentrated on listening outside that I don't catch it.

"I've sent an officer. They are on their way," I finally hear her say as I refocus.

"Thank you!" I cry before hanging up.

It's not stopping, and whoever is trying to get in is going to succeed. My body starts to shake. I know it's a man... What if...what if he found me? What if he's here to do what he said he would? *How* could he have found me, though?

"Let me in!" the man shouts and I lay my head on top of my scrunched-up knees. I try to decide if I know his voice, if it's Rory's, but I can't tell, not through the panic and sobs.

The tears fall faster, hitting my bare thighs, and I sit here for several minutes, unable to move as the man continuously tries to get in.

I can't die.

Not like this.

I tilt my chin up, scanning the room for anything I can use as a weapon, standing to my feet in an instant when I spot the lamp. I rip the cord out of the wall, tilting it upside down as I inch out of my bedroom. I suck up the tears, trying to gain an ounce of composure if I'm going to try and put up anything close to a fight. The handle jiggles one last time before headlights shine through the strips of my windows on either side of my door. I exhale deeply at the sense of relief. I hear a car door shut, headlights still beaming bright. And a familiar voice that follows.

Dutton.

He made it here first.

My shoulders relax as I try to listen closer. Then a knock at my door, followed by his voice again, jolts me nearly out of my skin. "Kaiton? Open up, it's me."

I walk to the door, unlocking it before carefully twisting the handle. Dutton stands before me, in sweatpants and a hoodie, his hair disheveled. He towers over an elderly man at his side, in a long blue night robe that nearly swallows him.

"Kaiton, this is Mr. Fitz. He used to live here. This is who I built the deck for," Dutton says calmly. I can't speak, the words won't slip from the tightness of my throat. "Mr. Fitz got confused, and thought he still lived here."

Red and blue lights bounce off the pines in the darkness as the cops come over the hill. No sirens, just the sound of tires hitting my gravel driveway. I stand in my doorway, my eyes swollen from crying, my cheeks wet with tears, a lamp held upside down at my side. I realize I'm not wearing pants.

No pants.

Just an oversized Chicago Bears T-shirt that belonged to my dad. I'm mortified, adding to the immense range of other emotions.

"I'm going to bring Mr. Fitz over to the police. I'll be right back. Go sit down." He points back inside my house.

I stand still, unable to move as he gently grabs the man by the arm, guiding him down the stairs to the two officers standing in my driveway. I watch as they talk for a moment, until my knees buckle slightly from underneath me. Turning around eventually, I take a seat at the dining table, my eyes fixated on the doorway. Time passes slowly—my head in my hands, elbows rested on the wood. My mind races with a thousand thoughts per second, but I can't focus on any of them. *It's not Rory. It wasn't Rory. I'm safe. The police are here. Dutton's here. I'm okay.*

My phone buzzes from my bedroom floor but I don't move to grab it. I can't move. My body is frozen, except for this damn bouncing leg I can't control.

"The police are taking Mr. Fitz back to his house." Dutton walks through the door, carefully shutting it behind him. "His niece lives with him. I'm not sure what happened but they live about two miles down the road, must have been a long walk for him." I don't say anything, my head still resting in my hands, my eyes now fixated on the multicolored brown wood of the table.

"Are you alright?" he asks softly as he walks around, placing the flat of his hand on my back. I lift my head to answer him, but no words come out. Instead, those same warm tears fall as I start to cry again. I cover my face with my hands, shielding myself. "Hey, Kaiton, it's okay."

He pulls out the chair next to me, sitting down with his hand still on my back, lightly rubbing it in a small circle. "Kaiton, can you look at me?" He gently tugs on my arm, trying to get my hands unglued from my face. I give in, letting my arms fall to the table, and look at him. I can feel the warmness of my face and the mucus that wants to run from my nose. I try to suppress myself from crying further, but my chin quivers as I do so.

"You're shaking." He grabs my hand. "Come here." He wraps his arm around my body, pulling me into his chest as his other arm wraps near my waist snugly to keep me in place. I can't help but cry more, right into his sweatshirt. I feel stupid, embarrassed, scared, and I don't know why, but I can't stop weeping. He holds me in his arms until I finally calm, breathing in the scent of his fresh laundry detergent. I can feel my body relax, the pressure and worry floating away. I stay wrapped in his arms, not wanting to move, desperate for some kind of comfort.

"Who did you think it was, Kaiton?" he asks softly after some time. The hum of his words vibrates through his chest as my ear stays pressed on him. I lift my head up slowly, straightening my body away from his grasp.

"I thought it was Rory, my ex."

"And you're *that* terrified of him?"

"He just...said some things—"

"What did he say?"

"He said..." I take a breath. "He said if I left him, he would kill me, then kill himself."

"Jesus Christ." He sighs and drops his head. "And he has no idea where you are?"

"No. I mean, I don't think so."

"What can be done? Can the police do anything? Has he ever hit you? Has he ever abused you?"

"Not physically," I say quietly, deciding to leave out our last moments together where I thought he might break my wrist.

"Fuckin' hell," he breathes, his deep voice shooting even lower. "Who knows you're here?"

"Just my parents and my best friend, Layla."

"And none of them would ever tell him where you are, correct?"

"Right."

"Listen, this is a hard place to find. You're essentially in the middle of nowhere. One of my good friends works at the sheriff's department, I called him on the way over. Want me to see if he can drive by some nights just to make sure everything's all good over here? Would that be okay?"

I nod my head.

"Do you want me to stay a bit? Is there anything I can do?"

"No, you can go home. I'm sorry to wake you up."

"Don't apologize, I wasn't sleeping yet," he says, but his appearance tells another story. "You sure you don't need anything?"

"I'm sure," I say, trying to give the best grin I can.

"Okay." He taps his hands on his knees before standing. "Just...call me if you need anything." He starts to walk to the door.

"I will."

He pauses as he starts to walk out, holding the frame. "If it *was* a bear at your door, what did you want me to do? Fight it?"

"Yes?" I grin tilting my chin to the side and giving him a weak shrug.

He scoffs with a smile. "I would have." He gives the door a little tap, then turns back to walk out, closing it behind him.

I take a deep breath, getting to my feet so I can lock the door. My hands still shake slightly but I close my fists tight to stop it. I grab my phone from the bedroom floor, looking at the screen that shows the numerous missed calls and text messages from Layla, my mom, and Ellie. I dial my mom first, explaining what happened. I feel at ease just hearing her voice—her simple reminders of how I'm safe, her words of affirmation, telling me not to think about the what ifs. She calms me. That is, until my father gets on the phone.

"Kaiton, listen." His voice is forthright, direct, and to the point. "I talked to Officer Allenda, you know, Leslie's dad..." He waits for me to respond.

"Okay, and?" I finally say after the longest pause.

"Well, Kait, he said there really isn't enough tangible evidence for you to have a case here. You don't have anything in writing of him threatening you?"

"No, I don't." My tone grows softer.

"Honey, I'm sorry. He basically said the judge would throw it out. Texts of him just being an asshole aren't going to be enough."

I sigh into the phone. Every emotion I want to feel right now is blocked. I have no words, no reaction. I'm drained, tapped out.

"It's fine, Dad. I'm okay. There's an officer here who can drive by occasionally and check on the house for me. Just don't let anyone know where I'm at. Okay?"

"Okay, sweetie. I love you," he says gently.

"I love you more, Dad."

As soon as the call ends, I text Ellie and Layla, explaining the situation repeatedly. I'm tired, on edge, and just need sleep. I don't know why I got so afraid. Rory hasn't laid a finger on me before, other than that morning. But there was something in his eyes then. Something I had never seen before. He meant it, with every fiber of his being, *he meant it.*

I lie in bed, covers up to my nose as I bury myself in the blankets, mentally and physically exhausted from this day. The hum of my mom's words run through my head as my eyes drift shut.

"*Worrying won't change the future, the what ifs won't change the past. Live in the now, Kaiton. You're safe,*" I hear her say.

  You're safe.

CHAPTER
SEVENTEEN

THE SUN BLASTS through the empty space in my blinds, shining directly on my squinting eyes as I wake. I slept like hell, tossing and turning for what seemed like every second of the night. My phone buzzes on the pillow next to me and I groan as I turn my body slightly to reach and grab it. With fuzzy eyesight, I type in my password, pulling up the text I missed.

DUTTON BECK: Good morning.
Let me know when you wake up, please.

My eyes widen seeing Dutton's name on my screen. My body shoots up straight as an arrow as I text him back.

ME: Morning. I'm up now.

I clutch my phone in my hands as the "read" receipt pops up underneath my text. No sooner does he read it than my phone starts to ring.

"Hello?" I say, my voice slightly cracked from the dryness of my throat.

"Hey, listen, if you've got some time this morning, my friend Henry—Officer Lewis—wants to meet you. I can be there too, if that makes you more comfortable. I think he just wants to hear about your situation and see if there is anything he can do besides check on you every so often."

"Oh, um...yeah, that's fine. I would like you to come too, if you can." I press the palm of my hand to my eye, rubbing the sleep out of it.

"Great, can we come in like fifteen? I have to open the store in an hour."

I pull the phone away from my ear, checking the time to see how early it is. "Yeah, that works."

"Okay see you in a bit," he says softly before we hang up.

I yawn and stretch my arms high above my head, trying to wake my body. Eventually, I leave the sheets and waddle to my dresser to find something more appropriate than just my T-shirt.

"Fuck," I mumble, catching a glimpse of myself in the small mirror. I run my hands through my hair, combing through the nest I feel beneath my fingers to see if I can salvage my appearance.

It's hopeless.

The knots from my restless sleep make me look like I've been electrocuted five times over, and there's no way in hell I will allow either of these men to see me like this. I bolt out of my bedroom, starting the shower in my bathroom as fast as I can. I scramble back to my room, grabbing the first set of clean clothes I can find before hopping into the scalding stream of water flowing from the rusted shower head. I make it fast, washing myself as quickly as possible before jumping out, and throw my clothes on with just a minute left before a knock sounds from my front door. I shake my hair with my fingers—it's still sopping wet, but at least it's combed through.

"Hi." I beam, opening the door. Dutton stands next to a thicker man, shorter than him, but one I recognize from the blues festival.

"Hey, I'm Henry. Nice to meet you," he says, extending his hand for me to shake. I smile, introducing myself before I motion them both inside.

Dutton whispers a small "hello" as he moves past me, gently placing his hand on my arm as he walks over the threshold.

We sit at my dining table, a seemingly perfect gathering spot since I don't have chairs anywhere else—unless we all wanted to cozy up on the couch together.

"So, Dutton tells me you've got a bit of an issue with an ex back home. Is that right?" Henry asks. His mustache is thick, nearly hiding his entire upper lip.

"That's right." I nod.

"Are you afraid he may find you here?"

"Yes," I reply timidly, pausing beforehand because my real answer seems too complicated. "I mean...yes and no. He threatened me and it had me rattled enough to leave my home. Then he chased me in his car for a long time."

"He what?" Dutton presses, and I realize there's so many finer details I've left out.

"Yeah, I, uh, I got away, and I don't know if he's looking for me, or what he would do if he found me. I think part of the reason I left was for him to cool down—hopefully find someone else to fixate on, so I could go back home."

"Can you tell me what the threat was?"

"He said if I left him, he would kill me, then kill himself. That was it. I mean, he's said numerous times he would kill himself if I ever left him, so that wasn't anything new. This was, however, the first time he said he would kill *me*. And I don't know...I—" I pause a moment. They're both looking at me. "I believe he will."

Dutton's fist clenches tight on the table while Henry asks another question.

"Has he ever hurt you?" he asks calmly, his hands clasped together as they rest on the table.

"The only physical pain he's put me in was when he grabbed my wrist before I left. Other than that, no."

"What about emotionally? Was he ever emotionally abusive?"

"I'm...I'm not sure. I don't really know what that would look like." Only, I think I do. I bet it looked like him needing to know where I was every second of the day, watching everything I wore and where I wore it, mocking what I ate, keeping me in check with "our dreams", "our future", "our needs".

"That's okay. Is he—or *was* he—controlling at all?"

I blink, lost in my own thoughts.

"Miss?" he presses, and I quickly decide to tell the truth.

"Very," I say, almost in a laugh. "I wasn't allowed to go to certain places without his permission, hang around non-approved friends, wasn't allowed to drink—but that's okay, it's not really my thing anyway. The only thing he wasn't controlling over was my finances. We had separate accounts, thank God, but agreed to have joint accounts once we got married."

Henry nods, listening intently as I speak. "Is he an angry person, generally?"

"Absolutely. Something small could flip his switch in an instant. I had a lot of holes in my apartment walls because of it."

"From his fists?" he asks.

"His fists, remote controllers, my phone—I had to replace a couple of my phones because he threw them into the wall, and they basically shattered on impact."

I glance at Dutton, his jaw clenched tight, lips pressed firmly together, eyes locked on me.

"Okay." Henry pulls out a notepad and pen from underneath the table, either hidden in his sweatshirt pocket or his jean pocket, I can't tell. "What is his name and birthdate?"

"Rory Keppner, June tenth, nineteen ninety-seven."

"Do you have any photos of Rory, by chance?"

"I don't. This is a new phone so he couldn't track me." I pick my phone up off the table and wave it slightly.

"Could I pull him up from social media or somewhere online?"

"Yeah, you could try," I say.

Henry unlocks his phone, scrolling and typing for a moment before he shows me a profile on social media I've seen before, except it's changed to strictly all photos of Rory—some of which are photos he took with me that I'm cropped out of.

My stoic expression hardens. "That's him," I say, disdain flowing with my words. Maybe he has moved on, finally, and I'm just sitting here balling over a poor, helpless man jiggling my doorhandle at night.

Henry looks back at his screen, observing all of the photos of Rory's perfectly manicured blond hair, styled and swept while his "I'm pretending to be rich" sweaters get the love and recognition he so desperately hoped for all over the internet.

Fuck that guy.

Dutton leans over slightly, sharing Henry's screen with him as I watch his face twist. He looks repulsed, his brows pulling down and pinching together as his eyes narrow on the photos Henry swipes through.

"What kind of vehicle does Rory drive?" Henry sets his phone down.

"A black Jeep Grand Cherokee."

"Okay." He nods as he writes in the notepad. "I'm going to show a couple officers these photos of him, and we can help keep an eye out around town. I've got all the information I need right now. If I have any more questions or see anything suspicious, is it okay if I give you a call?"

"Absolutely."

"I know this is probably a difficult time for you," Henry says gently, his eyes softening as he speaks. "But trust me when I say, this town is small. Anyone comes here who's not from here, were gonna know about it. Hell, the second you came here, there was buzz already," he says, and not a second later, Dutton's fist hit Henry's leg under the table.

"For me?" I laugh lightly, shocked at Henry's words.

"Yeah, you." He chuckles. "The Ridge doesn't make women as pretty as you. I think I can speak for everyone when I say that."

Dutton groans as he hangs his head, rubbing his hands on his face to shield himself, probably out of embarrassment for his friend. I smile awkwardly, not used to the compliment, and unsure if I should find it weird that an officer thinks of me like that, then remembering he's still around my age.

"The point is"—Henry still gawks and smiles at me as he talks with his hands—"anyone comes around here who doesn't belong, we'll know about it. You don't need to worry. Falton isn't a place that attracts tourists. It's essentially a ghost town in the grand scheme of Montana. A little hidden treasure, if you will. You're safe here. Just try to enjoy your time at The Ridge, and of course, if you hear any weird bumps in the night or need some help, call either one of us." He motions between them both.

"Thank you," I say as my lips curl into a small grin. Henry nods and lightly slaps both hands on the table before he stands, prompting Dutton to rise, too.

"Listen, were going to Neddy's tonight if you don't have anything to do. Might be good to get out, take your mind off things. It's dollar burger night, and they have karaoke too. Should be a fun time," Henry says as I follow them to my door.

"The burgers aren't that great," Dutton chimes in. "But they're cheap."

"Well, maybe I'll see you guys later, then." I smile while they walk out.

"Nice to meet you, Kaiton!" Henry shouts from my driveway as they walk back to Dutton's truck.

Dutton raises a hand to me, not speaking, only grinning from ear to ear with closed lips, showing off his dimples underneath a five o'clock shadow. He makes it hard to not smile back. I wave one last time as they reverse, pulling out of my driveway, then stand in the doorway until they crest the hill—far enough for me not to be able to see me—before I close the door behind me. I walk to my phone resting on the table, texting Ellie to see what she's up to today. I don't have to work, and I have enough groceries for the week, so sitting home alone and moping all day doesn't sound much fun.

ME: Good morning

ELLIE BOONE: Good mornin!
How you feeling sweets? Did
you get any sleep?

ME: Eh, not really. But it's
okay. Got any plans today?
I have the day off.

ELLIE BOONE: No plans.
Wanna come over and ride
the trails in an hour? Might be
good to get out, clear your mind.

ME: Sounds perfect.

I set my phone back down, moving to my room to find the only pair of jeans I have, slipping them on once I locate them folded neatly in the dresser drawer. Then I slide on a pair of socks under the Ariats Ellie bought me. I'm not sure what the forecast is today, so I keep my white crop top on, grabbing a dark green hoodie to bring just in case. I finish my hair, blow drying and lightly curling it to get the biggest loose waves I can. Then I run my fingers through to the roots, fluffing and shaking out the strands for a fuller effect. I only add mascara and lip gloss before I check my phone again, realizing I've already spent thirty minutes getting ready. I pop a bagel into the toaster sitting on my counter, spreading it lightly with butter before sticking it in my mouth, clenching it between my teeth, and grabbing my crossbody bag, keys, phone, and head out. Luckily, getting to Ellie's ranch is pretty simple: only two turns the whole route. I finish eating my bagel as I make the first turn and it's only a matter of time before I'm pulling on to the long dirt path, spotting the familiar wooden fence that houses her gorgeous animals. I practically crawl down her driveway, slowly rolling my tires to not kick too much dust up for Bunny and Poppy—and Ellie, who seems to be saddling them both. When I was here last, she let me give them carrots and apples. But for some reason, I had this pull, this gravitation toward Bunny. She's silky brown with equal amounts of white spots and patches. Her coat is visually stunning. But I don't think it was because she was noticeably beautiful that pulled me to her. It seemed to be the fact that both of us had lost something. Like a piece of each of our souls was gone. For her, it was her best friend and for me, well...for me, I guess the same.

"I got somethin' for you!" Ellie shouts after I park in front of her garage and get out. "It's on the porch!"

I squint, and a cocked smile rests on my face as I turn my head to her porch. A cowboy hat sits on top of the stairs, and I walk over to grab it.

"This?" I yell back as I hold the hat up.

I see her nod as she finishes saddling Poppy and I place the light brown hat on top of my head, fixing my hair as I push the tresses in front of my shoulders. I walk up to her, the dirt and rocks crunching under my boots.

"Come on in," she says as she points to the gate down the way. Her infectious smile beams bright under the rim of her own cowboy hat. "Which one do you want to ride?"

"Bunny?" I question, hoping she didn't want to ride her first.

"You got it." She nods.

I smile and shove my hands in the back pockets of my jeans. I walk down the fence to the gate, unhooking the black latch from its position.

"Have you ridden before?" she asks as I get closer to her.

"When I was younger, my parents paid for some lessons. Didn't really stick with it though."

"Well, don't worry. We won't be riding rough today. I'll just let you know a couple of the basics and you'll be good to go. You ready?" she asks as she pats Bunny's biggest white spot, near the center of her belly. I nod eagerly. "Put your left foot in this stirrup, and carefully swing your right leg over. If you can't reach the saddle horn, grab onto what you can."

I twist the stirrup slightly, reaching my arms up high before hiking my leg and placing the ball of my foot inside. Grabbing her coarse mane with my left hand—something I faintly remember from my lessons—and the swell of the saddle in the other to hold me in place, I hoist my other leg over, careful not to slam back down on her. Bunny stays still for me, only bowing her head slightly as I adjust myself.

"Keep some slack in your reigns," Ellie says as she mounts Poppy. "When you want to slow down or stop, tighten them. Okay?"

"Okay." I nod.

As Ellie instructs some more, Poppy trots over to me, circling behind Bunny and I. "When you squeeze her with your legs, she'll move. Remember to steer with your reins. Take it to the left if you want to go left, take it to the right if...you get it." She smiles.

I give Bunny a little squeeze as I bring my legs in, and the hollow sound of her hoof hitting the hard ground fills my ears.

"You ready?" Ellie asks.

"Ready," I say, assuring her with another nod.

Bunny and Poppy move simultaneously as I follow Ellie's lead toward the barn, squeezing through an open gate. We move around the backside of the large red structure, and I'm greeted with rows of thick pines in front of the mountains. We haven't even left her backyard yet.

"What a view," I mumble, mostly to myself under a breath.

"It's really something, isn't it?" She smiles.

I tightly bunch the reins in one hand, freeing my other to run the flat part against Bunny's silky bourbon-colored coat. I take in the air, the quiet—relaxing the buildup of tension in my body, just swaying with the movement of Bunny's gait. I sit up straighter as we enter a clearing through the scattered trees, riding side by side on a two-track trail.

"You okay after last night?" Ellie says softly.

"Yeah, just...tired." I sigh.

"I know I already told you, but I'm really sorry I didn't answer. I tried to call you back as soon as I saw it. Rod and I almost just booked it to your house, but I figured you would call back if it was important. Just figured you might have fallen asleep." Her voice remains delicate.

"I know." I nod and smile faintly. "No apology needed."

"I'm glad Dutton was able to be there, though."

"Me too. He came over this morning with Officer Lewis."

"Oh, Henry? Sweet boy. Dutton, too."

"Does everyone know everyone in this town?" I giggle slightly.

"Well, we're all kind of connected with the city—business owners, police, brick and mortar shops. But Rodney and I used to be great friends with the Becks. Dutton and Belle pretty much grew up with each other, even though he was already about seven when she was born."

I listen as the wind blows slightly and we climb in altitude, the mountains on full display as I look at her.

"Shame what happened to them. They really would have been proud of the man he's become." Her eyes are heavy, her lips press in a thin line. "And Henry…" Her voice raises as her eyes widen. "They ran around together ever since they were young boys. Both of them would be at our farm from sunup til sundown." Her smile grows. "Oh! We're coming up to my favorite part. Follow me, the trail gets tight through here," she says as Poppy trots faster to get in front of us, her hooves hitting the ground in heavy thumps as they dig into the dirt.

I follow as the track becomes narrow and the pines thicken, trailing her for what seems to be a mile, just admiring the beauty of the land, until we get to her favorite part. Which admittedly, is probably going to be my favorite part, too. Ahead of us is an open river, the sun beaming bright on the rocky water and the forest around it. It's a large clearing, deep enough to hit our horses' knees as they trot into it. The sloshing sound of the river echoes in the open space as both Bunny and Poppy nearly take off when they're in it. Ellie and I laugh as our horses pick up pace, water splashing us on all sides. I grip the reins tighter to steady my balance. We cross the wide river, leaving my jeans with specks of wetness that dry completely by the time we finish our ride. I help Ellie take the tacks off once we're back, brushing them both and freeing them back to the pasture as Bunny takes to the ground. She dips her shoulder and rolls back and forth, nudging her head against the grass before coming back to her feet, shaking her whole body. Poppy comes trailing behind her, rubbing her neck on Bunny's croup.

I didn't know horseback riding would be so therapeutic. It might have saved my parents thousands in counseling had I stuck with it. The scenery helps, I'm sure, but this was everything I needed today. And I can't thank Ellie enough.

Bunny included.

CHAPTER
EIGHTEEN

I HIKE UP Ellie's too-small-for-me jeans over my ass, trying to suck in my cheeks, if that's at all possible. I don't know why she thought I could fit into these—her frame is much smaller than mine, with only one of my thick thighs being the size of her entire body. She said they were stretchy, and didn't fit her well, so she handed them over to me to wear tonight for Neddy's dollar burgers. Once they are successfully snug around the curve of my back, I suck in my little tummy pouch and button them up, only feeling *slightly* like a stuffed sausage as the material stretches and conforms against my skin. They flare at the bottom, with a rip on each thigh big enough to fit my hands through. I keep my white crop top on, along with my lightly muddied boots, then fix my hair from today's ride. I hold up the turquoise-stoned belt Ellie gave me with the jeans, knowing damn well I don't need it, but realizing the higher waist of the fit looks almost incomplete without it. The silver metal outlines every large stone, and I clasp it tight once I feed it through each loop, stepping back as I try to fit my frame into the small mirror on my dresser. I cock my head to the side, pursing my lips as I wrack my brain, wondering what's missing. I gaze at the end of the dresser where the cowboy hat Ellie let me use today, sits. I grab the top of it, fitting it snugly on my head as I look back into the mirror. Grinning as I give a sharp nod to my reflection, I know the look is complete. I check the time on my phone, realizing I should have left about five minutes ago. I'm just meeting Ellie and Rod there, but I don't want to have them waiting on me too long. I grab my keys and phone, taking my wallet out of my purse and shoving it into the back pocket of the tight jeans before heading out. Rain droplets fall from the clouds, scattering the gravel with small specks, and I look up at the sky, noticing the dark haze that's rolling in. As the light rain falls on my windshield, I drive into town, successfully arriving inside of Neddy's before it starts to pour. The soft yellow lights bounce off the entire wooden space, creating a dim cast over the bar. Mounted deer heads decorate the walls and stapled dollar bills coat the wooden planked ceiling above me. My eyes wander through the packed crowd until I spot Ellie and Rod sitting on chairs around a table made of repurposed barrels. The singer on stage is loud, but the hums and murmurs of other patrons are louder. I smile as Ellie's glance catches mine, and I head her way.

"Have you eaten here yet?" Ellie says loudly over the music.

"I had some things to go, it was pretty good." I smile back.

"It is," she agrees.

"Their burgers aren't that great," Rod chimes in.

"Rod!" Ellie slaps his arm.

I can't do anything but laugh. "So I've heard."

"Babe, you can't go around saying that—they're good customers of ours." Ellie laughs, scolding her husband as he just smirks. His large frame takes up half of the side they sit on. "Neddy and Tina have bought and sold a lot of properties through me, and Rod here did all their plumbing. So, forget he said any of that," she says to me as she waves her hand over him.

"Deal." I giggle and give her a little nod.

The hard clack of the billiard balls startles me and I shoot my eyes over to the pool table. Two large men stand around it, holding their cue sticks at their sides. It's even more shaded in the corner they stand in, but the red Budweiser light hanging with chains above it casts just enough brightness for them to play.

"Henry! Dutton!" Ellie shouts as she looks past me.

I shift my body more to see both boys standing behind my chair. Dutton's eyes fall down to mine as he gives a little smirk before directing his attention back to Ellie.

"We saw you guys come in and just wanted to say hey," Dutton raises his glass slightly.

"Come sit, come sit." Ellie waves them in.

Both boys shake hands with Rod before scooching into chairs beside me. Henry sits closest, nearly touching arms with me as they fit.

"Glad you came!" Henry cheers, looking at me.

"Me too." I smile. "I haven't been in here yet. It's pretty cool."

"Good evening, everyone! My name is Lana and I'll be your server tonight. Can I get you started with something to drink?" our waitress says, standing to the side of the table.

"Yes, I'll take a Miller Lite and Rod...what do you want?" Ellie says.

"Jack and coke, please," he responds in his usual gruff tone.

The waitress nods, then looks at me. "I'll just have a water, please."

"Sure thing."

Henry's elbow taps my arm. "Is gettin' drunk on a Tuesday not your thing?" he jokes.

"She doesn't drink, Henry," Dutton reminds him low under his breath.

"Oh." Henry slaps his head. "Sorry, I forgot." He smiles.

"Shit, Hen. Our burgers are done." Dutton points, lifting in his seat to see food sitting in front of their empty bar stools.

They both push back their chairs, Henry taking a sip of his beer while Dutton says, "Rod, you getting up there for karaoke later?"

"Yeah, right." Rodney chuckles.

"Ellie?" Dutton questions.

"Dutton, everyone's ears would bleed if I got up there and sang anything," she replies.

He taps his hand on the back of the chair. "Enjoy your guys' food," he says before both men make their way to the bar.

Dutton glances back at me, his grin enticing, but it happens so quick I could have missed it if I had blinked at just the right time. The waves of his dark hair fall perfectly in place, like he just ran his fingers through it. I smirk back at him before I shift my attention to the waitress as she sets our drinks down and takes the rest of our order.

The music thumps through the speakers and a slightly tone-deaf woman sings Shania Twain, then our waitress eventually comes back with another round of drinks and our food, refilling my water for the third time tonight. We all giggle and critique each singer as they step up—some seemingly professional as they get on the microphone and sing better than the artist themselves and some who should probably only stick to singing in the shower—but props to them for the confidence.

"Eight," Rod rates the last singer as they step off.

"Really? I was thinking more like a six," I say.

"Definitely a six," Ellie agrees.

The drinks keep flowing for Rod but Ellie takes a break, deciding she's the one driving tonight. I offer to take them both home so she can have some fun too, but she declines, thanking me generously for the offer.

At this point, I feel I've drank enough water to keep my body hydrated for a week straight, all without going to the restroom. But two hours of sitting here, holding it, has been long enough. "I'll be right back." I glance around quickly, trying to locate where the bathrooms could possibly be in this busy bar.

I stand up, crossing the dance floor as I weave into the small hallway, pushing through to the women's bathroom. The music blasts so loudly I can still hear the booming of the bass through the worn-out grey stalls while I finish up. I walk out, keeping my head down as I continue to dry my hands on my jeans since the paper towel dispenser was out. My body slams into that familiar wall of stacked brick and I look up, realizing I just bumped into Dutton's chest.

"I'm sorry." I laugh. "I should have watched where I was going."

He smiles as the song changes, and his eyes light up once he hears the first chords of the music.

"I love this song," he says with glossy red eyes. "Let's dance." He gently grabs my hand, pulling me to the middle of the dance floor, where only three other people sway to the music.

I can't contain my smile as he spins me around so quickly I need to hold on to the top of my hat. He keeps ahold of my hand as his arm fits snug around the curve of my lower back, swaying me side to side with the music. I look around, seeing if anyone notices. But Ellie and Rod are too wrapped up in their conversation to see us. Dutton sings in a low tone, right along with the man on stage, and my smile hasn't faded as I look at him, seeing his eyes have grown a little more bloodshot.

"You good, buddy?" I ask curiously as the corner of my mouth curves up.

"Oh, I'm great." He tilts his head down slightly, closing his eyes as we move with the music.

My hat nearly takes up all the space between us, but I try and lift my head to get his attention. I can tell by his movements he's anything but stable, especially with the dopey gaze in his eyes.

"Wanna sit?" I giggle. He laughs and nods as I take his arm in mine and walk him back to his seat at the bar next to Henry.

"Where did you go?" Henry shouts as he slaps Dutton's back so hard I could hear the thump.

"Did you hear it? It was my song!" Dutton exclaims.

"I did! I figured you were out there dancing by yourself, so I ordered another round."

"Well, I wasn't by myself." Dutton stops mid-sentence, focusing as the realization hits that he grabbed *me*. His mouth hangs slightly open as his eyes widen, like he's too stunned to speak. Or just now realizing the way his hand stroked the small of my back as we danced may have crossed some universal line between a boss and his employee.

"I'm going to get back to Ellie and Rod. You boys have fun," I say with one hell of an awkward smile as a way to dismiss myself. I don't want to make Dutton any more uncomfortable than he seems to be looking right now.

I don't mind. I didn't then, either. It was nice to be held for a moment—disregarding the status of our work relationship, of course. But it's been a long time since someone has asked me to dance, I think that's why I'm sulking back to the table, feeling like I'm on some walk of shame from the night before. Although I've never experienced that, I can imagine this is what it feels like. Did he really not realize who he was dancing with? He looked right at me. I mean, just because his lights were on doesn't mean anyone was home, I guess.

The minute I sit back down at the table, our check arrives.

"Rod's drunk. I gotta take him home," Ellie whines. "You ready too or are you gonna stay a bit?" she asks.

"I'm ready." I nod. "It's getting late. My bedtime was like...three hours ago." I laugh as I look at the time on my phone. "Let me get this." I grab the check, digging in my back pocket for my wallet.

"Ellie, take that from her. Don't let her pay," Rod slurs.

"We'll get it, Kait, don't worry about it," she says.

The tab is one of the cheapest I've seen. In total, it doesn't even hit thirty dollars. If I was going to contribute anything, at any time, I would prefer it to be this bill.

"Let me get this one," I insist.

"Kaiton, you better hand that over," Ellie warns, teasing me with a mischievous grin.

"Just this once," I beg.

"Absolutely not, now...give it up," she says as her outstretched hand motions in a beckoning fashion.

I sigh, defeated once again as I hand over the tray with our receipt to her.

"Next time, I get it."

"Fine, fine, whatever," Ellie jokes.

Rod looks like he's half asleep already, so I get where the urgency lies to take him home.

"Thank you," I say.

"Of course." She smiles.

Ellie lays her cash flat on top and lets the waitress know we don't need any change. We stand and give hugs goodbye before we walk over to the bar. Ellie and Rod get to the boys first but the entire way, Rod stumbles when he moves, leaving Ellie no choice but to head straight for the door as she issues them a simple wave.

"You boys have a good night," I say as I place my hand on the center of Dutton's back, leaning in to both of them as they rest their elbows on the bar.

"Kaiton," Henry mumbles. "You think you could possibly take us home tonight?" he asks sweetly as his top lip curls up, hardly noticeable though with how thick his mustache is.

"Absolutely." I nod.

Not to say I find it odd, but seeing a police officer get shit-faced at a bar is equivalent to seeing a teacher out in public. Although, I've never seen him in uniform yet, so maybe it's not *too* out of the ordinary. I snap out of my thoughts as I see Henry's mouth move. I was so zoned out, I didn't even hear him speak. He looks at me with an eyebrow raised and a shit-eating grin on his face.

"So?" he begs like a four-year-old trying to persuade his parents to give him candy for breakfast.

"Sure?" I say, but it comes out more as a question. I didn't hear a word this man said, but he seems really excited.

"Woo! Shots!" he exclaims to the bartender.

"I'm not doing shots." Dutton laughs, leaning back on the barstool, his arms crossed in front of his broad chest.

"Come on! We got a ride," Henry says ecstatically.

I giggle as I roll my eyes, taking a seat at the empty barstool next to Dutton.

"What kind?" the bartender shouts back at Henry.

"Uhh, give me tequila!" he yells back.

"I am not doing tequila." Dutton shakes his head as he sits straight up. His arms still cross over his chest, wrapped up in his dark crewneck.

"Fine," Henry replies to Dutton. "Make it Jameson!" Henry shouts back at the bartender. "Last drink. That's it. Then we can get you home and tucked into bed," Henry says as he pats Dutton's chest.

The bartender smacks two shot glasses against the woodgrain bar right in front of them. "Close it out?" he asks Henry.

He nods back and the bartender takes his glass.

"Let's go," Henry chants as he raises his glass to Dutton.

Dutton just sighs, looking up at Henry as he stands. Dutton takes his glass, clinking it against Henry's, then they bring them to their lips, tipping back the whiskey as they swallow nearly at the same time. Henry blows out air as his face twists slightly, like he's trying hard not to grimace at the taste. The bartender hands Henry's card back to him before he looks at me, cheesing so hard the apples of his cheeks practically hit his eyes.

"Yep. I'm gonna fuckin' puke!" Henry cheers with a nod. He is still smiling, even though he knows his fate is sealed.

I just giggle as Dutton laughs too, and we all walk out together. The rain still falls and I take my keys out of my pocket, unlocking my car as we quickly approach. Dutton slides into the passenger seat while Henry folds himself into the back. He manages to cram his legs in, even though my seat is almost all the way up to the wheel. I take my hat off, tossing it into the back seat next to him before I run my fingers through my hair to try and fix the current state of the half-wet, half-flat mess I'm sure it's in.

"Where to first?" I ask as I start the car.

"I'm closest," Henry groans from behind me.

Dutton leans his head back, closing his eyes gently as he gets comfortable. I glance at him first, before shifting my body more as I back out of the parking space.

"Which way?" I ask.

"Just...go up to the light, take a left."

The music plays softly, and the car remains quiet. I turn left at the light and drive some more, waiting for any instructions to ring from the back seat.

"Right at the stop sign, then I'm the first house on the left," he says. "Thank you, Kaiton, for taking us home."

"Yes. Thank you, Kaiton," Dutton says as he lifts his head, opening his eyes to look at me.

"No problem, guys. Anytime. I promise," I say, slightly regretting the way I enunciated the *anytime* part.

I slow down for the stop sign, turning right once I'm in the clear. I pull onto a concrete driveway. A small wooden cabin with a garage next to it waits at the end. As soon as I'm in park, Henry's hand comes around the seat, tapping me on the shoulder.

"Thanks again, Kaiton. You're the best," he says before opening the door.

"Dut!" he calls as he gets out.

"Hen," Dutton says as he gives him a little nod.

Henry shuts the door, and I wait until he's inside before I start to back out.

"You're next," I say softly to Dutton while I look out my back windshield.

"You can pull out of here and take a right. You'll go for a couple of miles before you have to do anything else."

I nod to him as I drive, only the road in front is visible from my headlights. The dark night covers everything at my sides and I try to navigate the best I can with the downpour of rain that suddenly picks up pace.

"How was your burger?" Dutton asks after some time with a little smirk.

I laugh lightly. "It was kind of shit."

"I told you." He chuckles. "Take a left at this next road."

I flip on my blinker, turning slowly as I approach. My headlights shine on the small green sign that reads, "Eagle Ln" "as I turn.

"I'm the last house on the right," he says, eyes still facing forward.

I'm not entirely sure why this car ride has been mostly filled with silence. My guess would be either he's embarrassed about dancing with me, or he's drunk enough that if he makes any sudden movements, he'll hurl up his entire dinner. But I don't question it any further as we come to the end of the road.

"This one," he says softly.

I pull into a drive twice as long as mine until we finally get to the small structure. I can't see much with the darkness outside, but with the light above the garage, I can make out some roof peaks and brown stonework. I put the car in park, sitting back in my seat as I rest my hands on my lap and turn to face him. He reaches over, eyes drawn down as he unbuckles himself. He tilts his chin up, staring right at me as I hear the click. I see his chest rise and fall as his breath deepens.

"I hope I didn't make anything weird by dancing—" he stutters until I interject.

"It's fine, I promise." I smile. "It was fun."

"I just..." He leans in a bit closer to me, minimizing the space between us created by the center console. "I don't know..." The corner of his mouth cocks up, like he wants to smile, but doesn't. It's almost like half of him is ashamed but the other half couldn't give two fucks. I notice the way his eyes trace over me, inch by inch, even though he doesn't say another word.

"It's okay," I say as I bring my hand to his arm, gently tracing back and forth on the cotton material of his sweatshirt.

His eyebrows pinch together slightly as his gaze remains still fully intact with mine. His breath shallows even more, nearly on the brink of shaking. And in a matter of one split second, his hand caresses the side of my face, his skin as cold as ice. He delves under my hair, his fingertips grasping the base of my neck, pulling me in closer to him. His soft lips collide with mine and I close my eyes as my heart pounds with such force, I feel I may be on the verge of a heart attack. He tastes like honey and whiskey, and I kiss him back, wanting to keep the flavor of him on my lips longer. My mind races. Thoughts flow a million miles per second.

What am I doing?

What are we doing?

I'm not ready for this.

I place my hand on his chest, gently pushing him away from me until the last hold of his bottom lip releases from mine.

"I'm so sorry," I say quietly. Our noses nearly touch with what little space is left between us. "I'm not...ready."

"Oh my God." He sighs and his eyes fall, remorse washing over him. "Kaiton, my God, I'm so fucking stupid. Please forgive me. Holy shit." His breath picks up pace.

He brings his hand to his head, gripping his own tresses as he hides.

"No...I want to, I just..." I try to form the words, but I have none. A part of me could have stayed in this car all night, tasting the sweet whiskey from his lips. But the other part of me—the naive, trusting idiot part—can't look past the fact that it hasn't even been a month since my entire life was flipped upside down. I gave my *all* to one man. *My fucking all.* And he lied. He made me believe he loved me as much as I did him. My heart hurts physically just thinking about it. And I can't shake it. I can't get rid of it. Because no matter how bad I want to, I don't know if I could ever let myself fall again, or even try. Even if I wasn't a mess from Rory, the doubt burns me. The way Dutton's lips felt on mine and every moment we've had up until this point...I know I'm just gearing up for another gut-wrenching heartbreak.

"No. Please, please, forgive me. I'm so sorry, Kaiton. I promise, that will never happen again."

"Dutton."

"I should go."

His eyes go distant, like he's trying to hold in every emotion he wants to let loose.

"Thank you for bringing me home. I'm...so sorry." He shakes his head, opening the door before stepping out.

I don't even have a moment to say anything before his door shuts and I watch him walk in front of my headlights. I sit dumbfounded, replaying everything that just happened picture by picture in my head. The way his expression looked before he pulled me in, like he was begging for me, just with his eyes. The way his pouty bottom lip felt hugging mine as we teased the tips of our tongues together...

I run my fingers along my lips, trying to pick up any remnants of our kiss until his front porch light kicks on. My eyes flutter up, realizing I'm still parked here. I reverse in the open area, my headlights shining on a pole as I turn and drive the entire way home, not listening to anything on the radio. I stay in a clouded haze, trying to taste the last bits of honey whiskey I can.

CHAPTER
NINETEEN

I COULDN'T SLEEP, which isn't anything out of the ordinary since I've been here. Usually, it's the faint creaks in the old wood. Or the rustling trees that dance with the wind. Last night, however, was for a very different reason.

And his name is Dutton.

I think I would be lying to myself if I said I didn't enjoy the kiss, even for a moment. Physically, he's attractive. The way his hair forms perfect waves, flipping at the nape of his neck, falling gently in place into a messy but not disheveled sort of way. The way his deep emerald eyes give the softest stare, never harsh or hard. His body is a whole other beast...and I've never been one to objectify a man, but goddamn. I can tell he's worked hard for it. Sometimes, when his arms flex, a vein runs right through his bicep, similar to the one that leads down underneath his boxers. Not that I've wanted to notice these small details, but it's hard not to when it's right in my face. But if I'm being really honest, he's more than that. His voice is deep and smooth like that whiskey he was drinking and when he speaks to me, it's always kind and gentle. He problem solved in a split second for me during the Battle of the Businesses, when I thought I might be a burden to the team. He rushed to me in a time of need. A person I hardly knew was ready to handle whatever—whoever—was trying to break into my home. I could think of plenty of other ways he's made me feel safe without saving me, but the longer I lie here wrapped up between the sheets in my bed thinking about him, the more I'll want to kiss him again.

And I don't need that.

Not right now.

There's no way I could possibly have anything left to give someone when I haven't had the chance to heal myself.

I stare at my ceiling, observing the ridges and bumps of the popcorn texture. My alarm sounds again, for the second time after I've hit the snooze button, and my body stretches as I try to coax myself into getting up out of this bed. Slowly, I make my way out of my room, getting ready at the same speed paint dries. I have a couple hours before I need to be at the store, and I plan on using every last drop of the seconds I have left to remain in the comfort of my house. It's not that the possibility of seeing Dutton is haunting me, it's just...if I do, I might not be able to focus on anything other than his lips. But who knows, he might not even come in, given the fact that he's probably embarrassed as hell about last night.

I make myself a simple breakfast, my honorary bagel and cream cheese, before my time has officially run out and I'm needed to open the store. My stomach feels weightless and empty as my nerves kick up slightly and I lock the door behind me, looking at the sky and walking to my car. The clouds form into large puffy balls above, and the sun peeks out slightly behind them. The radio's on as I drive, but I'm not listening to the music. I should have called Layla last night. I should have told her what happened, ran my thoughts past her. That's what best friends are for, right? Maybe I wouldn't be stuck in my own head if I had just gotten everything off my chest. But I know Layla, and I know what she would say. Something like, "Why did you push him away? You have one life to live. Go back there and fuck his brains out." Well, she probably wouldn't have said all of that, but it's pretty damn close. And that's not what I need to hear right now. I guess I could have called my mom, but I'm not one to talk about kissing boys with her. We're close, but that's just a little too close for me. Time has run out for me to be lost in thought anymore as I pull into the parking space behind The Wright Tools.

I open the shop, flipping on every light before I get the register up and running. Once nine o'clock rolls around, I flip and turn on our signs, mentally preparing and secretly hoping for a slow day. And as if a genie granted me my wish, I successfully pull off three hours with not a soul waltzing through. That is, until my game of solitaire on the computer gets interrupted by the bells above the front door.

Exiting quickly, I peer over, my stomach full-on falling into my ass as Dutton's body pushes open the door. A large bag of cement is thrown over one of his shoulders as he pushes through.

"Stock day," he says in a strained voice as he walks to the stockroom.

"Oh, shit," I murmur to myself as my feet hit the floor and I push off the stool, practically racing outside to be greeted by Colby and the swing doors that are open to the back of his truck.

Bags of concrete mix lie stacked on top of each other. Some bags are labeled sixty pounds, others labeled ninety. I opt to grab the lesser, heaving it in my arms with one pull as it slams on my chest, nearly knocking me back a step in the process.

"I can get these." Dutton's low groan rings right in my ear behind me.

"I can help," I reply as I push through the front door, dropping the heavy bag on the stockroom floor once I haul it there.

Dutton's already pushing past me with more bags and hardly making any eye contact in the process. *I try.* I try to look in his eyes as we pass. I try to see if there's any expression on his face other than the stoic one that's in place. I want to see his little smirk, the one where his eyes crease in the corner as he smiles. I don't know why I was nervous to come here, because having him right next to me as we pull these heavy bags out has me wanting to drop them on the floor by my feet and sit down and talk.

He shouldn't feel embarrassed. He shouldn't feel sorry. It's not like I hated it, I just...hate myself for enjoying it so much. His plush lips against mine, it was like his mouth surrounded me, but not in a heavy way. His kisses were light, wet with his tongue—goddammit, just the thought of it has me wanting more. But I know I'm not ready. Physically, maybe I am. God, it's been so long since I've had sex, I completely forgot if I even like it or not. But something tells me just by the way he kisses, he isn't at all bad in bed. Emotionally, though? I'm ruined. Fucking finished. I'm spent, and I just have this gut feeling that if Dutton's mouth lands one more time on mine, there's no coming back from it. But how am I supposed to tell him this? How am I supposed to put these words into something simple for him to understand?

"I'll get this last one." Dutton pushes through the front door, heading back outside to the truck.

I weave around the counter, blowing out heavy breaths as I sit back down. I should really get my ass to a gym. There is no way someone my age should be this out of shape.

I feel a bead of sweat drip from my forehead, running along my temple until it reaches just below my ear before I wipe it away. I'm not sure why all of a sudden it got so fucking hot in here, but the moment Dutton barges back through that door, another heat wave begins. The latching of the stockroom door causes my heart to race as the sounds of his footsteps get closer.

"Kaiton?" he asks softly, approaching the desk, and my eyes fall to his. "Listen, I'm incredibly sorry about last night. I mean, after everything you've been through and everything you told me... I can't believe I was so stupid." His eyes fall to his hands, his head shaking back and forth, and I can tell regret fills every piece of his soul as he keeps speaking. "Please forgive me. It was absolutely unprofessional of me. And if working here is uncomfortable for you, I understand completely. I can promise you it will never happen again. I'm just so fucking sorry." The last bit of his speech comes out nearly breathless. He doesn't just look *sorry*, he looks *devastated*.

"Dutton, I—" I try to form my thoughts into words but the moment I speak, Laura pushes through the front doors.

"Good afternoon!" her voice rings through the empty store in the most chipper tone.

Dutton clears his throat as he straightens his body before he whispers one last time, "Let me know if you need to resign. I can call some other businesses around and give you a great referral."

And with that, he leaves. He moves past Laura, rubbing the scruff on his face as he pushes right through the front door, not taking one last look behind him.

Does he want me gone this bad?

I didn't even get a chance to tell him what I felt. What if I wanted to apologize for pushing him away? I mean, I did…in a way. But I didn't even have the fucking chance.

"Sheesh, what's gotten into him today?" Laura scoffs with a crooked smile as she glances back at the front door.

I let a breath out through my nose, forcing a pressed smile. "Not sure." I shrug my shoulders, knowing damn well it's because of me.

Laura's here for the second shift, and I try to not make it obvious that I'm packing my things up at the speed of light to hopefully reach Dutton before he drives off. But it's too late. The moment I step outside, his truck is gone. And I'm left standing on the sidewalk trying to breathe in the thick air that surrounds me. I pull out my phone. If anything, he should know that this doesn't affect my ability to work here before he goes ahead and tries to find me another job.

ME: I still want to work here, if that's okay.

DUTTON BECK: Of course.

I hold my phone in my hand, fingers wrapped tightly around its rectangular body as I try to decide what more I can say. This isn't a conversation that should be held by text. I would prefer to tell him my fucked-up range of emotions in person. So, I leave it at that, and hope at least sometime soon, I'll see him again. And next time, it'll be my turn to apologize.

CHAPTER
TWENTY

THE MASON JAR glasses clink against the tray with every step I make as I carry it carefully down the hill. A glass pitcher of lavender lemonade rests between them and the weight of it all nearly has my arms shaking. I walk around the chairs by the dock, resting the wooden tray on the small table that sits between them both.

"Is this your famous lemonade?" Ellie asks as she sits upright from the lounging position she was just in.

"Sure is." I grin.

I pour a glass for her. The yellow liquid spills over the ice in her cup and I hand it to her once it's full. Pouring one for myself next, I finally sit down, ready to spill the beans.

I'm a firm believer that you have friends in your life for certain things. Most of what Layla and I gossip about is things I would never discuss with my mother. And heartfelt mom talks are things I wouldn't particularly discuss with Layla. However, in my most recent situation, I feel my two closest confidants wouldn't understand the magnitude of my emotions. Layla is too strong minded, my mother too soft for what I need right now. So that's why I asked Ellie here. Not that I necessarily need advice... I just need to get this shit off my chest.

"I'm so disappointed I won't be here for your birthday weekend," Ellie says.

"Oh, it's okay. I have to work anyway."

"I know, but we'll celebrate when I get back. Alright?" she says as her smile beams bright. "Oh my God, this is delicious," she adds after she takes a sip.

"It's lavender simple syrup, honey, and just regular old lemonade."

"My God. It's fantastic." She takes another sip. "So, what's been goin' on? You sounded like something was bothering you on the phone."

I keep taking small sips of my drink, trying to figure out how I want to start this off.

"Well." I clear my throat slightly. "For the sake of staying anonymous, let's call this man I met, Ted." I pause, waiting for her to say something, but I'm faced with more silence as she stares blankly. "Ted...kissed me unexpectedly." My teeth clench as I press my lips, finding it extremely hard to even keep a straight face with my choice of name. After all, the tall, gruff, mountain of a man whose lips were on mine doesn't resemble a 'Ted' in the slightest.

Ellie stays silent, just listening to me speak as she takes another sip of her drink.

"I pushed him off and told him I wasn't ready yet. And he immediately apologized. Like, profusely apologized. Even promised it would never happen again. But what if I want it to happen again?" My heart is thumping through my chest as I recall the memories. Just one fucking kiss has my stomach turning into mush. This is how I know I would be severely fucked up if anything between Dutton and I went any further.

"Do you?" she asks.

"Do I what?"

"Want him to kiss you again?"

"Yeah. I mean, no. I—"

"Let's take it slow here." She sets her glass down back on the tray. "Why did you push him away?"

"I said it was because I wasn't ready yet."

"That's what you told him. But why did you really?"

I sit and think, trying to gather my thoughts together from the jumbled mess they've been in the last couple of days. "Because I'm afraid."

"Afraid of what?"

"Getting hurt."

She nods, biting at the inside of her lip before she talks again. "And you think this 'Ted' will hurt you?"

"I don't know. We hardly know each other. But one thing is for certain, and it's that I'm naive. I'm fucking...*stupid*. And too trusting. But I'm not going to be that anymore. I have a guard up, this wall that I'm building. It's not even finished yet. I can't have someone break it down already. There's just something about him. I could have kissed him all night, Ellie. I really could have. I can't explain the safety that I feel in his presence. But I've felt that before.

That security, that warmth. Rory made me feel the same at one time. And I got royally fucked, excuse my language.

Ellie gives a little laugh. "Kaiton, please promise me one thing. Never, and I mean *never*, call yourself stupid again."

I sit back a little, relaxing my shoulders at the bite of her words.

"But that's how I feel."

"Why? Kaiton, you are a bright soul. And it pains me that you have been led to believe you are anything but. Sometimes in life, you place your trust in the wrong hands. It happens. But not everyone will be quick to betray you. I agree, maybe you need some more time. Sort your feelings out before getting involved with anyone. But a kiss is a kiss. I kiss my girlfriends all the time." She laughs, trying to lighten my mood as I'm sure she sees my eyes gloss over. "A little fling doesn't need to involve complex feelings. Haven't you ever had a fling before?"

"Not really."

"No flings? No casual sex? Nothing?"

"I've only been with two people before. And they were both long-term boyfriends, well...one became my fiancé."

"*Ex*-fiancé," she clarifies before taking another sip of her drink. "I think you can allow yourself to have some fun. At your own pace, of course. If you're not ready, you're not ready. You don't need to explain yourself to anyone on that. But don't feel wrong for wanting to explore either. This is your fresh start, your new beginning. Don't feel ashamed for wanting to break free and let your hair down."

I snort. "Let my hair down. God…I haven't done that since high school."

"Well, now sounds like a fine time to start." She raises an eyebrow, her lips hiding behind the mason jar as she swigs another sip. "So, tell me, what are your birthday plans?"

"Nothing." A small chuckle escapes my lips.

"Nothing? Come on, it's your twenty-fifth, it's a little milestone."

"I don't usually have good luck with birthdays, so when Laura wrote up the schedule, I asked to work that day." I can't help from sinking my teeth into my bottom lip, trying not to remember the last couple years of misery this day has brought me.

"Now I'm even more pissed I'm not going to be here. Maybe I should just tell Rod we can visit my family next weekend."

"Oh no, please don't do that. I promise I'm fine. When you get back, we can celebrate." I raise my glass a little to her, offering a sort of cheers.

She purses her lips, still slightly displeased. "Fine. But I will call you at midnight tonight. Just a forewarning."

I laugh, a deep one rooted in the pit of my stomach. "You remind me so much of my mom."

"I'm glad to hear it. Your mom sounds like a beautiful, intelligent lady." She winks.

"She is." My smile grows wide as I nod.

I think if it weren't for Ellie, I would have already gone back home with my tail between my legs, waving a white flag at Rory, *just* so I could be near my family. It seems silly, I mean, I'm practically a grown woman, although the word "adult" seems fallacious. But I haven't left home for this long before. It's just nice to feel like I have a piece of home here, with Ellie.

The wind is calm over the water as the sky becomes mixed with streaks of lilac and Ellie and I nearly finish off the entire pitcher of lemonade. Before it's too late, Ellie heads back home to pack up for her weekend getaway to Memphis where the rest of her side of the family lives. And I treat myself to a homemade dinner of Tuscan orzo and the hottest, longest shower I've had since living here—which subsequently only takes thirty minutes before the hot water runs out and I'm left with conditioner in my hair, trying to rinse it out under the icy stream in a hurry. I wrap the towel around my body, sitting on the couch while I turn on the TV, and pick up my phone. It's already almost midnight, minutes away from a day that has brought me nothing but bad luck, and once the clock finally strikes it, my phone begins to ring.

"Happy Birthday, baby!" my mom's voice blares through the speaker on my phone.

"Thanks, Mom."

"Happy Birthday, K. Love ya!" my dad says, his voice further from the phone than my mother's.

The other line beeps as Layla tries to ring in, followed by Ellie after. This is the only part of this God-awful day that I like. *The midnight phone calls.* After that, the day usually goes to shit. Let's hope this one is different.

New year.

New town.

New *me*.

At least this year I don't have to worry about my significant other forgetting to wish me happy birthday.

So already, I'm off to a great start.

CHAPTER
TWENTY-ONE

WHEN I OFFERED to work a double, I didn't take into account how long and drawn out the day would be with hardly any customers. When I first opened, there was an immediate rush. Five or six people practically lined up, hitting me with questions left and right about lawn mower accessories, circuit breakers, and grass seed—all of which I had zero fucking clue about, but got everything figured out nonetheless. Since then, not a soul has waltzed through. But that hasn't stopped me from breaking a sweat. I've singlehandedly tidied and organized every nook and cranny this place has to offer and let me just say, I did a hell of a job. The bells chime against the frame of the door while I'm stuck in aisle fourteen, wrapping up the chains and ropes I had taken from the shelves to clean. I set them down, peering into the center aisle to get a straight view of the door. The familiar face of the woman from the flower shop next door stands smiling from ear to ear.

"Hi!" I grin.

"Kaiton?" she asks as she walks toward me, holding in her hand a bouquet of flowers similar to the one I purchased weeks ago from her shop. One that has unfortunately withered away to nothing.

"Mhm." I nod as I meet her in the middle of the store.

"Happy Birthday! These are for you." Her grin never fades as she hands me the fresh-smelling flowers, still wet with light water droplets from their morning mist.

A card wedged between plastic prongs on a stick touches the tip of my nose as I raise it up to take in the sweet smell.

"Thank you." I smile.

"Anytime. If you ever need anything, I'm right next door."

I bring the vase to the counter while watching her leave, then set them down carefully as I grasp the card between my fingers. Knowing my parents, this is probably their way of gifting me something today since they're over a thousand miles away. How ironic that they chose practically the same bouquet I bought myself when I first arrived.

I open the small, folded card, the chicken scratch letters catching my eye first.

I know this handwriting.

This is the handwriting that signs my time slips.

Happy Birthday, Kaiton.

— Dutton

My cheeks run hot as I stare at the letter. He didn't just call and place a delivery order. He went in, picked these out, and wrote the card himself.

Fuck.

"Happy Birthday!" Laura's singsong voice calls the second she walks through the door.

I snap the tiny card shut, clutching it in my hand as I try to slow down the rushing speed of my heart rate.

"Thank you." I smile but my voice is not far from breathless.

"Oh, pretty flowers." Her eyes grow wide as she touches an orange petal on one of the roses. "Jesus, it's so clean in here." Her focus shifts back as she glances around the entirety of the store.

"Yeah, it's been pretty slow today. Didn't have anything else to do."

"Dutton's going to be thrilled. This place hasn't looked this nice in years." She chuckles. "Well, anyway. I'm here to print off end of the week numbers and run them over to the boss."

"Oh." My voice trails off. "I could do that for you."

"You wanna work *after* work...on your birthday?"

"It's practically on my way home, anyway," I say, even though it's not. At all.

"I mean, that would be great. Would save me a trip for sure. I've got my grandbaby staying the night tonight so I'll just get her even sooner. Are you sure, Kait? You really don't mind?"

"No. Not at all," I say, keeping my grin. "Could you just show me what I need to bring?"

"Absolutely," she says as she whips behind the counter.

She makes a few clicks on the computer and I try to follow along. Soon enough, the printer below starts spewing page after page.

I wanted to talk to Dutton. I wanted to explain my feelings. But the more I think about it, the more fucked up it makes me seem. He just kissed me, for God's sake. He wasn't asking for my hand in marriage. If I tell him I'm afraid of getting hurt, he's going to look at me like some serial monogamist who can't stand the thought of being single.

I can *do* casual.

I can *be* easygoing.

A single kiss can't make me fall in love. So, fuck it. I'm twenty-five now. I can make my own decisions without feeling guilty. I will, however, apologize to him. I don't want him to feel like I pushed him away because he's hideous. He's anything but. What I won't tell him, though, is that for every night since he kissed me, I've fallen asleep to thoughts of it going further—him pulling me into his house, letting his large hands roam over every inch of my body until—

"And that's it!" Laura exclaims as my focus shifts back to her and not on Dutton undressing me again.

I grin as she hands me the stack of papers, unsure of where she found the mound of receipts she has fastened with a paperclip. I was so lost in my head that my vision blurred out. My eyes might have been staring right at her, but I only saw my burning desire to live a little.

"I'll get this over as soon as I lock up." I give her an assuring nod.

"Awesome, I appreciate it. Have a great rest of your birthday, Kaiton." She leans in for a hug.

I wrap my arms around her, embracing her warmth before we let go and she's back out the door. The rest of my shift drags on but the moment I begin to close, my stomach is tossing, turning, and flipping like it's some Olympic medal winner. I don't even know what I'm going to say to him. A proper "thank you" for the flowers seems like a great start. I can exclude the part about this being my very first time receiving them from a man who wasn't my father, though. That might throw some red flags his way.

My phone buzzes in my back pocket and I pull it out to see my favorite picture of Layla and me, puckering our lips to the camera as my blonde curls mix with her auburn strands.

"Hello?" I say, unable to contain my smile.

"Hello, birthday girl. Are you busy?"

"Just closing up the store right now."

"How exciting. Are you having a good day so far?"

"Yeah." My voice raises an octave as I answer her. It hasn't been terrible. In fact, this hasn't even come close to the worst birthday I've had so far. So honestly, it's going great.

"I'm glad to hear it. Got any big plans for tonight? I miss you. Wish I could celebrate with you."

"I miss you more. No big plans, just have to run some things over to my boss's house."

The line goes quiet for a moment. So quiet I question for a second if I lost signal.

"Dutton's house?" she asks, her voice rupturing with optimism.

"Yes. Dutton's house," I say, tucking the phone between my ear and shoulder as I reach up to flip over the sign.

"Okay, girl. Get it."

"Layla—"

"I'm not saying anything!" she quickly retorts.

"No, I want to ask you something." I grab the phone between its pinched place and hold it in my hand instead, switching to speakerphone as I walk to the computer to shut it down.

"Fire away, K. I'm all ears."

"Is it easy to have casual sex and not catch any feelings?"

She coughs like she just took a sip of a drink and choked. "Who are you planning on screwing? Your boss? Are you finally going to make a move?" A giggle flows with her words.

"No, I— Just answer the question."

"I mean, I do it all the time. I've had plenty of sex with men I don't like, personally. Just think of it like a business transaction, if that helps you. You're a woman, you have needs. Sometimes you just want a good lay after a stressful week. I mean, you like sex, right?"

"Yeah, I...well, I don't really know. It's fine, I guess."

"You guess? I thought Rory was good in bed. It's one of the reasons I thought you stayed so long."

"Layla! I mean, it was good, I think. I don't have that much experience. You know this." I stumble over my words, trying to figure out the right ones to choose. Layla and I never really talked about my sex life, only hers. She's respectful that way. Never prying about sex inside of relationships, only dishing out on the one-nighters *she* had.

"What do you mean?"

"Well, at the beginning of our relationship, things were more exciting...from what I can remember. Sometimes we'd even have sex during the day. But as it went on, it kind of became less and less—only before bed, one position, and of course after we both had showered. But then I seemed to be the only one initiating it. You know what I mean? And even that was usually met with a huff and a sigh, like it was...some chore he had to finish. He was always tired from work, or just 'not in the mood.' Eventually I stopped trying, so that, combined with the lack of effort with anything from his side...we didn't really have much sex by the time I left. Unless, on rare occasions, he came home drunk from a night out with his friends. But I don't even think I could consider that sex since it lasted less than a whole minute."

Layla burst into laughter on the other end of the line, cackling like a lunatic so loud I debate for a second on turning the volume down.

"I don't mean to laugh, I'm sorry. It's not funny. But the minute thing. That got me. I can so see it. I'm sorry." She tries to calm her giggles by clearing her throat and I can't help but crack a small smile.

"So how long do you think it's been then?"

"Since?"

"Since you last had sex?"

"Hm...I don't know. Maybe right when we got back from our trip to Michigan when we all went last summer."

"Kaiton..." Her voice trails off. "That was a fucking year ago."

I blink, a mindless expression on my face as I realize just how long it's been. The hurt of it all comes racing back.

"I guess...I hadn't realized."

"Don't you like...buff the muffin?" she asks.

"Buff what muffin?"

"You know...polish the pearl?"

"What pearl?"

"Kaiton! Do you flick the bean?"

"Layla, please. I don't know what the fuck you're talking about."

"Don't you masturbate?" Her voice shoots louder and it echoes throughout the store.

"Oh. Uh, no."

"No? Kaiton, please tell me you're kidding?"

She sounds like I personally killed her cat and she just now found out it's buried in my backyard.

"Layla, I'm not kidding. I'm really not a sexual kind of person. I think I used to be... I remember a time when I enjoyed it, but that ship has sailed. And I'm fine. Trust me."

"Girl, get fucked. And I don't mean it in a 'get lost, go away,' kind of sentiment. I mean literally go out and get fucked."

"Layla." I lower my voice even though I'm the only one in here.

"Kaiton, listen to me. That fucking imbecile of a man has probably been trotting around sticking his dick wherever that little baby carrot of his will fit. Which is just about anything. What an idiot he is to not have been putting in the work with you every night. I don't mean to get all up in your shit right now, but Kaiton, believe me when I say you have a body that makes every woman jealous."

"Layla—"

"I'm not done. Your tits sit so perfectly I would have put money on it that they were fake if I didn't know you any better. Your ass single-handedly could shake an entire county if you moved it. Your thighs could crush a fucking watermelon. I mean, literally, I could go on for hours. What I'm saying is that you're smoking fucking hot. And any man on planet Earth should feel lucky enough to get to have his dick anywhere *near* you. Go out. And get fucked. You deserve it. And if you find that you still don't enjoy sex, don't do it anymore. Just...make sure to be safe. You know. Wrap it up. Use all the protection. And *no*, the pull-out method is not sufficient."

She ends with a long-winded sigh, like every word took her last breath.

"Thank you," I finally say, after being dumbstruck on the compliments. "But don't you think it's a little soon?"

"K, baby, I love you, but please. Rory fucked someone while you were *together*. I think you're good to go ahead and get laid by someone else weeks after you've broken it off."

"Okay. Thanks. I appreciate your words of wisdom."

I don't know what I expected out of my question. I think I could be capable of having sex without that emotional pull. Maybe I just needed the 'go ahead' from someone else too, even though

I've gotten it twice over now between her and Ellie. Not that I'm planning on fucking *Dutton*. It could be anyone. Whenever the time is right, I guess.

We finish up our call by making all kinds of plans for when I'm back home in Illinois before I finally shut the lights off and lock the front door behind me. I clutch the papers tight to my chest, trying to balance them and my bouquet as I walk to my car. Storm clouds roll in as the air becomes thick with humidity and a dark haze falls over the town even though it's only a little past five. I click in my seatbelt and back out of my parking space as I try to remember how to get to Dutton's as I pass Neddy's bar. It only takes me a few turns before I see that familiar green street sign and the obscenely long driveway. The same brown stonework I saw in the darkness lines the bottom of the house and I see Dutton swinging an axe above his head as he splits a log in half, right in front of the large barn. Me pulling into his drive isn't what catches his attention. It's the sound of me shutting my car door that perks his head. I flash him a smile, even though we're too far apart to read each other's facial expressions. My steps are timid as I walk forward, pacing myself as the wind makes a vicious blow, not at all changing the temperature of the muggy air. Chills run up my spine at the barking of a dog.

I'm already on edge.

Even the slightest bit of commotion is stirring me up.

Dutton stills, watching me as I approach, when a golden retriever comes zooming out from inside the barn, darting its way right at me. I can't help but smile as I see its tongue stick out, flopping with the wind, until it finally reaches me. The dog weaves in and out of my legs, causing me to step carefully as I try to push closer to Dutton. I laugh, leaning down and giving in because this dog would rather get attention from me than go anywhere else. I run my hand along its back, a teal collar jingling as I scratch behind its ear. It licks at my hands, licks at my jeans, and wherever it can get to me. Dutton whistles and both of our gazes shoot right to him. The dog runs back to his feet, and I straighten myself up, continuing toward him.

"Where's Laura?" is the first thing he asks.

Not a "hello", not a "how are you", not a "happy birthday".

"Uh, I offered to bring you these today," I say, trying to mask my tense state.

"Oh," he says as he grabs the axe handle, and in one swift motion, slices it down the center of a new log. His muscles strain as he swings, and lines of different veins poke up from just under his skin. He takes a long breath as he tosses the axe on the ground, reaching his hand out to grab the papers from me.

"Thanks for the flowers today."

"Yeah, no problem," he says as he flashes his stare between me and the pages he's reading. "Are you having a good birthday so far?"

"Yeah, probably the best one yet," I let out with a sigh.

Dutton stops, lifting his eyes from the paper to me, cocking an eyebrow while lines scrunch on his forehead.

"You worked all day. That was your best birthday yet?"

I flash an awkward smile. To anyone else in the world, I'm sure that seems peculiar, so I get it. "Yeah, very relaxing I guess," I say, trying to make it simple to understand.

"Hm." He huffs as he draws back slightly. "Alright. Well, thanks for this." He holds the papers up, giving me a small smile.

This is almost as awkward as when he was in my house nearly naked. I can't think of how to start off any sort of conversation with him. But as my luck would have it, I don't need to think for too long before that retriever comes bolting back to my feet.

"Hi!" I squeal in my doggy voice. Similar to a baby voice, but less annoying, in my opinion.

I bend at my knees, giving the dog a stepping stool to get to my face as it kisses my cheek.

"Birdie. Down, girl!" Dutton calls.

"She's fine, I kind of asked for it." I shimmy my hands at her sides, roughing up her hair as I scratch near her stomach. Her tail wags from side to side as she pants heavily in my face.

"Sorry, she needs attention twenty-four hours a day. I'm almost certain she thinks she'll die if someone doesn't pet her constantly." Dutton laughs.

A real laugh.

Deep-rooted and full of richness.

Finally, some genuine emotion.

I peek to the side from behind Birdie's face, smiling at Dutton when I look up at him. I straighten my legs, letting my hands go from her body before I wipe her loose hair against my jeans.

"It's okay, I miss my own. I needed to get some pets in anyway."
I grin.

A boom of thunder rattles the ground before the first of the raindrops fall, and almost simultaneously, Dutton and I look to the sky.

"Fuck," he mutters under his breath as I watch him hastily fold up the papers and shove them into his back pocket.

He moves quickly, gathering up bundles of small, chopped logs in his arms as he practically runs to throw them in the barn.

"Need help?" I call out as he quickly moves.

"Sure." He grabs some more wood from the high pile stacked on the side of the building.

I walk over, grabbing one log at a time until I fit all that I can cradle into my arms. The rain drops faster, and I hurry to throw these on the smaller pile he's creating inside.

I dart around him, grabbing three more before I toss those on the second stack. The rain seems to plummet harder the faster we work, and it doesn't take long until every strand of my hair is completely wet. My white tank top sticks to my skin as I move, and Dutton has to slick back all the pieces of his hair that want to fall in front of his face. He exhales in a loud huff, and I watch the water fly in specks from his pouted lips as he grabs the biggest log he has yet to chop. His biceps flex as they hug the thick width of it and with ease, it's up off the ground. I follow behind him, carrying the last four small bits of wood as he slams the stump down inside.

"Fuck!" he groans as his arm shoots up to cover his eye.

I drop the wood in my hands, watching him work his fingers into the corner of his eyelid.

"Are you okay?" I ask with his back still facing me. He only grunts as he continues to dig.

I glance around quickly, seeing what I can do to help and spot a five-gallon bucket in the corner. Grabbing it by its sides, I waddle it back over to him.

"Here. Sit, I say as I flip it over, holding onto his arms to guide him down. He takes a seat, still poking and prodding his finger into his eye. I grab his hand, pulling it away slowly as he clamps his eye shut. "Let me see," I say and gently pry his lid open, immediately seeing the smallest sliver of wood right on the white of his eye. I run my finger against it, pinching the small piece between my index and thumb before I pull it out and flick it off my fingers.

"I got it." Our bodies are still close as he opens both eyes to look at me. He blinks rapidly for a moment and gives it one more rub, digging his knuckle into the corner. I straighten, still holding his gaze while Birdie prances and jumps around us.

"Thanks," he says, the side of his mouth tilting up into the sexiest smirk I've ever seen.

My heart thunders inside my chest and I can't seem to figure out for the life of me why being this close to him almost brings me into cardiac arrest every damn time.

"You're soaked," he voices with a deep laugh, his Adam's apple rising and falling with every pitch.

"*You're* soaked." I smile, eyeing him up and down. His silky strands now drip with water while fully formed droplets still rest on his face. His light grey T-shirt looks almost black, and we could probably fill this bucket he's sitting on just by ringing out our clothes.

"Do you want to dry off?" he asks.

My heart hammers even faster. "Sure." I nod slowly.

"Let's go in," he says before he's up on his feet, whistling at Birdie and glancing back at me before he raises his eyebrows. "Come on." He nods his head toward his house and in a split second, we're dashing to the door, running through the torrential rain again. It's a straight downpour from the sky as if God himself opened up a floodgate. Birdie runs between us, following Dutton's lead as he leaps up his front steps. I'm right behind, laughing like a kid in the schoolyard until I'm finally under the roof of his wraparound porch. He opens the door and Birdie runs inside first, shaking her body vigorously as the water flies from her coat. Dutton walks in and I follow, shutting the door behind me. He looks at me, my back against the door as I take him in. His shirt clings for dear life against each curve of his muscles and his suntanned skin looks even more golden under the few bulbed lights he has in the corner of this dimly lit living room. My breathing picks up pace as I keep my back pressed firm on the door. I take a quick glance down at my soaked white tank top, only now remembering which bra I chose to wear today. The peaks of my nipples push against the fabric, not leaving much to anyone's imagination. Then I tilt my chin back up to Dutton, noticing his hand rubbing at the sharp line of his jaw as his chest caves in and out with every deep breath.

He stands there, soaked from head to toe, with eyes so wild they make my knees weak.

I want him.

I want to taste him again.

Right here.

Right now.

My body nearly lunges toward him without hesitation. His strong arms wrap around my frame and he grabs the hair at the nape of my neck. My hands fall to his face, rubbing against his edged-up beard he's been letting grow. My lips land on his first. They're soft and plush, just how I remember.

"Are you sure?" he breathes against my lips between the kiss.

I only get a chance to nod before he kisses me back slowly, sweeping his tongue against mine. I moan into him. The feeling of his hands all over me, gripping me tight, makes me nearly feral. I haven't been touched like this in so long. I haven't been *kissed* like this in so long. The feeling is unfamiliar, but I don't want it to stop. Our rhythm picks up—faster, longer, drawn-out kisses as our tongues intertwine and the force of my body against his pushes him backward to the fireplace mantle, rattling everything on it. His hands glide down my body, rubbing over the curve of my ass before he grabs tightly and lifts me up. I wrap my legs around his waist without a single thought as if I've done this a million times over. He sinks his teeth into my neck gently as his tongue runs with it, and I tilt my head, offering more access to the skin exposed. He bites at the strap of my tank, pulling it down from its position on my shoulder. His firm grip on my ass never lets up while he still holds me as if I'm weightless. He squeezes, pushing my pelvis hard onto his. I can feel him through his jeans as I grind my hips slowly against him. He groans in a low sigh, like thick molasses, as he kisses the top of my breast before dragging his tongue *just* underneath my ribbed tank, making it almost to my nipple that's only covered by the loose lace of my bra. I lift my head to face him, trying to give him a hand at pulling the rest of my shirt down until my eyes lock on a photo behind him, resting right on the mantle in a silver metal frame.

A photo of Dutton, in a tuxedo.

Standing next to his *bride*.

"What the fuck?" I gasp as I push against his chest.

Dutton stops to look at me as I wiggle my body free from his hold.

"What?"

"You're fucking married?" My tone grows louder even though I'm certain it feels like an elephant is sitting on my chest.

"Kait—"

"No!" I throw my hand up to his face "I— I—" No fucking words will form. No matter how hard I try, I can't speak. I close my eyes, my heart pounding, and I keep shaking my head as I quickly stumble backward.

"Please—"

"Save it!" I shout as I finally grip the handle and yank open the door, not even closing it behind me as I sprint to my car.

"Kaiton!" he calls from his front porch.

I don't look back.

The rain falls just as fast and heavy as my tears, and I can't even make out the difference of them on my face as I pull open the door.

Dutton is standing in the middle of his yard, calling for me as the raindrops thump against my car. I hang my head in my hands, weeping into them. How could I have been so careless? He's fucking *married*. And she's beautiful. Picture-perfect stunning in her thin-strapped gown with Dutton cheesing happily by her side. I'm a fucking idiot. And a homewrecker.

A homewrecker.

"Fuck." I sob. "Fuck!" I scream as I punch my steering wheel.

I know how it feels. I know how it feels when the love of your fucking life steps out, and now I'm going to be the reason she stays up at night. I'm going to be the reason she can't trust a single soul again.

I'm mad at myself for being so reckless.

But I'm even more mad at him for making me the last person I would ever want to become.

"Kaiton, please!" Dutton's voice is muffled as he raps his fist against my window.

I give him the best "fuck you" glare I can before I shove my keys into the ignition, cranking it hard in hopes it will start faster. I throw it into reverse the quickest I ever have and slam on the gas as my tires skate across the dirt. I don't even bother looking back in the mirror but that doesn't stop my phone from buzzing. One missed call after the next. I can't pick up. I don't want to pick up. I don't give a fuck what he has to say. Because in this very moment, I hate him.

Almost as much as I hate myself.

CHAPTER
TWENTY-TWO

I SHOULD HAVE KNOWN. It's the fucking day. It's cursed. *Although...it wasn't the most awful.*

The worst birthday I probably had was only because it was the most embarrassing. I had told Rory about the dinner plans I made for us. He started right off arguing about what restaurant I had chosen. That wasn't the half of it, though. On the way to dinner, he had to stop for gas. *My fault for not filling it up beforehand.* I had run in to pay since Rory didn't like doing that. Me, dressed to the nines in a beautiful black silk dress. A *backless* dress that crossed at the neck, not exposing any cleavage. *God forbid.* My heels were tall and strappy and I felt so pretty with my dainty gold jewelry and a slicked-back bun. It was elegant, timeless, *expensive.* And here I was, standing in line at Starkey's, waiting to put forty dollars on pump two. A man walked in to stand behind me, probably in his late fifties, roughly around the same age as my dad. He told me I looked pretty when our eyes met, and asked what the occasion was. I let him know it was my birthday, to which any sane person on planet Earth would reply, "Well, Happy Birthday." I smiled and thanked him. And God, had I wished a thousand times that night that I had gotten gas earlier. I was accused afterward, *loudly*, in front of every patron in that restaurant—accused of flirting, accused of cheating. All because he saw me chatting with a man through the glass of the gas station. Then, the kicker. Our waiter came over. He asked for our drinks, to which I replied, "A glass of champagne, please."

Wrong thing to do.

I got told off like a child. Napkin thrown in my face. How dare I want a celebratory drink? Women who drink, cheat.

Or so he would say.

The people around us froze. They stopped talking to each other, they stopped laughing, they all just *stopped* to watch. I was mortified. That was the last time I asked to go anywhere for my birthday.

We stayed together for three more years.

It's my fault for not leaving sooner, I know. At first, the jealousy made it seem like he really cared about me. Like he was worried. Afraid of losing me because I was *it*. I was his world. The good times were *so good*. But when they were bad...they were awful. I found myself making pros and cons lists constantly, always seeming to come up with just a few more pros than cons, validating my decision to stay.

Maybe he will get better when we have a child. Maybe he will see I'm not doing anything behind his back. Maybe he'll understand I don't want anyone else but him.

I tried. Really tried. I gave him my all, I gave him everything. Lost so much of myself that I just ended up a shell of the woman I used to be.

I think the infidelity hurt. But it wasn't different from any of the pain he'd already caused me. It all ached the same.

But if this new incident wasn't a sign of how I need more time, I don't know what else would be. Dutton is *married*. Or at the very least, just starting to file for divorce. He can't already be divorced. The way that photo was so proudly displayed on the clean mantle in the very front room says otherwise. They both looked young, like they've been married for quite some time. And God was she beautiful. Brown wavy hair that ended in the middle of her back. She had the most breathtaking smile I think I've ever seen another woman have. Her dress looked so simple and sophisticated the way it clung to her small frame, and Dutton's arm was placed tightly around the lower part of her back.

It's been two days of mostly wallowing in my self-pity, flopping between my bed and the couch. Dutton has called a total of eleven times. Six of them were between when I left his house and when I got to my own. I have texts from him, too. Only a couple. But I don't want to hear him out right now. My skin is crawling enough from my own doing. I can't hear some poor excuse for his behavior. That'll just make me want to claw at my own eyes in hopes I never have to see another man again.

I already asked Laura to cover my shift tomorrow. I told her I had a stomach bug. I'm not one hundred percent lying. There definitely has been puking in this household over the weekend. But

I'm not entirely sure what to do about my shift on Wednesday. I have to quit. There's no doubt about that. I can't be the other woman and *still* remain his employee. What a gut-wrenching punch that would be for her.

Maybe I should call her.

I should let her know somehow. It's not fair to her.

That's what I'll set out to do tomorrow. Tonight, I'm staring at a bottle of whiskey that I bought before all this shit hit the literal fan. I bought myself alcohol for my birthday, with no one telling me not to. No one yelling at me, cursing at me, or accusing me of shit I haven't done. I didn't really have any intention of drinking it then—it was sort of a way for me to show *myself* what independence feels like. Now, with the circumstances, I wish I would have opted for champagne because if I bring this whiskey to my lips, it's going to taste just like *him*.

I've been playing music from an old stereo system that sits on a small table against the wall between the living and dining rooms. Thankfully, the iPod was already attached, but most of the songs I've never heard of before. There's one, though, that I've played for the second time in a row—"The Chain" by Fleetwood Mac. I've heard of the band before, but never this song. Something about the melody, words, and vocals makes me want to keep it on repeat. My arms hang over the back of the chair I'm leaning on, eyes locked on the glass bottle while I bob slightly to the music. I chew at the inside of my cheek as the song restarts again, my fingers now tapping along to the rhythm as I contemplate just having a sip. I don't think I like alcohol, but I can't even remember a time when I felt safe enough to ask if I could try it out, just to make sure. Now I *don't* have anyone to ask. I get to make my own rules. I get to decide what's best for me. And that freedom feels really fucking good right now.

I finally move from my hunched position over the chair and grab a glass from one of the open shelves. It's only a matter of seconds before I'm pouring the amber-colored liquid straight into my cup. I bring the glass up to my nose, not even having to inhale before I get a whiff of its pungent spiced caramel smell. My nose twists up at the shock of it. It's fierce, almost bitter, with just how smokey it seems. I gulp, swallowing nothing with how dry my mouth is, before I bring the glass to my lips. I close my eyes as Fleetwood Mac sings the chorus I'm finally learning the words to, and tip my head back slightly, letting the whiskey hit my lips as I part them. The room-temperature liquid slides down my throat as if it has knives attached to it. It burns, and it's even more malty than it smells. I do everything but gag as I finally swallow and without a second thought, slam the half-filled glass on the dining table.

"Not for me," I say out loud.

Although the aftertaste is nothing like how it went down, I still am not enticed to pick it back up. It's sweeter now, but my eyebrows pinch and I grimace at the thought of what I'm tasting.

Honey. *Fucking honey.*

I brush the thought off as fast as it comes. I'm tired of giving men the power to make me sad. I'm over it. Fuck that and fuck them.

I just drank alcohol, and my ass didn't get reamed out for it.

A triumphant smirk gradually stretches across my face. I bob my head and sway my hips as the true feeling of freedom hits me in an instant like a heavy wave crashing onto shore. I take one last small sip, just solidifying the fact that I can do what I want, when I want, and this one goes down worse than the first. I cough, instantly gagging before tossing the rest into the sink behind me. A faint shiver rolls down my body and I shake it off before The Fleets—that's what I'm calling my new favorite band—start the chorus again. I nail down the words and scream along with them. Between the stereo blasting as loud as it will go and my cheerleading voice I know can travel far, it's a good thing I don't have any neighbors close by. Especially because my vocals resemble that of a shrieking donkey and claws on a chalkboard mixed together.

It doesn't take long until my hair is whipping around as I jump to the pounding of the drums and the ending guitar solo, fake microphone-hand to my mouth as I finish the song.

All I know is that between the sweat starting to form on my hairline, the headache I already feel coming on, and the pure exhaustion this weekend has brought, I may finally get a full night's sleep here for the first time since coming to Falton Ridge.

CHAPTER
TWENTY-THREE

MY HEAD THUMPS to the beat of a knocking sound, pulsating at the same time each hit slams against the butter-yellow wood. I groan in misery and desperation as I turn and pull the pillow over my head, trying to muffle the God-awful vibrations. The knocking doesn't let up and it only clicks just now—someone is at my door.

I spring up, immediately throwing my hand to my head to apply pressure to the raging headache that won't go away. Another sign alcohol is just not for me. I haven't drunk in over three years, but if two swigs can make me feel like ass, I can't imagine what five or six would do.

"I'm coming, I'm coming," I say as I slide my legs out from under the sheets, my tone growing more agitated as the knocks continue.

I shuffle my feet across the floor as I drag myself to the door, yanking it open with one swift pull.

Dutton stands before me, one hand in his pocket, the other clenched tightly in that stupid fist he used to pound so unnecessarily loud.

"Nope" is all I say before I slam the door shut back in his face.

"Kaiton, please open up. I need to talk to you," he calls to me from the other side of the wood. It's muffled, but clear enough to make out.

"I don't want to talk to you!" I yell back to make sure he hears me.

"It'll take five minutes, then you can decide where you want to go from there."

"How 'bout I decide in three seconds? *No. Thank. You,*" I snarl back as I cross my arms tightly around my midsection.

"Kaiton, it's...it's not what it looks like."

I scoff and pinch my brows together. *Not what it looks like?* Who does this fucking guy think he is?

I swing the door back open, only so he can see the disgust that washes over my features. "What does it look like then? Hm, Dutton? You were definitely in a tuxedo. And she was one hundred percent in a wedding dress. What, were you guys taking modeling shots for a Sears catalogue? I mean, really. Not what it looks like? Then tell me, Dutton, what *does* it look like then?" I bark at him, tapping my foot on the ground and keeping my guarded stature secure with my arms wrapped tightly around myself.

"Can I...come in?"

"No. You may not. We can stay right here," I huff, feeling more comfortable with the screen door remaining shut as a barrier between us.

"Fine." He nods as he takes a seat on my porch, resting his back against the door frame.

I follow suit, sitting on my wood floor as I lean against the wall opposite him, treading carefully on the way down since I'm only wearing an oversized T-shirt and underwear.

Dutton clears his throat as I look at him. Even through the screen, I can tell the desperation pleading to me from his eyes. A look so desolate, I fear he may be on the brink of tears. He holds my gaze, and in his natural husky tone says, "Her name is Hailey. She was my best friend since I was a kid. We only became friends because I got picked on at the playground. She shoved a second grader into the dirt for giving me a wedgie. *We were in kindergarten.* She had a very 'take no shit' kind of attitude. She was a fighter, always scrappy. I liked being friends with her because I felt like she could pretty much beat up anyone who looked at me funny." He laughs lightly before his eyes fixate on his fingers as they fumble together, resting on his scrunched-up knee. "Then she got sick, but the only thing that changed was her physical strength. She was still as feisty as ever. Always had a positive outlook on every fucked up situation she was dealt. She battled leukemia for about six or seven years. It wasn't until she was in her twenties when that leukemia spiraled into an even bigger beast of stage four, when it spread to her liver. At that point, she was only given two weeks as her final prognosis." He clears his throat once more, eyes still weighing heavy behind his lashes. "As kids, we would make this sort of...bucket list. Things we wanted to do before we died, kind of thing. Mine had crazy shit like skydiving over an ocean and meticulously landing on a yacht full of supermodels." He laughs as he shakes his head, knowing how ridiculous it sounds. "And riding a camel through an actual desert, that one was for sure on there. But hers were simple. More realistic, obtainable things. In a way, I think she decided to make it like that because of some crazy foreshadowing sense of her future. Kissing a boy was number one, obviously." He smirks, his head now lifting to capture my gaze again. "But we checked that off with Henry. We were all like, eight years old at this time, too, so...go easy on me wanting those supermodels."

He sidetracks, holding his smile, and I find it hard to contain a small laugh, fighting through the tears that rim my eyes. "She also had things on there like swimming in the ocean, going to Disney World, reading ten books in one month... I helped with that one," he says proudly as his eyes beam brighter. "When she was too weak to pick up her hardcover books, I read them to her, a series of five excruciatingly long fantasy novels. Don't ask me anything about them, though, because I've chosen to block out everything I read. She was seventeen or eighteen then, and never in my life would I have thought that fairy porn would be a type of book." He nearly shivers at the memory before taking a deep sigh. "When she left that doctor's appointment with her prognosis, we spent the next two days crossing off every last item we could, until we got to the very end. "Get Married" was what it said on the twentieth line of her list. Now, Hailey and I were the best of friends, but in no way did we ever think of each other as anything more. Never kissed, never held hands, shit...I don't even think we hugged each other. But it was kind of a no brainer for me. I looked right at her as we stared at her list jotted down on a very old, crumpled-up piece of notebook paper and I kind of just shrugged my shoulders and said, 'I'll marry you.' It took her a day to finally agree. She felt bad that I would 'waste my first marriage on her' and I hated when she said that. To me, it wasn't a waste. I mean, people tell you to marry your best friend all the time. We quickly made the plans, had a small ceremony on her parents' farm, and that was that. She was extremely weak at the time, so we didn't have a proper first dance, but everything else was the same—a true officiant, bridal party, wedding dress and tux, the whole nine yards." His smile starts to fade and he swallows hard. "She ended up dying four days later. We were both twenty-two, so...it's been almost nine years since then. I have our wedding photo up because it's the only picture I have of us together. And even then, it was kind of a process to take. She couldn't stand for very long, so we had to make the photos quick." He pauses, looking at me as he finishes, but I don't want him to see the tears rolling down my cheeks. I don't want him to see how my face is tomato red from trying to hold back my sobs. I feel horrible. For *Hailey*, for thinking every repulsive thought about *him*. For everything.

I feel horrible for everything.

"I'm not this awful guy, Kaiton. I know it's hard to believe, and God do I want to hit the asshole who made you think that all men are like that, but I'm not. I'm not that kind of man."

"I'm so sorry," I finally say as I slowly stand, bringing my hand to my mouth to hold in the sobbing sounds that want to thrash out. I open the screen door and as Dutton comes to his feet, I wrap my arms around his neck and stand on my tiptoes, squeezing him tight. "I'm so sorry," I say again, only this time in a whisper.

"You don't have to apologize."

"I do. I was terrible to you, and I said some really horrendous things about you over the weekend."

"Oh, yeah?" He smirks and pushes me away only slightly so he can look at my face.

"I mean, yeah, it was pretty bad." I giggle as the tears still well inside my eyes. "Do you want to come in? Maybe you can tell me some more about Hailey?" I offer.

He only nods, but the corner of his lip curls up. His hand stays on the small of my back as I lead him inside. He clears his throat behind me, and I turn to see him pointing to the whiskey bottle on my dining table. "Did you, uh, have company over?"

"No. It's mine. I tried it. Alcohol really is not for me." I chuckle. "Let me put some pants on. Do you want some breakfast? Coffee? Anything?"

"Coffee is good, when you're done." He pulls out a chair to sit on.

I nod before darting to my room, rifling through my drawers to find what I'm looking for.

I feel like such an asshole. I immediately stuck him into some fucked up narrative in my head. Cursed his name for three days straight. I was quick to judge, had all these preconceived notions about him as a person, about his character. I was wrong about everything. I acted out of anger and a heartbreak he didn't cause. That wasn't fair—to him, or to Hailey.

"When was her birthday?" I shout from my bedroom as I dig through my bottom drawer.

"March fifth," he calls back to me.

I smirk, gearing up for my next question about her. "What was her middle name?"

"Louise. Hailey Louise Wright."

I perk up from my drawer, holding my soft waffle-knit shorts between my fingers as I stand, poking my head out from my bedroom.

"Wright as in The Wright Tools?"

He nods with a grin and I tuck back into my room, slipping my shorts on as I grab the matching sweater. I lift my shirt over my head, my breasts on full display before I tug the sweater over my head, no time to pull it all the way over my stomach before I'm out of my room.

"Her parents', or?"

"It was her parents', yes. They retired and handed it over to me. I've been the sole owner for almost four years now."

"That's really cool. Do you still talk to her parents? I mean...wait, that's probably a stupid question," I say as I move past him to my kitchen counter. I grab two mugs before starting on the coffee.

"It's not a stupid question," he says, turning to watch me. "We're really close. I lost my parents when I was young. The Wrights basically took me in and haven't been able to get rid of me since."

I carefully bring the mugs to the table, setting Dutton's down first. "Maybe you can tell me about your parents at a later time. I'm sure I've put you through enough already asking about Hailey." I purse my lips toward my cup, the pecan-colored coffee rippling as I blow.

"I don't mind at all, Kaiton. You can ask me anything." He takes a sip. I know the coffee is scalding hot, but he swallows it like it's ice cold. "I was fourteen, at a friend's house for the night. His parents got a call at around two a.m. about a fire at my house. We didn't have many details other than it was caught too late. They kept saying that over and over again. *It was caught too late, it was caught too late,* and I didn't understand the magnitude of the situation. I was sleep deprived from staying up until midnight playing video games. I was barely a teenager with raging mood swings and terrible impulse control. I kind of brushed it off. Asked if my dog was okay, not even thinking of anything else. We got in the car, and as soon as we turned onto my road, it was packed full of police, firefighters, and ambulances. I saw my neighbors' houses on both sides from the distance, but I didn't see mine in the middle. I think that's when it sunk in. My house was gone. The whole thing. Nothing left but a crumpling frame, completely charred. For a half second, I suspected my parents would come running at me from the crowd gathered around. I thought maybe they got out in time and had to watch their house burn down. That would be an awful thing to experience. But that thought came and left once I saw it in the neighbor's eyes—they all looked at me with pity. Remorse and guilt washed over them as I pushed my way through the mosh pit they'd made. It took a lot of years for me to fully come to terms with the entire incident. That's why I don't mind talking about it now. It's a part of who I am. My aunt was granted custody and luckily, she only lived a block over. So, I didn't have to move far or change schools. She was a lot older than my mom was, so any chance I got, I was over at the Wrights', or Ellie and Rod's." His gaze stays fixated on mine, never wavering even though tears stream silently from my eyes. "I don't want to make you cry any more today so I'm not going to go on, but if you ever have any other questions about my family or Hailey, just ask. I have to go into work around one o'clock today, so what can I do before I leave to make you happy again?" He lets out a soft chuckle.

"I'm fine." The words come out in nearly a squeak as I try to hold it together. I wish I could suck up my tears before they fall. He's spilling years of trauma, and I'm just sitting here sobbing uncontrollably like a lunatic. "Do you want some breakfast? I like to cook. That would make me happy," I ask with a warm smile before I sniff my nose, trying to clear it so I can breathe better.

"How about I make you a deal?" He smirks, leaning back in his chair, holding the coffee mug close to his lips. "How about you make breakfast, and I'll make dinner?"

"Tonight?" I ask.

"Yes, tonight."

I nod as I smile back, using the sleeves of my knit sweater to mop up the remaining tears on my cheeks. I rise to my feet, getting ready to work my magic in the kitchen as Dutton also starts to stand.

"Can I help with breakfast?" he asks.

"Can I help with dinner?"

"No." He smiles.

"Then, no. Sit down. Blueberry brioche French toast or my specialty coffee pancakes?"

"My God. I'm warning you right now, I only have two go-to meals for dinner that I know how to cook. One is spaghetti, and the other is spaghetti with meatballs." He grins, showing off his pearly white teeth.

"That's okay, I love spaghetti."

"What do you like to make? What's *your* favorite breakfast?"

"Mine?" I slam my index finger to my chest to point back as confirmation and he only nods before taking another sip of his salted caramel mocha. No one's ever cared what *I* wanted for breakfast.

I take a moment to think, although it isn't a hard choice to begin with. "A bagel with cream cheese," I state.

"Perfect. Make that two, please."

CHAPTER
TWENTY-FOUR

LAYLA STARES BACK at me over FaceTime, dumbfounded and rendered speechless. She only blinks mindlessly and I can't tell if she's truly breathing right now or not.

"Kaiton Faye Riggs!" she finally snaps. "Are you telling me you kissed *your boss*?" Her lips curl up into a devious smile and I know exactly what she's thinking.

"I tell you about his wife and parents who all died in horrific ways, and that's your takeaway?"

"Oh yeah, that is traumatic as hell for him, and I feel awful. We can dive into that later but I knew this was going to happen. Can I just say... told you so!"

There it is. I knew it was coming.

"Yeah, yeah. Anyway, do you think this is okay to wear? I want to be comfortable," I ask as I pull at the white spandex material of my biker shorts.

"I think it's perfect. Easy to slip off, too." She winks.

"Layla!" I scold with a smile.

"What? You know it's true."

I stare down at my fingers holding the nylon blend fabric. Maybe I do want something a little more...accessible for tonight.

"So do I just tell him I'm not looking for anything serious or how does this usually come about with your one-night stands?"

"Well, we usually don't discuss a lot of things before it happens. You just do the deed and leave."

"I just leave right after?" I ask.

"Yeah, because it's embarrassing as fuck when they want you gone but don't know how to get rid of you. They'll say shit like "I'm so tired" or "I need to work really early tomorrow, but I'll call you", she mimics in a long, drawn-out way. "It's just easier to get up and leave without watching them try to conjure up some shameless lie."

"Okay. Fuck, then leave. Got it," I say, trying to process the steps of this hookup like a to-do list.

She nods with approval, like her training has finally paid off. "Your tits look nice today."

"I think it's this sports bra," I say, moving closer to the camera to show her the brown ribbed material. "Then I've got this matching zip up." I throw it on, zipping it only halfway so it can hang off one shoulder slightly.

"Yeah, love it," she says with a wide smile.

"Okay, cool. It's not like, too informal, right?"

"I think it's perfect. Text me when you get home tonight. If I'm up still, we can chat. Love you, K."

"Love you too." I smile as I blow her a kiss. And with that, we end the call.

My insides are turning like tires going ninety on the freeway, and I can't figure out if it's because I'm nervous or because I haven't eaten anything since breakfast. It's only until my stomach feels like it's waging a war inside with only pitchforks as weapons do I realize how long it's been since I've had any food.

I glance in my mirror one last time, fixing the strands of my hair that seem to have gone awry between me curling it and talking on the phone with Layla. I secure my small, thin, gold hoop earrings and slip on a couple equally thin gold rings before my phone buzzes on the dresser.

DUTTON BECK: I'm almost home. You can head over.

My stomach churns again before I send him a simple "okay" with a blushing emoji and walk out of the house. My nerves won't quit as I drive and I keep glancing in the review mirror, checking to make sure I still look the same as when I left. I wipe my finger under my eyes to grab any last-minute running mascara and the ten-minute trip feels like it's only been two when I pull into his long driveway. A couple deep breaths is all I need before I get the courage to make my way to his front door, but my chest starts to tighten as I get close.

I can do casual. I got this. No sweat.

I knock once, waiting a moment before he calls from the other side. "Come in!" he yells.

I push open the door, my gaze instantly falling to his as he peeks his head to the side from the half wall that separates the living room and kitchen. I walk in, closing the door behind me as the familiar, rich scent of burning timber and pine needles hits me. Birdie darts down the hallway, her nails clipping at the wood floor until she comes to a halt, nearly crashing into my legs.

"Hi, pretty girl," I coo at her as I pet her soft coat.

I only give her a moment of attention before slipping off my shoes. I walk and she follows me. Rounding the corner, I see Dutton forming meatballs with his hands on the butcher block kitchen island. His light blue graphic Tee clings to his biceps as he rolls the ground beef between his palms.

"Need some help?" I offer, setting my purse down at one of the bar stools on the other side of him.

"I couldn't help with breakfast, remember?" He smirks.

"Fine." I grin and shake my head slightly. "It smells really good already." The sweet smell of tomatoes and garlic invades my nose.

"My aunt's secret sauce. Can't tell you what it is, she'd kill me, but I can tell you I make big batches of it and stick it in my freezer so all I have to do is reheat it when I make spaghetti." He grins wide, that same grin that makes my stomach flutter every time. One side of his lip curls up, only showing bits of his teeth, and when he has a five o'clock shadow like right now, I can see the dimple that forms to the right of the smile. "I've got waters for us on the table, but if you want pop or juice, it's in the fridge. Or that bottle of whiskey you gave me this morning is over here." He chuckles lightly as he points to the corner of the counter where the hardly drunken bottle sits.

"Oh, God," I groan in disgust at the remembrance of that sharp liquor taste. "That whiskey was terrible. I don't know how you do it."

He just laughs. "Why *did* you get whiskey to try? Over everything else? I mean, you might have liked a seltzer better. Or a sweet wine."

My breath deepens as I inhale slowly. What am I supposed to say? That I was bamboozled from the taste on your lips? So much so that I thought all whiskey would taste the same? I start to speak—some petty lie about how it was the first thing I saw on the shelf—when he cries out in a sort of nipping yelp.

"Ah, fuck!" He jerks his hand back, shaking it back and forth as the meatballs pop in the hot pan.

The oil keeps popping as he jumps to each side, trying to dodge the little fireballs as they score his skin. He laughs at the madness. I laugh because it looks like he's trying to learn the salsa, but as someone with zero rhythm.

"Let me help you." I place my hands on him, moving him out of the line of fire. I reach to turn down the temperature of the stove from high to medium-low. "Once it calms down, you can bring it back to medium and keep cooking them like normal," I say as I give him a couple pats on his arm.

"You got it, boss." He winks and I swear my heart skips two beats with how fast and subtle the gesture was.

As I sit on a barstool, my stomach grumbles and gurgles, loud enough to get Dutton's attention. I wrap my arm around it tight, in hopes of hushing the noise, but to no avail.

"Hungry?"

I just nod as he holds my gaze before focusing his attention back on the food. While I'm not technically lying, I think my stomach issues this evening have more to do with anxiousness than anything else.

I'm nervous.

Being around him gives me the same jittery feeling I had on my first day here at Falton Ridge. I'm exhilarated and highly strung all at once.

I nod along as he talks more about his aunt and the recipes she *tried* to teach him, with only this particular one sticking. The way he describes her, I imagine she stands at four-foot-nothing, toting a shotgun in one hand and a pack of cigarettes in another. He beams bright when he speaks of her, and I can't bring myself to ask if she's still alive or not. I don't think either one of us wants to endure a night of me sobbing over more of his family trauma.

He occasionally glances back at me with a crooked smile while he tells his stories and I just gawk at him in appreciation when he turns back around. His broad shoulders take up half of the stove space—I can hardly see what he's doing in front of him. He towers over the counter, just like he towers over me. Even at my best, standing as tall as I can, I only reach his chin. I've never been with anyone as masculine, as strong as him. The memory of him holding me in the air as if I were weightless comes creeping back into my mind as I watch him drain the pasta. He tips the pot to the side and his arms flex tight. The veins in his large hands protrude as I watch them rise on his arms. That's something I never thought I would find sexy.

Veins.

How fucking odd.

I want to touch them. Run my fingertips against his skin. Feel the ridges and hills of each line. He also has them on his lower stomach, right in the middle of his carved-out hips that point in a V.

"It's done," he says as he grabs two plates out of a cupboard.

I force myself to snap back to reality as the clanking of the dishes nearly jolts me out of my seat. "Looks really good." I slip off the stool and move closer, resting my arm on the counter as I lean slightly and wait for him to finish plating.

"We can sit." He holds both dishes, nodding his head to the side, motioning us over to his dining table.

I follow his lead as he sets the plates down and I sit in the chair next to his. "Thanks for making this," I say.

"I'm happy to." He grins.

I twist my fork into the spaghetti, wrapping each noodle around it until I get a heaping bite. We dig in, and I admit—it's pretty damn good. The sauce is spectacular, and the meatballs are perfectly seasoned.

"This is delicious." I beam as the first bites go down.

"I'm glad you like it, I was nervous."

"Why?" I exclaim with wide eyes.

"After my breakfast choices this morning, it sounded like you know your shit. This is literally the only thing I know how to make." He laughs. "This and burnt toast."

"I just follow recipes." I smile and shake my head. "I'm not like a chef or anything. I like cooking, it's relaxing to me."

"Relaxing?" he jokes. "What about when tiny oil missiles are flying at you from the pan?"

"I mean, yeah, that part's not usually fun." I giggle. "But you did a really good job, I'm proud of you."

"Thanks, Kaiton." His lips curl up in a smile so big his cheeks raise and his eyes crease at the corners.

"By the way," he says between bites, "the store looks fucking fantastic. Laura said you cleaned and reorganized everything. You didn't have to do that."

"Oh, great. I'm glad you like it. We were really slow on Friday. I didn't have anything else to do."

"Well, thank you. It really looks great." His smile is warm and inviting as his eyes burn right into my flesh.

Every time he glances at me, I swear he looks directly into my soul. His eye contact never waivers, it just seeps right into me, absorbing me like a sponge.

I run my fingertips along the oak table, following the curves of the live edges as we continue in conversation. It seems handcrafted in nature, like one big slab of wood that sits on trestle legs. I'm intrigued and would bet money he probably made this himself. My eyes continue to wander between bites and curiosity gets the best of me as I keep finding more rustic touches throughout.

"Did you make this?" I ask as I point my index finger down on the tabletop.

He nods with a mouthful of food.

"And those cabinets?" I point toward the small kitchen area with cabinets constructed in the same wood as the table.

"I did," he says once he swallows.

"What else did you do here?" I raise a brow.

He takes a breath in, gearing up for the long list he seems to be checking off in his head. "Well, let's see." His eyes roam around. "When I bought this house, I had to rip everything to the studs. Insulation, drywall, paint—all of that was me. The added things like the stonework around the fireplace, the cabinets in here and this table, and the wooden beams on the ceiling, I did as well. Rod did my plumbing, and a buddy of mine helped with the electricity. Other than that, I pretty much did the rest."

"Where did you learn to do all of this? Like, I wouldn't have any idea how to build *this*"—I point to the table first—"let alone *that*." I gesture to the wooden beams above us.

He just laughs in a shy sort of way. He tilts his head down and to the side as if it's nothing spectacular. "I don't know really. I just have been doing odds and ends type of shit for so long that I have a very 'it can't be that hard, can it?' kind of attitude. It might take me a couple tries, but I think I could build just about anything."

I don't know why I find it so sexy, a man who can be so handy. I've never dated anyone like that. So useful, so *skilled*.

I've nearly cleared my entire plate at the same time Dutton has and he offers to take it, but I decline. Instead, I bring my dishes to the kitchen, helping him put away the leftover spaghetti as he washes the plates by hand. Once I stick the containers in the fridge, I take my place next to him, drying off each wet piece of silverware before sticking it back in the drawer. He looks at me, his eyes dark and smoldering as he wipes his hands on a towel. I face him, leaning back on my knuckles behind me as they grip his counter. He doesn't say anything, just takes one step closer to me, limiting the space between us.

"So, you never told me why you chose to try the whiskey over anything else." His voice is low and gruff as he quiets his tone.

I swallow hard, tilting my eyes up to his as he towers over me.

"I, uh—" I try to form another lie, but my stalling is already a dead giveaway. "I liked the taste of it on your lips. I thought it would be the same from the bottle," I finally let out.

"What did it taste like?" he asks curiously, grin stretching even further.

"I don't really remember." I tug at my bottom lip, trying not to smile and give away any more of my secrets.

He squints like he doesn't believe me. And why should he? I've always been a terrible liar.

His arm raises next to me, crowding me in the tiny space between his body and the vent hood above his stove. He opens the cabinet next to my head, pulling out a short glass as he sets it down on the counter. Reaching next for the whiskey in the corner, he pours it into the cup, slowly bringing it to his lips to take a sip. My mouth hangs open slightly as I watch his every move.

"Can you tell me what it tastes like now?" he asks as he moves in just a bit closer to me.

I nod slowly, still looking up at him through my lashes as my teeth continue to try and hold onto my bottom lip. My heart thumps through my chest and I push up on my toes, gaining more height to reach his mouth. I place my parted lips on his, just a peck that creates a small smacking noise.

I lick my lips slightly, tasting the remnants of the bitter whiskey on his lips. "Vanilla," I say once I'm flat on my feet again.

"Anything else?"

I try hard to suppress my smile, although it's useless. I lift up once more, placing another gentle kiss on his lips as he parts his a little wider for me this time.

"Honey," I say.

He nods as he leans in, placing both hands on the counter behind me so our eye contact is level.

"That's it?" he asks with a head tilt and a cunning smirk that sends a chill down my arms.

Every breath he takes is hot on my skin, and without words, I nod. My innocent eyes burn right through his as he cocks his half-smile.

"Maybe you should try one more time. Just in case." His gaze narrows and his low groan seeps into my soul, warming my core to its highest temperature until I'm nothing but a shallow puddle.

I grin as sly as I can while my heart seems to think I'm in a relay race, pounding as fast as possible against my chest.

I run my fingers against his cheek, brushing against his stubble as my hand cups his face. I pull him in just a touch, before he makes it the rest of the way himself. Our lips collide and we both inhale. His hand grips the side of my neck, holding me in place as he claims my mouth. He rolls his tongue slowly against mine as I taste him, then groans softly through our lip lock before backing away. Birdie dances around his feet, trying to work her way into the middle of us. I giggle when we look down and he shakes his head as he bites his bottom lip, smirking all the while.

"Birdie, out," he demands, pointing to the side.

She wags her tail, spinning in circles as her nails clip at the floor. Dutton grabs my hand, trailing me behind him as we move around the kitchen and into the living room. He opens the front door and Birdie takes off, darting out and making a sharp right.

"Is she going to run away?" I ask with my eyebrows raised. If I could see my face right now, I would imagine it's one filled with an uneasy smile and terrified eyes.

"She won't leave the property. She's fine."

"Are you sure?" I ask, and at the same time, I feel extremely foolish.

Of course, he's sure.

It's *his* fucking dog.

I'm sure they've done this a million times. It's like my word vomit is topped out when I'm anxious and I can't stop myself from spewing idiotic thoughts.

He just keeps his grin, tugging me outside to stand with him on the porch. He looks to the right, trying to find an unobstructed view of Birdie on the side of the house.

"Come here," he says as he starts down the stairs.

"I don't have shoes on." I look at my feet.

"Get on." He stands on the bottom step, offering me his back to jump on.

I grin, squeezing my hands on his broad shoulders as I hop on, securing myself with my arms around his neck. He walks me effortlessly around the house, toting me into the backyard until we see Birdie lying in the grass near the edge of the trees.

"What's she under?" I ask.

"A bird bath. It was here when I bought the house. It was the first thing she ran to when I brought her home. She'll lie there all day waiting for the birds to come so she can play."

I watch her, head lying the grass, waiting. She seems lonely out here, just waiting for someone to come play and chase her.

"She needs a friend," I state.

"Oh, yeah?" Dutton smirks up at me.

I can't help but grin, tucked into Dutton and feeling the chill of summer coming to an end, while we watch Birdie lie and roll in the grass under the weathered concrete basin.

Dutton whistles loudly and Birdie flips upright, perking her head up when she hears his call. It's only a matter of seconds before she scrambles to her feet and rushes to us.

"Told you she wouldn't leave." He tilts his head up to look at me.

"I've never had a dog that didn't at least *try* to run away. I just got worried in the split second I saw her take off." I giggle, although it's more out of sheer embarrassment.

Dutton opens the front door, still carrying me, until he reaches the couch.

He bends slightly and I slide off. "Find us a movie. I'm going to get more wood for the fireplace."

I grab the remote on the table and take a seat on the dark brown sofa as he walks outside once more. I click on the power button before flipping through to find any sort of watchable channel. There seem to be about eight hundred buttons on the remote and I can't exactly figure out how to get where. I just keep pressing in hopes I land on anything that isn't static, finally flipping to the entertainment channel that's streaming a rom-com with Sandra Bullock. Dutton barges in with three small pieces of wood in his hands and I get settled into the cushion, scrunching up my legs as I hold myself to keep warm. It's not unbearably cold in here, but I can tell the strong heat is dying down from the embers that glow inside the fireplace. He tosses a log on the fire, rolling the other to the back. The embers fly and swirl around inside as he makes room for the other logs to fit. He stands to his feet, walking toward me before fitting snug on the couch.

"You cold?" he asks as he grabs my legs that are now tucked inside my zip up. His hand rubs gently against the outside of my thigh as he tries to warm me up with just his touch.

I stare at him in awe and wonder. How in my life have I never experienced this kind of man? He's caring, and gentle, and so fucking *nice*. I'm sure this is crossing some sort of invisible line for the employee/boss workplace relationship protocol but I just don't give a fuck anymore. *I want him.* Just like I've wanted him from the second I slammed against his body in the doorway of The Wright Tools. Even though I've admittedly tried denying it to myself every day since.

He grins at me, still warming me up with his callused hands. They aren't soft by any means, but goddamn do they feel just as exceptional. They're hands from a *man*. And I want them on much more than just my leg.

I wrap my arm around his neck, running my fingers against the bottom of his tresses. Dutton leans in to kiss me, planting his plush lips on mine and I flatten my legs, my knees slipping out from underneath my sweatshirt as his hand runs higher up my side. His tongue dances with mine and the pace of our mouths colliding picks up as he reaches for my other leg, spreading it apart and right over his lap. His fingers gently graze the insides of my thighs and my lips are wet from his kisses as I pull away slightly.

"Dutton," I whisper against him. "I'm leaving in a couple of months, remember?"

He sighs gently as his fingers slow down their soft touch. "I know," he says in a low, somber tone.

His breath brings heat to my lips, and neither one of us moves, but I can't take it any longer. *I need him*, desperately. I place my lips back on his, parting them with my tongue, and he doesn't take a second longer to trace his fingers over my inner thighs once more. He rides over the ridges of my shorts, drawing over the outline of my pussy, and I quiver the instant he slides over my clit. I can feel him smile beneath our kisses and I buck my hips, not because I thought to, but because my greedy body has a mind of its own now.

I start to move my hand to my waistband, hooking my thumb between my skin and the fabric before Dutton's fingers stop stroking me and help pull them down completely. The brown material hits the floor and I sit as the cool leather pricks my bare ass. Dutton grabs my leg to move it back to the same position before pulling me back to taste my lips again. His soft tongue drags against mine, and my pussy tingles at the thought of his fingers dragging against it bare. His hand travels down, grazing gently across my skin so softly, I giggle the moment he touches my hip.

He smiles between us as the tips of his fingers now run over my thigh down to the crevice separating my leg from my pussy. I suck in a breath the moment his finger traces over my slit, right in the center. He drags it gently, circling my clit as his tongue works against mine. I whimper into his mouth, finding it hard to keep my body from already convulsing. I forgot what it was like to be touched like this. To feel the chills and tingles as they travel up my spine, to feel the need and want seeping out of me as he touches me ever so lightly.

"How do you want to be fucked, Kaiton?" he groans against my mouth while his finger still plays with me.

The looming thought throws me off guard. "I-I don't know," I whisper against him. "It's been a really long time," I finally say, and once the words spill out of my lips, Dutton's hand freezes.

"How long?" he asks in the same quiet tone.

"A year," I say in a breath as my body starts to slump.

Dutton clenches his jaw, not waiting long before he grazes his lips against mine, teasing me with a kiss.

"How about we figure that out tonight? What you like and don't like, okay?" he murmurs against my skin, still toying with me with his touch.

I only nod, and he finally presses his lush lips fully to mine, circling my clit once more before dragging it to my center, slowly pushing it inside me. I gasp at the pressure of his finger filling me.

"You like this?" Dutton whispers as his mouth moves to my ear, nipping at it softly before his tongue runs against the skin on my neck. I can only groan and nod as my core tightens and my eyes roll unwillingly to the back of my head. He pumps his finger inside me, going as deep as he can while his tongued kisses don't miss any bit of skin on my neck. He slows the pace of his finger, bringing his lips back to my ear as he commands in a whisper while tugging on my clothes, "Take this off and lie down."

I do as I'm told, unzipping my sweatshirt before his fingers dust my skin, helping me pull it off completely. I reach for the hem of my sports bra when he does, and I raise my arms high as he pulls it up. My breasts bounce as they fall, and something in my core flutters as I hear Dutton's groan. I lean back, propping my shoulders against the armrest as I watch his gaze darken.

"Fuck," he murmurs, nearly breathless as his eyes roam over my naked body.

He slowly drops down, grazing his lips against my skin as he trails kisses to my breast. His hand rubs up my stomach before grabbing a handful, and his eyes tilt up to mine, his mouth merely inches from my skin.

"How about this?" he asks as he sweeps my nipple into his mouth, swirling his tongue over my taut pink peak.

"Uh huh." The sound comes out in a breath from my tight throat, and I sink further into the couch as he continues.

"What about this?" He nips softly, tugging it between his lips as he sucks.

"Yes," I sigh.

"What about them together?" He alternates the two, running his tongue in circles as I watch from above. He wraps his lips around my nipple, sucking as he flicks.

I whimper loudly as my head falls back and my hands run through his hair, gripping his soft waves between my fingers. The feeling of his warm mouth and flat tongue sends heat to my core and my pussy contracts as he flicks at my nipple some more before he moves over to my other breast, taking as much care as he did with the first while his finger rubs gently over the other, making sure I'm stimulated from both. I buck my hips against his jeans and I'm finding it hard to not scream how badly I want him inside of me.

So long have I gone without intimacy. So long have I gone untouched. Dutton has hardly done anything, and I feel like my body is unraveling at every second. I'm craving him and it's only getting worse the longer he teases and toys with my breasts. I grind my hips again. My movements are uncontrolled, my body reacting without thought, and I don't dare try to stop it. He releases his mouth from my nipple, only to trail soft kisses down to my belly button. My body flinches at the gentle touches, and I watch as he keeps moving lower. His arms hook under my legs so they rest on his shoulders, and he drags his lips across the skin just above my hip. His eyes flicker up to mine through his lashes as he lets out a breathless "fuck" with a smile as he stares at my bare pussy.

His finger runs up the center of my slit, and I nearly gasp at the sensation, going totally breathless the moment his tongue drags in the same fashion. His lips close around my pussy as he kisses, and before I know it, he consumes me, swirling and flicking his tongue around my clit as he moans. I arch my back, fighting hard not to scream as I grab onto the back of his head. He grips my hips, burying his face into me as I pant and groan.

"Do you like it fast?" he whispers against me as his tongue flicks at my clit quickly. "Or slow?" He slows the pace of his tongue, dragging it gradually and rolling it like he's licking ice cream from a cone.

"Fast," I pant and he picks up pace again without hesitation, flicking and sucking at my clit as I grind my pussy further on his tongue. It's wet and warm, and I don't remember a time when my body has felt this fucking good.

He releases his mouth from me as he moves his hand to my center, running his finger against my slit, and my wetness coats him. He rubs on my clit, circling lightly with his finger, and I cry out before he slides his finger deep back inside me. I let out a loud grunt that was buried down in my chest. The pressure of his finger has me clenching around it as he pumps, and I can't keep my hips from grinding against him. He nods his head up and down as he shifts his body, bringing his lips closer to mine.

"That's it, ride my fingers." His voice is so low it nearly shakes as his breath heats my skin. "I want you to come for me." He nods slowly as the tips of his lips graze mine. "You're doing so good, keep riding my fingers, Kaiton. Come all over them."

I can't do anything but moan as he plays with my pussy, thrusting and pumping his finger relentlessly before taking it out and swirling it over my clit. My core starts to tense, and I grab onto his bulging bicep when it does. My pussy starts to contract and for fuck's sake, I haven't come in so long I think every pent-up emotion is pouring out of me at once. I cry out as my orgasm unleashes, long and hard as I shake. I grip him tighter, holding myself up as my body trembles.

"You're so fucking perfect," Dutton says as he grazes his nose against me before pressing his pouty lips on mine.

My breath is audibly loud as I gasp for whatever air I can feed into my lungs, and my body slumps into the couch, all the while my core still quivers from the aftermath of my orgasm.

I'm a puddle, *a goddamn puddle*, because of him.

He's careful when he gets off the couch, sliding his arms under my naked body before picking me up and cradling me as I remain dead weight in his hold. I sling my arms around his neck, hanging on as best I can while he carries me with ease past the kitchen, down the hallway, and into his bedroom. I'm exhausted, parched, and sweaty, and I'm sure my cheeks are flushed as red as a cherry tomato. But I don't care. I'm ready for him, and however else he wants to ravage my body tonight.

CHAPTER
TWENTY-FIVE

I JOLT UP FROM HIS BED where he laid me down gently just seconds ago, pushing my hand against the top of his head to unleash his mouth from my sensitive clit as he dives back in for another taste. My core trembles still from how weak he left me on the couch, but the only way I can force him off is to sit up in this half-crunch of a position.

"I already came, you don't have to do it again," I pant.

"Once isn't enough for me," he nearly growls before his mouth suctions back on me.

His tongue drags up and down my slit as he pushes my legs up higher, and I gasp at the feeling of his firm tongue against me, licking from ass to clit. I'm powerless as I cry out while he works on me. I can't remember the last time I was eaten out, but I can count how many times I've been eaten like this.

Zero.

He's acting like he can't taste me enough, like he's devouring his last meal on earth, and it just so happens to be his favorite. I stay in this sitting position just to watch him, small whimpers escaping my throat. His eyes flicker to mine once he hears my moans, and a smile wipes across his face as I watch his tongue circle around my throbbingclit. I can't help but grind against his scratchy beard that feels so good between my thighs, and I can tell he enjoys when I do that, too.

Every time my hips move, he grips me harder and moans right into my pussy. It's the hottest fucking thing I've ever seen in my life and that's just enough to push me over the edge once more. My hands grip his hair as I fall back onto his mattress, but he keeps going at that same perfect pace.

"Do you want my fingers inside your pretty little pussy?" His low groan rumbles through my body.

"Yes," I whimper as I relax even further, sinking into the grey duvet cover.

His hand grazes my leg before he slips it underneath, toying with the sides of my pussy as he caresses outside of it in a V.

"Tell me," he groans. "Use your words."

"I want—" I sigh breathlessly as he works on me, still teasing me with his gentle touch everywhere except where I crave him. His eyes flash up to mine through his lashes as I watch his wide tongue flick my clit and he nods up and down as his tongue moves with him.

"I want your fingers inside of me," I finally let out in a breath before he drags them over my center, shoving two right into my core.

I let out a deafening moan that can't be contained and at that exact moment, my soul leaves my body and hands itself over to him on a silver platter.

"Come on my face," he demands.

I can't even breathe with the sensation I'm feeling. Never in my life have I felt this ecstasy, this *euphoria*. His fingers stay deep inside while he curls the tips of them, building the pressure while his tongue flicks at my clit continuously. I'm out of body, watching myself from an elevated level as I die and meet a higher power.

"You can do it," he groans. "Show me you can do it."

His voice trembles up my spine, sending a shockwave through my bones and I can't suppress the feeling any longer. I bear down, riding my orgasm out as my pussy contracts over and over again. My cries grow louder by the second, and Dutton doesn't let up until my shaking ceases and I push his head off me again.

He hovers over me, bringing his gaze up to mine as his face glistens under his dim bedroom lights. I can see my wetness all over his beard, glimmering over his grin before his lips land on my neck, kissing me softly as his tongue runs with it. I groan while my hands tug on his shirt, trying to lift it up so he can take it off. He kneels, bringing his hands to the hem before lifting it over his head. My eyes trail over his chest, memorizing every crevice and every detail of his chiseled body. I follow the lines of his abs, and my gaze flickers down to his belt as he unfastens it. He moves off the bed just to the side of me as he pushes his jeans down to the floor, making sure his boxers tug along with it. I watch as his cock springs the moment it's released from his cotton boxers, and he takes it in hand, gripping onto the thickest dick I've ever seen. I don't know why, but looking at him stark naked in front of me has me wanting to beg—beg him to fuck me, beg him to let me to suck him off.

And I hate sucking dick.

God, do I hate it.

But not right now.

Not in this moment.

And certainly not with him.

I scramble to my knees the best I can, given my weak state. It's only a moment before I wrap my hand around his girth, taking his cock in my hold as I come to eye level with it. I look up at him through my lashes and see his devilish grin before I stick out my tongue, running it on the underside of his cock nice and slow before taking him as deep as I can until he hits the back of my throat. Almost to the base I run my tongue as I suck, and he makes the sexiest noises I've ever heard come from a man—his sighs, his moans, his "oh Gods" that come out with every breath.

I can taste his salty pre-cum as it drips down my throat, and I focus on the head, swirling my tongue around it, picking up any last drops I possibly can.

"You're doing such a good fucking job," he groans as his hands run through my hair, pulling any loose strands out of my way.

I run my hand along his shaft, gripping tight as I pump back and forth while still rolling my tongue and sucking on the tip.

"Fuck," he drags out in a loud moan as his hips gently thrust into me. "Just like that," he pants.

I keep going, not slowing as his head falls back, and he lets me go on only for a moment longer before jolting his hips back and releasing my grasp from him.

"You're gonna make me come if you don't stop that." He smirks with a ragged breath before opening his bedside table drawer and pulling out a condom.

He brings the corner of the wrapper to his mouth, clenching it between his teeth as he rips it open. I watch him closely as he rolls it over his cock, and once it's all the way down, he crawls on the bed, pushing himself right between my legs as I fall on my back once more. His fingers gently run against my pussy again, making sure I'm still wet enough to take him. I suck in a breath at his touch which only gives him more motivation to make me squirm again. He shoves two fingers back inside me. I grunt but he only pulses inside a couple of times before pulling them back out and straight to his lips.

"I just wanted another taste." He smirks after he sucks his fingers.

My heart is thumping through my chest, and I stay lying on my elbows just to watch him as he takes ahold of his cock, running it between my folds a couple of times. My head falls back and I moan but he doesn't stay for long, and the second he pushes inside of me, my head springs back up. He shoves himself in slowly and we sigh at the same time. His arms fall next to my head as he hovers over me, moving steadily at first, dragging his cock against my walls unhurriedly as I dig my nails into his back.

"You're so fucking tight," he says, picking up his pace, pounding me faster and faster until my little moans are just gasping breaths.

He kisses me so passionately our mouths are wet from our flailing tongues. His momentum never lets up, and I swear my pussy feels swollen with the need and want he's making my body obsess over.

"Come here," he says as he wraps his arm under me, flipping us over so I'm straddled on top of him.

I don't know what to do.

I haven't been on top before.

I just sit still as he adjusts himself, propping his back against some pillows so he perches more upright. He grabs my hips, guiding me as he raises me a bit before pushing me back down, making sure I take every inch of his cock. I get the hint and bounce a little by myself, crying out every time he's fully inside of me. The pressure is unimaginable, and the pleasure is so intense I don't even remember what my own name is. I bounce faster, trying to chase the feeling of me slamming back down on him. His hand grabs my breast while the other remains gripping my hip.

"Fuck, Kaiton." He sighs.

I lean forward, resting on his shoulders for more control, and I bounce my ass up and down as he moans right into my ear.

"Grab the headboard," he instructs before my hands reach up, gripping the dark linen material.

He wraps both arms around my back, squeezing me tight as he drills his hips into me. I don't have to move with him doing all the work but it's not like I could even try—he leaves me paralyzed with the way he pounds each long stroke into me.

"Do I feel good buried inside of you?" he asks as he slams his cock deep in my pussy before holding it there.

"Yes!" I manage to cry out between the gasping breaths.

He grunts before pounding into me harder over and over again as fast as he can as he drives his hips into me.

I don't think I can get any louder with my cries and I feel on the brink of exploding again between the pressure of him filling me and the way my clit rubs against his skin on impact.

"Fuck, you're so wet." He drags out in a moan as rough as gravel.

My mind goes blank. I can't form a single thought. I can't form a single word. The only noises I'm making are sounds I've never heard slip from my lips—mixes of grunts, cries, whimpers, and whines.

I can't control it.

Dutton lifts me up slightly to kiss me, running his tongue with mine the best we can given the ragged and jolting movements.

"I'm gonna fucking come right in your pussy." His groan is strained as I bring my hands to his head, gripping onto his hair that's laced with a touch of his sweat.

His thrusts become harder as he grunts with each forceful pound, and we lock our gazes, our lips nearly touching.

"Fuck," he draws out in a loud, low whimper, his eyes nearly rolling to the back of his head as he plunges inside of me with longer strokes. His body quivers under mine until he's finished coming and I can't do anything but keep my body draped on top of him.

I'm weak, exhausted and disoriented, and I didn't even do any fucking work. Dutton's arms stay wrapped around me, and he squeezes tighter before running his hand gently up my back, tickling me softly with his touch. He's still rock solid inside me, and I know this is when I should be getting up to leave but I'm powerless, nearly numb in some state of seventh heaven. I wait for him to make the first move, maybe fidget underneath me or start to push me off, but he doesn't. He just continues softly dragging his fingertips against my goosebumps. I lift my head up, making eye contact with him as he just grins with the same dopey smile I'm sure I have on my face. He brings his fingers to my cheek, brushing a wispy tendril off my face and tucking it behind my ear. He strains his neck, placing a gentle kiss on my lips before he whispers against me.

"You're so beautiful," he says before placing another small kiss on my lips. I smile underneath his touch. I'm not used to compliments like this.

"So are you." I grin before my eyes grow wide. "I mean...you're so handsome." I giggle.

He laughs, patting my ass with one tap as he says, "Come on, let's get up."

A pain shoots to my heart, a familiar feeling of disappointment. "You're right," I say, trying to hide the misery in my voice as I move off him and stand to my feet. "I should get going."

"Going?" he asks as he sits on the edge of the bed behind me. "No, we're getting in the shower." He stands, gripping my hip with his hand as he presses his semi-hard cock firm to my ass. His breath is hot as it dusts my ear, and I can't help but get the same tingling feeling in my pussy as he speaks. "Round two is in an hour."

CHAPTER
TWENTY-SIX

"ARE YOU SURE I HAVE TO GO TO WORK?"

"Dutton." I giggle. "You're the boss. Yes, you have to go to work."

We've been bickering back and forth for thirty minutes. I lie on my stomach while he plays with my ass—grabbing it, biting it, kissing it. He's buried between my cheeks but what he needs to be doing is getting ready to open the store.

His store.

He groans once more, and I just laugh as I bury my head into my folded arms. He spreads my cheeks apart, running his tongue between them, and my giggles turn into groans as he works it against me. I arch my back, pushing my ass closer to his face, driving his tongue deeper inside me. But the more I react to his touch, the more worked up *I* get. I never thought I would be one to love anyone's tongue in my ass but when he got on his knees in the shower last night, it changed my mind completely.

"Dutton." I peek my head over my shoulder. "You need to get going."

He groans again, but it's more of a huff mixed with disappointment.

"Realistically, how am I supposed to leave you like this? Leave knowing you're here in my bed, naked? Kaiton, I can't do that. I'm sorry. The Wright Tools is closed today." He chuckles and slaps one cheek lightly.

"I can't stay here all day anyway, remember?"

"I know, but you're coming back after. Right?" He perks his head up as he gives me another good squeeze.

All morning, he's begged me to stay right here, in his bed, butt-ass naked. As tempting as it is because, let's face it, his memory foam mattress is a thousand times more comfortable than the knobby spring piece of cardboard I sleep on, I have to leave for at least some time today because I promised Ellie I would come over. Belle isn't able to come visit this summer, so the Boones are going to travel to Oregon to see her instead. Ellie asked me to watch the horses while they were gone, said her normal farm sitter isn't available and they were in a bind. I didn't mind at all, not like I have much of anything going on, plus I get to spend extra time with Bunny. The only problem is that I don't know what to do with them. So today, Ellie is going to show me the ropes before they head out next week. I suppose I can do that, then come right back here to the most comfortable mattress my naked body has ever had the pleasure of lying on.

"Right." I smile as I keep my head rested on my hands, still lying face down as he gives my ass a couple more kisses, eventually giving in and getting off me to put clothes on.

I stay, lazily flipping over and pulling myself under the sheets as I watch him rifle through his closet. It's a shame to have him cover up his faultless body with articles of clothing, but a split second of jealousy runs through my mind at the thought of anyone else seeing him like this—naked and rugged with his scruffy beard, sleep in his eyes while his disheveled wavy hair still falls so effortlessly.

"I'll be back right after five," he says as he fits his large arms through a flannel, not securing any buttons so his dark grey T-shirt is fully exposed underneath. I nod , not doing much of any other movement as I stay snuggled between the pillows with the covers just above the tops of my breasts. "When you leave, you can lock up the house. Key is under the mat. Then, if you come back before I do, just let yourself in. Birdie might need to go outside by then. Just let her run, she'll be fine." He makes his way closer to me, hooking his finger under my chin and tilting my head up to give him better access as he closes in. His pouty lips press against mine and I tease him a bit, running my tongue gently against his lip as my hand cups his face.

"I'm not even kidding. I will stay here all day and fuck you senseless." He grins between us.

I give him one more final peck before I pull away. "Go to work." I beam. "I'll just be here...playing with myself in your bed while you're gone."

His hand falls to his mouth, shaking his head while he wipes it down. "You're being mean.".

He knows I'm fucking with him, but my God is this fun. I can't explain how powerful it makes me feel. But a part of me is reluctant. Is he just some guy that only thinks about sex all day, every day? How many other girls has he done this with? How many other girls has he begged to stay? My stomach knots and I eventually flip to my side after we say goodbye. I hear his front door shut and my first immediate instinct is to grab my phone before my envy and resentment get the best of me. The FaceTime tone rings as I see my reflection in the screen. My cheeks are cherry red, flushed to the max, and if my hair doesn't scream "I had sex all fucking night" then I don't know what else it could be saying.

Layla picks up, giving me a few blinks and utter silence before she speaks.

"That's not your bed," she says.

"Great observation, Layla. Has anyone told you that you would make a great FBI agent?"

She laughs. "Oh boy, this is not good."

"Not good at all," I say as I press my lips in a firm, thin line. I adjust myself, sitting against the headboard as I keep covered up with the duvet.

"So, you didn't go home. And are still not home."

"He begged me to stay."

"Casual!" she shouts. "What happened to casual, Kaiton?" She's fighting hard to not let her smile break, but I can see it's on the verge, just like mine.

"I'm trying!"

"Oh, are you?" She raises a brow. "Are you naked under there?"

I tuck the covers up closer to my neck.

"You *are* naked under there, aren't you?" she yells.

"I'm so fucked."

"Yes, you are," she agrees. "So...how was it? I know what you look like when you wake up. But this morning you have sex written all over you." Her smirk finally breaks fully.

"I–" I try to find the words. "Hot" is all I come up with. "It was fucking hot."

"Oh my God!" she screams as the phone shakes.

"If I would have known that's what sex *should* feel like, I would have been begging for it constantly."

Her mouth drops as she stares. "I'm so happy for you. Now, get the fuck out of there before you catch feelings."

I just groan, burying half of my face in the covers as I feel the soft cotton sheets rub against my bare legs. "I do have to get going soon. I'm heading over to Ellie's to learn how to take care of the horses while she's gone. But..." I trail.

"But what?"

"I'm coming back here after."

"My God." Her hand falls to her forehead as she shakes it, still with an unwavering grin. "You're so fucked."

"Okay, well, good chat, Layla. I'm going to put some clothes on now."

"Wait! You're not going to give me any details? I'm dying over here. It was your first sexcapade in over a year, what the hell! You can't leave me hanging!"

"Secret." I grin.

"Kaiton, I'm begging. Give me something."

I pucker my lips, twisting them to the side as I think. "You know the movie *300*? With the Spartan warriors?"

"Yeah..."

"Imagine the best body on that screen, times it by a hundred, and then think of him fucking you into some sort of blissful stupor—gentle and rough at the same time and *all* while praising you and your body. Then picture the most earth-shattering orgasms you've ever had, four times over."

"Four times?"

"Goodbye, Layla." I smile. "Love you," I say before we hang up.

I keep my phone in my hand as I lie in his bed and stare at the ceiling. I keep having flashbacks of last night. Him in the shower, washing my hair, washing my body. He didn't want to keep his hands off me. I've just...never experienced that kind of intimacy with anyone before. No man has ever obsessed over me in that kind of way. The compliments, the praise, all of it is just so...new. It doesn't make me feel any better, though. I'm supposed to be keeping this thing between us easygoing. Because what this is and all it can be is just temporary.

My phone buzzes in my hand and something in my gut tells me it's him before I even look at the screen.

DUTTON BECK: You still in my bed?

ME: Yep. Running my
fingers down between

my thighs as we speak.

DUTTON BECK: You're killing me.

DUTTON BECK: Actually killing me.

DUTTON BECK: I swear to God if
I was there you'd need the jaws of life
to get my mouth off your pussy.

ME: Lol, shut up.

DUTTON BECK: I'm not kidding.

DUTTON BECK: I wish I could
feel how wet you are right now.

ME: Want me to tell you?

DUTTON BECK: Please.

ME: Really. Fucking. Wet.

DUTTON BECK: Fuckkkk.
That's it. I'm coming home.

DUTTON BECK: There's no use
for me here anyway. Mr. Debowski's
in and I'm bricked up behind the counter.
Can't even help the poor guy out.

ME: Lol Dutton! Focus. I'll be here
by the time you're off work. Okay?

DUTTON BECK: Good. I'm speeding
back home. Might fuck around and lock
up five minutes early.

ME: Lol I'll see you later.
Don't speed. And don't
miss me too much.

I click the side of my phone, shutting it down as I take a
long-winded breath, psyching myself up to get out of this bed.
I was just fucking with him. I didn't actually touch myself,
I just wanted to get him riled up. It makes me feel powerful
somehow—that I can say one little thing to him and off he goes.
But I guess it works both ways. I can't act like I'm not melting into
a puddle anytime he whispers into my ear. He could say, "Kaiton,
take out the garbage" in his low, gruff tone while his fingers dance
on my skin and I bet I'd be as fucking wet as Niagara Falls.

I hop out of bed, tossing my clothes from yesterday on before
attempting to remake Dutton's bed.

I shrug my shoulders at the finished product and make my way
to the kitchen where Birdie lies on her bed. Her head whips up
when she hears my footsteps and I smile at her as I call her name.

"Want to go outside?" I ask, and it doesn't take long until she's scrambled to her feet, following me to the living room as I open the door for her.

She darts out, and I slip on my shoes to follow her, rounding the side of the house only to see her already taking her position under the bird bath already. I give her a moment, letting my eyes wander around Dutton's property. There's a substantial amount of space between the neighboring properties and he's lucky to be the last house on the road, giving him only one actual neighbor. His yard is massive, maybe three or four acres of land. Manicured grass and a healthy tree line in back. His landscaping is clean. Not filled with weeds or bare patches of any kind. He takes pride in his home, and it shows.

I watch Birdie get up, sniffing and circling a spot in the grass before relieving herself. I call out to her once she's done. I don't know how to whistle so I hope to God my call for her works. She cocks her head, hearing my voice, but she doesn't move right away. I clap my hands against my thighs as I call her again and soon enough, she charges right for me.

"Good girl." I beam as I pet her.

I get her inside, closing the door on my way out as I reach under the welcome mat for the key, texting Ellie that I'm on my way right after.

I know I'm playing with fire coming back here later. I can't imagine staying another night is going to help my feelings for him dissipate. I'm only going to be hurting myself. Maybe I'll just tell him this has to be the last night we can sleep together. That we need to keep this more on a...friends with benefits kind of basis.

Yeah, that's what I'll do.

I just need to forget that everyone I've ever had feelings for also started off as friends, too.

CHAPTER
TWENTY-SEVEN

"YOU THINK YOU CAN HANDLE IT?" Ellie's voice rings of excitement.

"Yeah, I've got this." I smile.

I mean really, how hard can it be? Come here twice a day for four days just to feed the girls, brush them every so often, and smother them with all the love and treats Ellie's going to leave me. I've got this in the bag.

"We're going to have some workers around the house while we're gone, too. Some of our siding flew off during the last storm and I've got some odds and ends around the barn I need taken care of. So don't be alarmed if you see strange men around the property while you're here." She giggles.

"Got it."

"Let's sit. I haven't talked to you since your birthday. Did you have a good weekend?" she says as she motions us to her front porch swing.

I let out a weak laugh. "It was...eventful," I say.

"Let's hear it." She smiles and rests her back against the navy throw pillow.

I settle myself in the corner as I tuck one leg in, letting my other hang off the side of the cream cushioned swing as we sway gently from the shifting in our seats.

I never got to tell Ellie what happened over the weekend. When she texted back, I just chalked up my questions about Dutton as nothing more than pure curiosity.

"Well...where to start. Um..." I say as I wipe my clammy hands against my biker shorts. "I learned about Dutton's wife and his parents after a few days of wallowing in rage and dejection. Then he invited me over for dinner, and I haven't left him...until now."

"It's ten o'clock in the...*oh*." Her pitch ends in a higher octave as her eyebrows lift. "So, he talked to you about Hailey?" Her face relaxes and her eyes become softer. "That boy's been a locked box ever since she died. I'm surprised he was so open about it after not knowing you very long."

"I don't think I gave him much choice. We sort of...kissed on my birthday and I saw their wedding photo. Freaked the hell out and dodged his calls the rest of the weekend. He showed up unannounced yesterday and just told me everything. Or at least everything he wanted to share at the time."

"I knew there was going to be something there when you told me he kissed you after Neddy's." She grins.

"We're just friends," I lunge out quicky, as if saying it faster solidifies the statement.

"Mhm." She hums. "Sure, you are." She pinches her brows and purses her lips. "Listen, back in the day, Dutton used to be a real ladies' man. I'm talking girls all over his arm, sneaking in and out of his house late at night, gettin' caught in the back of the car with..."

The horrendous look on my face must make her stave off her passing thought.

"I'm gettin' there." She smiles. "Once Hailey passed away, that was it. He became guarded like you're trying to be. Kept mostly to himself. Worked on the business. Helped around the community. Really put his nose to the grind and grew up. "Yes ma'am" this, "no sir" that... You get what I'm saying. He's a good kid. There's not a cruel intention in his body. I saw the way he was dancing with you at Neddy's. Usually, he's up there dancing himself or with the oldest broad in the place, trying to make her feel young again. But I saw you both. He grabbed *you* because he wanted to. That boy hasn't shown an ounce of interest in a female in years. And you know Hailey and him were never an item. Even at their ceremony, they kissed on the cheek." She giggles. "I know you're planning on going back home once the middle of fall is here, but plans change. Don't be afraid to change with them."

Her words hit my chest like a bowling ball rolling down the alley, striking every pin. I understand what she means. But I have a plan and a promise to myself that I need to uphold. I can't be naïve anymore. That ship has fucking sailed. That doesn't mean, however, that I can't have some of the best sex of my existence in these few months I have left here. I just have to be careful.

Cautious, even. Protecting myself is my number one goal. So I can't get carried away.

Ellie and I chat some more as the crisp sixty-degree air swirls around us. I tuck my hands into my zipped-up sweatshirt pockets as she tells me her plans for Oregon and two hours and a pot of coffee later, I make my departure. Between Dutton and I texting back and forth, it's been decided I'm making dinner. Even though it pains him for me to do so. I was the one who offered to cook, he just didn't want me to. That's odd in and of itself to me. I always had to cook dinner for Rory. Fresh and hot, for when he got home. And God forbid if it wasn't ready the *second* he walked through the door, I'd hear about it. And if I burned something, that took the cake. I would have never legitimately thought a man would break an entire plate for the bottom of the biscuit being a little darker than it should. But despite that, cooking for people I care about just became a part of me, but Dutton looks at is as labor for me. That's just one of the many differences between those men that I can't seem to wrap my head around.

I return to his place around four o'clock and Birdie flies out the door the minute I open it, prancing and jumping at my legs like I didn't just see her hours ago. I let her loose as she runs through the yard and I chase after her around the side while I watch her dart over to her usual spot, except this time, there's a bird waiting for her, perched right on the edge of the basin. I observe Birdie and her gentle nature as she walks carefully to the red-bellied Robin. And it's only a little while of waiting before the bird flies in a circle around her, nipping at her wet nose. Birdie rolls to her back, and the robin dances in the air around her.

My cheeks warm as I grin, and I leave them be while I bring the groceries in, checking every so often around the corner to make sure Birdie hasn't gone too far while I find the pots and pans needed for dinner. I rifle through a cabinet, trying to find a grater for the cheese, and as my hand flails around in the darkness, my fingertips graze against a folded-up piece of cloth. I pull it out, the white vinyl of a chef's hat laced between "Kiss the Cook" printed on the front and as I unfold it, the apron expands. A split second is all it takes for the idea to pop into my head, and I race back to the front door, calling Birdie in before I slip into Dutton's bedroom and take off my clothes, tying the apron around my naked body. I walk back to the kitchen, swiping my phone from the counter as I lift it up, snapping a photo that gives an ample amount of side boob but enough visibility to make out the words on the front.

ME: Attachment: 1 Image

DUTTON BECK: FUCKING HELL
DUTTON BECK: Don't even start dinner yet.
I have plans the second I walk through that door.

ME: Aren't you hungry?

DUTTON BECK: Starving.
But I already know what I want to eat.

I grin at my phone like some seductive siren who knows what she does to men. I've never sent a photo like this to anyone before, but somehow, I knew his reaction would get me just as excited. The minutes drag slowly as I lean on the counter, scrolling through my phone mindlessly while I wait for him to get here and just as I'm about to text Layla, both Birdie's and my head pop up at the same time.

Right when we both hear that front door open.

Our eyes lock the second he steps foot in, and he grins so wide I have no choice but to smile back. His strides are long as he makes his way to me, running his hands to the side of my face and through my hair as he cups my cheeks, pulling me in for a long-awaited kiss. He rolls his tongue gently against mine before drawing away and dragging his eyes down the length of my body.

"I almost threw this apron away when I got it as a gag gift. Thank fucking God I didn't do that," he says with a devilish smirk as his eyes wander back to mine.

His hands roam and his lips sink back into mine. His grip on my hip is firm as his other hand roams higher, tucking underneath the cheap cotton while his fingertips graze over my nipple, teasing me with his gentle touch. I let out a small whimper and instantly, I can feel him smile beneath my lips. My legs all but tremble as he pinches my sensitive bud between his fingers and the hand that was clutching onto my hip ever so tightly travels south. It works its way under the apron as he dusts his finger over my bare pussy.

I gasp at the immediate sensation, and he lets out a breathless "fuck" as he slides right between me. I try to kiss him back the best I can, but my tiny gasps for breath keep my mouth hung open as he lightly circles my clit. I part my legs slightly to give him more room to play, remembering what his plan was all along. He drops to his knees, lifting the apron up as he takes a moment to admire my pussy before his mouth suctions to it. I cry out as his cold, wet tongue runs against me, and my hands find the locks of his hair, grabbing a fistful. I close my eyes, letting my head fall back simultaneously, and my brain doesn't even compute what I'm doing until I realize it. My hips drive into him, riding his face as I put more pressure on my clit. My body moves unwillingly, and I just let it, succumbing to this newfound sexual desire. I can already feel the buildup, the tension that rises in my core. I don't want to come yet, but I fear I'm helpless with his relentless tongue flicking and sucking at my clit. His hands rub against the backs of my thighs as he works his way to my ass, gripping a handful of each cheek as he squeezes. I tilt my hips into him, making him press his tongue into me harder and that is all it takes. I shatter against him. Unraveling at the seams, I come on his face. My groans become whimpers as my legs shake uncontrollably, and he doesn't let up until I physically push his head from me. My body slumps, and I rest my elbows on the kitchen counter. Dutton rises to his feet, his five o'clock shadow glistening under the recessed lights, and he grins cheekily as he leans in for a kiss.

"How can I help with dinner?"

My eyebrows pinch slightly at his question, confused as to why we stopped. "Don't you want to come too?" I ask.

He just smiles and shakes his head from side to side, placing another lush kiss against my lips. "All day, I only thought about one thing. And that was getting you off. I'm happy as hell just like this, unless...you want more?" He smirks. "If so, just say the word, boss." His tone trails quieter as he slowly leans into me, placing one last kiss on my lips.

I just smile, throwing my arms around him as his head falls to the crook of my neck. We stay like this, embracing for a while, until he lifts his head up, dragging his hands to my hips. I spin around, grabbing what we need for the recipe as I direct him to grate the cheese while I put my clothes back on. Eating dinner takes less time than cooking it, and even through the flowing conversation, I can't bring myself to let him know that I should be going home tonight.

I know myself.

And these little sleepovers with a nice boy whose only goal in life is to get me off will not help my chances of *not* having feelings for him.

But I'm weak.

I'm a sucker for the love and affection I've so desperately craved the past five years. That must be why I end up back in his bed for one last slumber party.

My head rests on his pillow as we turn to each other, and I finally work up the nerve to get out what I should have before I crawled under these sheets.

"Dutton," I gently say, lifting my eyes, gazing right at him as his fingers brush softly against my arm. My stammering words come out slowly as my breath nearly trembles. "Given my...previous relationship... and the fact that I'm going back home to Illinois in a couple months, I– I'm not really looking for anything...serious," I finally get out.

It takes him a moment and a hard swallow before he replies. "Okay," he says, blinking slowly.

"And," I start to say before his eyes darken, becoming glossed over the second I continue, "I don't think we should spend the night together anymore after this. Just to...keep it more casual."

"Is that what you want?" His tone grows colder, more gravely as he speaks, and his fingers stop in their tracks against my skin.

I just nod, pressing my lips together in a thin line as I assure him.

"Okay." He gives a terse nod back and I flash him a weak smile, trying to ease the tension he seems to be radiating before tucking myself into his warm body.

His arms wrap around me, holding me snug like a big bear, and I nuzzle my head on his arm, burying my face in his chest as he brings me in. I know I'm playing with fire, but being held is my security blanket, and if this is the last night we'll sleep together, I'm taking advantage of it. Dutton places a tender kiss on the top of my head, muttering "good night" as my eyes drift shut. I can feel the muscles around my mouth stretch as I drowsily smile but I don't sound any words back as I drift to sleep. My dreams only just begin before my phone buzzes on the bedside table beside me. I peel my lazy eyes open, realizing I've already turned, as my ass presses firmly into Dutton, his arm hanging over me. I untuck my hand from the covers and grab my phone. Once it lights in the darkness, my stomach lodges itself into my throat. I blink rapidly, trying to make sure the words on the screen are the same ones I'm replaying in my head and once my eyes return to normal from their dry state, I read it crystal clear.

LAYLA ARLO: Rory is back.

LAYLA ARLO: And he's looking for you.

CHAPTER
TWENTY-EIGHT

THREE DAYS HAVE PASSED since Layla let me know that I'm still in the forefront of this psychopath's mind. Shouldn't he be out trying to get some other girl or something? Since he had no problem when we were together, surely he doesn't care highly enough for me anyway. Since her text, my parents have called nonstop, worrying and losing sleep, begging me to come back home to stay with them. End this cat and mouse chase.

But I refuse.

I will no longer subject myself to submitting to a man on terms not in my favor—especially one like Rory. I'm free. And living by my own rules. Going back now, waving that little white flag I thought about doing for a moment, is long fucking gone. Although, I'm on the same losing sleep page as my parents. Every creak in the wood, rustle from the trees, or chirp from a grasshopper has my eyes springing back open every time I drift off. It's impossible to sleep, and it clearly shows on my face.

I pull on the bags under my eyes, trying to figure out how I'm going to cover this up as I get ready. Dutton invited me out with his friends to a bar thirty minutes away, in a town I've never heard of. I agreed because he's incredibly persuasive, and I need to do something other than work and sit in my house, lost in my head. I pile on the concealer, trying to hide any evidence of my lack of sleep and I opt for a brown smoky eye to match with the layers of makeup I spent an hour doing. Contouring this, highlighting that—all this work and I'll be surprised if Dutton even notices I'm wearing all of this. Rory never did.

My bedroom looks like a clothes bomb exploded by the time I finish, and I only manage to find one tank top that wouldn't pass for pajamas. The straps are thin and the corset clasps in front are too tight for me to wear a bra, but it's the dressiest thing I succeeded in bringing when I was blind-heaving clothes into my suitcases. I layer three gold necklaces to make up for the revealing neckline and call it a day once I clasp my hoop earrings. I stand straight, trying to admire my body without sinking back into the "not good enough" headspace. I could go on about how tight this top is, or that my jeans show my hip dips a little more than I would like. But I don't want to go there, and honestly don't have the time since I'm already running late as it is. The moon illuminates my driveway just enough for me to get to my car without the help of the weak front porch lights I should probably change. And in typical fashion, my phone can't catch a signal long enough for me to see which direction I should be going. Another five minutes and me lifting my iPhone up to the heavens waving it around for a single bar later, I'm on the road, heading north on the highway.

"Turn left" is the last thing the GPS voice says, and I groan as I enter the crowded parking lot.

The two-story bar has black iron railings securing the porch and rooftop deck and as I walk in, my eyes bounce from left to right trying to find a familiar face. I push in further, squeezing myself between the sea of people that mingle by the front door, and I see Dutton standing at the bar next to Henry, surrounded by women. At the same time the voice in my head starts to tell me to run, Dutton turns, catching my line of sight. I swallow hard before I take a step toward him, working up the nerve to squeeze between the wall of women on my way over.

"I'm glad you came," Dutton says, his smirk pressing tight. He's shaved since I last saw him, which only brings out the dimple beneath his stubble. "Kaiton, this is Emmett, Kip, and Cody. You know Henry, of course," he says as he raises his voice, making sure I hear him over the loud music playing while he waves his hand over each of his friends around him. And for each man in his group, comes two women ogling and gawking at them like they're endangered animals in a zoo.

"Nice to meet you." I grin and raise a hand, trying to play over which was which again.

"You can have my seat," Henry says as he gets up. "I've got to take a piss anyway."

I give him a nod as I walk over, replacing his warm bar stool with my body once he leaves.

Dutton leans his arm on the bar, fitting right between me and Kip and as the air moves between us, that same irresistible smell of sandalwood and leather hits my nose. It's warm—sultry, even.Especially when *he* wears it. A cologne that I swear was made just for him.

"What do you want to drink?" Dutton asks as he moves in closer to me. His eyes are like black ice as they pierce right through me, shining under the tinted blue lights that turn his irises into onyx.

"I don't know." I twist my lips and look up at him. "Something fancy."

Dutton glances at the bartender, raising only a finger as he catches the man's attention. "Can you make a fruity mocktail and put it in a fancy glass for her, please?" Dutton grins at the man and points a thumb in my direction.

I get a quick smile from the bartender before he agrees and fills a rocks glass with different juices and syrups before spearing a lemon and lime wedge with a pick, tossing it into my finished drink.

"Here you are," the bartender says. "Do you want to start a tab or—"

"Put it on mine," Dutton interrupts.

I snap my head to him. "You don't have to do that."

"I know." He smirks and brings his glass to his lips, letting that amber-colored whiskey slide down his throat. I watch his Adam's apple rise and fall as he swallows it down. My stomach warms, and my eyes stay focused on his as I try not to think about what his lips might taste like right now.

My thoughts are interrupted by the screeching laugh of a brunette who hangs all over one of his friends, and he's eating it up, too. Soaking in every minute as the drunk girl sways, using his shoulder to balance herself.

"How is it?" Dutton asks as I shift my focus back to him.

"Really good," I say before taking another sip of my cranberry and orange juice infusion. I spin on the stool some more, looking around the best I can through the swarm of people at the modern décor . "This place is neat," I say once my eyes are done wandering.

"It's pretty fun. I'd rather be home, though." Dutton lets out a soft chuckle.

"Well, why aren't you, then?" I tease him while we still speak loudly over the music.

"Because I figured I'd better do something with my life instead of sitting on the couch with Birdie eating my weight in takeout, bored out of my mind."

"You could have called me to hang. I wasn't doing anything, either."

He takes another sip of his whiskey, slowly bringing it down as he grabs onto the back of my chair, his hand merely inches from my ass. "I didn't want to overstep any." He leans in closer, his body towering over me as the heat radiates from him, his breath hot on my skin as he speaks softer. "Boundaries."

I start to speak, but the moment I do, Henry pops up out of nowhere to the other side of me. I tilt my head up, seeing his rose-colored puffy cheeks pulled up to his eyes as he grins from ear to ear.

"Hey, Hen."

"Kaiton, what'd you do to this poor man? He doesn't want to get shitfaced anymore," Henry jokes as he points to Dutton.

"I'm drinking right now," Dutton snaps, holding his glass up.

"No, you're babysitting," Henry teases. "I'm just playin', it's not your fault." He looks at me. "Dutton's just a pussy."

I find it hard to suppress my laughter as Dutton rolls his eyes and before I know it, the rest of the clan surrounds us, asking me questions about where I'm from, what I did before moving here—the whole spiel someone asks when they're trying to get to know you. Kip is shorter, with a backward baseball cap showing his light brown curls above the adjustable strap. He's more interested in why I chose to work at The Wright Tools. Emmett stands closest to me, his stature resembles that of an NFL player, athletic and tall, like Dutton. Only Emmett's nose is a bit crooked, like it's been broken a time or two. He's more curious about what a girl like me is doing in a town like this. Whatever that's supposed to mean. Cody's the skinniest, sporting a shaved head at the sides while his hair grows longer down the middle. He seems genuinely interested in me, asking about my hobbies and things I like to do when I'm not working for this "shithead of a boss".

His words, not mine.

I keep answering their questions, following up with my own as I keep glancing Dutton's way. All the while, his eyes never waver from me. The minutes go by as everyone but Dutton orders another drink and I still sip on my super-sweet mocktail through it all. Some girls push through, trying to enter the sphere his friends have made around Dutton and me, but leave after getting ignored for some time. I can't imagine my presence would make these men forget about the rest of the women at the bar, so I take this moment to excuse myself to the ladies' room, just to get a breather.

It takes a good push through a sea of people until I'm secure in the restroom, and I spend my time there fanning myself with my hand, running cold water against my skin. Anything to cool down. The bar itself is massive but when it's jam-packed and everyone is taking up oxygen, it makes for a stuffy atmosphere. Nonetheless, I'm glad I came out tonight. It's a hell of a lot better than spending a Saturday alone at home. And I *was* having a good time, until I step out of the restroom. My eyes fall on Dutton and a long-legged brunette whose hand caresses his shoulder, her body leaning all over him, and for a moment, I stop breathing. My mind goes black as I watch her, smiling and giggling as she bats her eyes at him. I can't see his face, or how he's reacting, but something inside of me is raging. A fire is starting that I don't know how to put out and now I'm pissed. For no fucking reason.

"Kaiton!" I hear Emmett's voice calling my name.

I whip my head to the side, just now coming to the realization I've been standing stark still shooting laser beams at Dutton, and Emmett's probably been watching the entire time. He stands next to the jukebox attached to the wall and waves, so I work my way to him, weaving between two-top tables and everyone else who can't find a seat in this place. "I'm changing this terrible fucking music. Pick a couple songs you like. I put five bucks in."

I touch my finger against the screen, swiping through as I pick a few of my favorites before stepping out of the way, letting Emmett choose some himself.

"So, are you and Dutton like, a thing or—" He scrolls through the set playlists, but I interject before he can rattle off any further.

"We're just friends," I state, using my very best matter-of-facttone.

"Oh." He smiles, glancing at me. "Really?" His eyes draw down the length of my body, taking a moment to stop and stare right at my breasts before his eyes flicker back to mine.

I inhale through my nose, drawing out a big breath as I quickly look at Dutton, his back now fully facing me. The only thing visible is that same brunette chumming it up with him.

"Yep," I snap back as I fully turn my body toward Emmett, trying to distract my wandering eyes from finding their way back to Dutton. I don't know why my tone came out bitchy. I can't stop myself. The feelings in my bones—I can't shake them. I'm fucking irritated. For no good goddamn reason. *I* was the one who told him we have to keep this casual. It just never occurred to me in that moment when I said, "I don't want you" that it certainly didn't imply "I don't want you to fuck other people". My chest starts to feel tight and my hands become clammy. I feel as though I may be on the verge of passing out. My head becomes weightless, and I knew my top was too tight, but Jesus Christ, it's suffocating me. I pull at the material, trying to loosen some of the pressure on my ribcage, but it's hopeless. This corset is locked like the Declaration of Independence in that stupid fucking vault it's in every night and

God, do I need to breathe right now. "I'm going to step outside."
I bolt out, not giving Emmett a second to respond.

I push through the front doors, the cold breeze of the night
hitting my skin, and I look from left to right, choosing the opposite
side of the smokers huddled in a circle. I lean my back against the
cool brick, taking a deep breath, letting the crisp air fill my lungs.
I focus on the cars in the parking lot, just the ones I can see from
the cascading lights next to the sidewalk. I should go home. He
probably won't even realize I'm gone until an hour from now. It's
like he barely noticed me tonight anyway, which is fucking wild to
me, because my boobs look incredible.

"You just out here starin' at your tits?" Dutton's voice hammers
through me.

I jerk my head up, slowly bringing my hands down my ribs as
I unlock them from their held position against my breasts that I
was just admiring. "Maybe," I say with a tone that comes out as
arrogant.

He chuckles lightly, shoving a hand in his pocket before he takes
a step closer. "You okay?" His eyebrows knit together.

"Yep. I'm fine," I quickly say. "I just...think I might get going.
I'm exhausted," I lie, swallowing down the lump caught in my
throat.

"Are you sure? I was thinking we—"

"Yep. I'm sure."

I start to lift my back from the brick, pushing myself off to head
to my car, but Dutton swoops in front of me, blocking my route.
"Kaiton." His voice is gentle but still gruff as he hoists his arm up,

resting his hand on the brick next to my face, trapping me in with his body like he did in his kitchen. "What is going on?"

"Nothing," I say, exhaling a shaky breath from my nose. I gaze right into his eyes, trying to keep a stern look on my face. I'm trying to play it cool but dammit, I'm tired of biting my tongue. "You'll be just fine without me here. There's a tall brunette waiting for you inside," I snarl, pushing off from the brick again, but not getting far at all as Dutton's other hand snatches my hip, keeping me locked in place.

He leans into me, our lips only inches away as he whispers, "You and I both know there's only one girl I want to take home tonight."

Our breaths mix in the limited space between us and it's taking everything inside of me not to lunge even a touch forward to feel his lips against mine. "You want to go? Let's go. I don't want to be here without you anyway."

"But that girl—"

"What about her? I was painfully waiting for you to come back to me, trying my best to ignore her, and when I had enough, I came looking for you myself." He releases the hold on my hip, bringing his hand up to the strap on my tank top as he fits his finger underneath, dragging against my skin down the length of it. "Do you know how fucking good you look tonight? My eyes were only on you. I couldn't look away even if I tried." He traces his finger against the neckline of my top, riding over the humps of my breasts, and chills run down my arm at his gentle touch. I lean forward, not able to take it any longer as I place my lips against his.

His hand fits around the back of my neck and his arm falls from the side of my head, sweeping to my hip as he pushes into me, diving deeper into my kiss, his tongue parting my lips.

"Just friends, huh?" Emmett's voice startles us out of a world of our own before we break away from each other. I rub my finger against my bottom lip, wiping the wet remnants from my skin as Dutton takes the lead.

"We're going to get going. Let the guys know for me, would ya?" He smirks as Emmette lights up his cigarette and the second Dutton extends his hand for me, I grab it.

"It was nice to meet you." I smile and Dutton pulls me away, leading me into the dark parking lot.

I follow him as he tugs me along, right to where his truck is. "Let me drive you, you've been drinking," I say.

"The two sips you saw me take inside were the only sips I had tonight. Didn't feel like drinking. Haven't felt like drinking. We'll get your car tomorrow, that okay?"

I only nod as the corners of my lips curl into a smile and he opens the passenger door for me, waiting until I'm fully inside before shutting it.

Dutton starts to drive as he hands me his phone. "Can you text Henry for me?"

I freeze, holding his phone in my palm, unable to move. He had no issues just giving it to me. I timidly find the messaging app, pulling it up as I look for Henry's name. I try not to snoop as I scroll through, but it doesn't go unnoticed that I don't see a single girl's contact information anywhere in sight.

"What do you want me to say?" I ask as I click on Henry's name.

"Say, 'Could you close out my tab...I'll pay you back Monday'."

"Okay. Done." I start to hand his phone back.

"Just keep it, in case he says anything else."

I bring my arm back, resting his phone on my lap. I don't know what to make of this. The couple of times I tried to use Rory's phone for God knows what, he acted like it was the end of the fucking world. Like humanity itself would cease to exist if I even so much as looked at it.

I shiver, visibly shaking the appalling thoughts that flood my mind, and I lean my head to the right, resting on the frame of the truck door as the soft country music plays and I look out the window. I've never noticed how stars light up the entire night sky, or that only the silhouette of the pines is visible against it. I've always been the one in the driver's seat for these night rides. It's nice to see it from this view.

Dutton reaches his hand out over the center console and rests it palm up. I look at him, catching his gaze as he softly smiles. I grab his hand, intertwining my fingers with his, and rest my head again, straining my neck to see if I can make out any constellations.

"Here." Dutton reaches up, pressing a button that slides the sunshade back, exposing the clear glass that gives me a better view of the sky above.

I move to the headrest, staring up while grinning from ear to ear. "I've just never paid this much attention when I drive at night. I'm usually panicking, making sure I'm not missing a turn."

Dutton laughs as he trails his thumb lightly against mine, still keeping his firm hold. The sounds of the truck hum beneath us, and I'm amazed at how beautiful everything looks with only the light of the stars and the crescent moon.

"Want me to take the long way home?" he asks.

I smile as I still look at the big sky, taking a moment to soak it all in. I tilt my chin down at him and nod, my grin never faltering as I try not to beg. "Please," I say before he gives my hand a quick squeeze, turning onto some back road as he keeps driving. I just sit, thanking every trial, tribulation, and broken road that has led me to this moment, right here...with him.

CHAPTER
TWENTY-NINE

I YELP AS HE GRABS ME, slinging me over his shoulder like a sack of potatoes.

"What are you doing?" I laugh as he kicks the front door shut with his foot before stomping all the way to his bedroom.

"I never got after you for getting yourself off. That's my job." He swats his hand against my ass and I squeal again.

He lets me down gently, grabbing onto my hips as he pulls me in closer to him. The soft cast of the moon shines in his bedroom and without that, I wouldn't be able to see a thing. I stretch my arms out, reaching around his neck as I play with the long waves of hair that flip up in back. He leans into me, dusting his nose against mine before our lips press against one another. His large, calloused hands rub up my back while mine fall to his belt and suddenly our motions become swifter. His fingers unclasp the hooks on the front of my top then mine fumble at his belt buckle. His tongue runs against mine and once he unhooks the last clasp, my breasts burst free.

His fingers skim over my shoulders, letting the straps of my tank fall until it's on the floor. I finally unhook his belt, letting him take the lead on unbuttoning his pants himself while I do my own as soon as our lips part. Only the sound of our heavy breathing fills the room and I hook my thumbs between my jeans and thong, pulling them both down to my ankles together. He only pulls down his jeans, but it doesn't take me a second thought before I fall to my knees, tugging his boxers down once I'm positioned in front of him.

His cock springs up in my face as the cotton material frees him and I grip him firmly in my right hand. My knees dig into the low pile carpet and he sighs, bringing his hand to my head as he wraps the loose strands of my hair out of my face into a messy ponytail. I rub my hand along his length, stroking him back and forth as I feel his hold on my hair become tighter. He lets out a deep, throaty groan as I run my tongue flat against him, circling the head of his cock before wrapping my lips around it. I still work my hand, only sucking and licking the tip as his breath quickens.

"Fuck." He sighs.

I catch a glimpse of my reflection to the right, and as I take him further in my mouth, my gaze shifts to the floor-length mirror hanging on the inside of his open closet door. I watch as his hips buck lightly into me. I watch as the veins on his forearm stand out underneath the moonlight that pours through the curtains while he grips a handful of my hair tightly. I watch *us*. So beautifully in sync with every rhythm.

I hollow my cheeks as I suck and run my tongue along him every time I do. His moans, his sighs, every noise he makes is like a symphony to my fucking ears, and I could listen to it forever.

My breasts pin between my arms as I take my mouth off him, spitting before I run both of my hands in tight fists around his thick cock as I stroke.

"Oh my God." He groans even louder. "Just like that. Keep going," he says in a breathless whisper.

I keep at it, tilting my chin up to him as I watch his mouth drop and his head fall back. I pick up my pace, pumping his cock faster, and he lets out an even louder groan, refocusing his eye contact back to me. "Get on the bed," he demands.

I slow the pace of my hands, not stopping completely. I wanted to get him off this way. I wanted to watch him come apart from my own doing. But his eyes narrow and the corner of his mouth curls up ever so slightly. He steadily nods as he hooks his finger under my chin before whispering, "Get on the bed, Kaiton. Don't make me ask again."

I stand up, using his arms for support and as I turn around, his tall stature presses right against me. His hard cock pushes against my ass and he plants a soft kiss against my shoulder. He guides me by wrapping his arm around my waist, sitting me on top of his lap as he sits on the edge of the bed. He spreads my legs, sweeping his fingers on the inside of my thigh before bringing them to the skin on my neck, brushing the loose tendrils from my shoulder. His mouth lands in that sweet spot right in the center of the crook in my neck and I groan, my head falling back effortlessly. The chill of his tongue against my warm skin shocks me to my core.

"Show me how you played with yourself," he mutters.

I stay still as his hands rub against me, finding their way to my breasts as he grips them both, massaging them as he takes care to slowly work on my needy body. I can't help but arch my back as his fingers nip and stroke over my nipples. He runs his tongue again, working his way to the back of my neck as icy chills and raised bumps form in patterns across my arms.

"Kaiton," he whispers again, his hot breath stinging my ear. "Play with yourself."

I timidly move my hand as slow as I can between my thighs. I swallow down every bit of dryness in my mouth as I stare at my reflection. He's too busy kissing and licking my neck to see the terror in my eyes but after one last kiss on my shoulder, his eyes flutter up, watching me through his lashes as he catches me stiff in the mirror.

"Just relax," he reassures me, and I give him a slight nod, our gazes still locked ahead. I drag my middle finger up my center, already feeling the wetness between. "Good." Dutton smiles before kissing me softly once more. I bring my wetness up, circling my finger over my clit lightly, like he does. I whimper at the feeling but somehow, it feels a hell of a lot better when he does it. He grips my breasts, still taking handfuls of them as he massages in the same fashion, working my nipples as I pick up the pace of my finger. I lay my head back on him, sinking into him to ease my tension, but my eyes don't stay closed for long. Dutton's hand rushes to my face, gently grabbing me, squeezing, and pulling at my cheeks and chin as he tilts my head back forward.

"I want you to watch. I want you to see what I see," he lets out in a low breath.

"And what's that?" I smirk as I continue working my finger against myself.

"See just how fucking beautiful you are like this."

I slow the pace of my finger, caught off guard completely. My chest feels like it's caving in and suddenly, I'm short on air. Right now, what I see are the rolls my stomach creates in this position. Is this what Dutton sees too? God, I hope his eyesight is terrible. This angle for me is not flattering in the least and it leads me to wonder if this is what I look like all the time, naked, in these fucked up positions. Is this the reason I wasn't enough for Rory? Is this why he didn't want to touch me, but had no problem touching anyone else?

My body stills, frozen in time like a shipwreck at sea, and I know he can sense something's off. His finger applies more pressure as he still holds my chin, and he turns my head to the side, forcing my eyes to find his.

"I– I don't..." My quiet voice shakes under each breath and I close my legs, still sitting on his lap as I turn my body.

"Kaiton." Dutton sighs and tips his head down, grazing the tip of his nose with mine. "Please believe me when I say you are the most beautiful woman I've ever laid my eyes on. "You're so..." His soft lips touch mine. "Incredibly..." He places another peck.

"Sexy." He seals it with a final kiss as his hands grip the sides of my face.

Running his fingers through my hair, he kisses me deeper. I can't help it, and the harder I try to fight it, the quicker it comes. A silent running tear escapes and I feel the warm liquid running down my cheek. I try to kiss Dutton back, keeping him close to me so he doesn't see, but it's no use. Without ever pulling away, he swiftly brushes his thumb against it, halting the tear from dropping any further. I run my tongue against his, trailing my fingertips down his arm as his kisses deepen and suddenly, my mind has shifted. The tears that were pricking at the back of my eyes, begging to come loose, have dried. My body sinks into his as my arm wraps around the back of his neck, and in an instant, I'm lifted up. He carries me to the side of his bed before laying me down and climbing on top. He leans up, kneeling between my legs as he reaches for his drawer, pulling out a condom and tearing it open. He rolls it down, keeping his hand on his thick cock as he presses it between me, rubbing and teasing me back and forth. I whimper at the feeling of him against my clit and I tilt my hips to get him in faster. He smirks like a handsome fucking devil before he gives in and gives me what I want, thrusting right into my center as I cry out. He falls on top of me, wrapping both his arms under my head as his large body nearly swallows me in this scrunched up position. His tempo is slow, and his deep thrusts come with so much pressure I can't help but moan. My nails dig into his skin while I twirl my tongue against his. Our kisses are messy, sloppy, and slow and I can feel myself getting wetter as the seconds go on.

I release my lips from his and my gaze falls between us. I stare while he thrusts and my core tightens as I see myself wrapped around him.

"Watch it, baby." His voice is as deep as his cock inside me. "Watch how you take me so well."

All I can do is pant, making little whimpering noises every time he's fully in me. I feel like I'm being stretched. No, *filled*. In the best possible way. And it's hard to form any thoughts, especially when his gruff voice rattles my bones every time he makes a fucking sound.

I feel like I'm on the brink of it. Right on the edge of that euphoria I know he can bring me to. But it's too slow. I need him in me quicker. Harder. I want him to pound me until I can't even remember my own name. Fuck. I just want *him*.

"Faster." I sigh.

And he does it.

Fucking me like I wanted, just like I imagined. His breath is heavy on my lips and both of our mouths can't stay shut as we gasp for air. His curved cock hits the perfect spot inside my pussy, and I feel like he's deep in my stomach with every thrust. Relentlessly he plunges, and I grab a fistful of his hair, holding on as the bed rocks from his rapid movement. His eyes glimmer with the moonlight and I stare into the dark pools of emerald, noticing a look I haven't seen before. They're intense, almost poetic, in a way. Like they're longing for something. Longing...*for me*.

"I think I'm gonna come," I whimper.

"Oh fuck." He sighs. "Come right on my cock. You can do it."

He pushes the loose strands of hair out of his eyes as the sweat starts to bead on his skin. I can feel the pressure rise in the pit of my belly and after only a few more deep thrusts, I explode, crumpling like rocks from a cliff. I cry out, wailing in a long moan as I ride my orgasm out.

"Good job, baby." He grunts. "Good fucking job."

And it isn't too long until he comes next, cursing as he spills inside of me, and God do I wish he didn't have a condom on. I sure as hell don't want kids any time soon but the thought of him fucking me raw until he comes drives me wild. I don't know why I've become this woman with these new sexual desires, but I don't care. He makes me want this. Crave this, even. He's created some goddamn animal out of me and I'm so fucking happy for it.

Dutton crawls beside me, letting his hand fall to my face as he brushes his fingers against my skin with the gentlest touch. He stares right into my eyes while the corners of his lips curl up at the tips and he doesn't say a word. I can't contain my smile or the laugh that runs past my lips when I ask, "What?"

"God forbid I ever lose my sight, I want to remember every little detail about you," he whispers. "The shape of your eyebrows," he says as his thumb rubs against them. "The small flecks of brown that you have in your eyes," he says as he runs his finger down the center of my nose. "And the way your mouth moves when you say my name," he finishes as his fingertip drags across my Cupid's bow.

I smile as I look at him. My heart flutters faintly and I bury my face into his chest, holding onto him tightly as I cuddle my naked body against his. I fit so perfectly here. My body conforms to his with every curve and he doesn't complain that his arm's falling asleep under me. He takes any chance he can get to touch me through the night, and I never knew I could have wanted anything more. My eyes are so heavy the only thing I can do is close them while Dutton's fingers drag slowly against my skin. And here I am.

Falling asleep in his arms once more.

CHAPTER THIRTY

MY EYES FLUTTER OPEN at the loud clanks and bangs that accrue from the other side of the door, and it only takes me a moment to adjust before regaining my perception. I'm still in Dutton's bed.

I've got to get out of here.

Fuck. I shouldn't have slept here.

Casual. My God, can I ever just take things slow?

I scramble out from under the covers and when my toes hit the grey carpet, Dutton walks in holding a small wooden tray with a plate and two glasses—one with a drink, and the other with an orange lily.

"Fuck," I mumble under my breath.

"Good morning." Dutton smiles as he brings the tray to me, setting it on the edge of the bed for me to see. A lump lodges in my throat as my eyes scan over the misshapen and disfigured chocolate chip pancakes sitting right next to two *almost* burnt strips of bacon.

"You made this...for me?" I swallow that lump down, looking up at him.

"Yeah." He beams with a light laugh. "Do you like it?" I had to watch a couple YouTube—"

"Dutton," I cut him off as I stand up. *Fuck. Fuck, this cannot be happening. I can't go through this again.* "I can't do this," I let out.

He stands motionless, dumbstruck as I push past him, just making it to his bedroom door before his hand grabs mine.

"Hey, wait!" he calls. "What are you doing? What's going on?"

"I can't, Dutton. I just can't."

"Can't what?"

"I can't do...this." I wave my arms between us. Birdie pounces next to me, thinking my hand movements are signals for us to play, and I expand my reach to his bedroom, where the breakfast he tried his hardest to make, sits.

"Why?" His tone hardens slightly.

My arms fall to my sides, grazing against the cotton material of the shirt I'm wearing, and suddenly I'm reminded that at four-thirty this morning, I was shivering. Dutton got up, put one of his shirts on me, and tucked me back in before holding me the rest of the night.

That is what I can't do.

Because the harder I fall for him, the harder I fall after he breaks thousands and thousands of endless pieces of my soul. That's not happening again, and certainly not with him. If this continues, I can't imagine the heartbreak it'll cause.

I'll never recover.

"Why, Kaiton?" he snaps again.

"Because it's not casual! Nothing about this says 'just friends'!"

"*Nothing* about the way we fucked last night said 'just friends' either, and you know it. Tell me this isn't what you want. Tell me right here." He takes a step closer. My body is powerless, and I can't do anything but stare at him. "I'm not okay with being just some hookup. I'm sorry. I can't do that. Not with you. I want so much more *with you*. I can't kiss you one night, then not see you for three more. I can't have you in my bed, then spend another night alone. I fucking tried. It's not fair. So, you tell me right here, right now, that you want nothing more than to be *just friends* with me."

"I just..." My voice shakes, quivering as I whisper, "I can't stay here, I can't stay here with you. That's insane, right? Yes! It's insane."

"Kaitlon—"

"No, it is! It's crazy. It's me jumping headfirst into something without thinking, just like I did with Rory, and look what he did to me! Look at who he made me! Until I came here, I couldn't even go out with friends without thinking about him, without texting him. He consumed me, and then he broke me. I am broken, and you—" I'm heaving, I can't breathe. The tears are going to choke me to death. "You're too good. You can't— I can't do this."

"Why don't I have a say in this?" A heat fills his voice. "You think you're the only one who's broken? What that fucker did to you, I can't change it, I can't fix it, but I can give you something he didn't. Something real."

"I can't," I say again, louder this time, needing to silence him before he says all the right things.

"Then neither can I." His tone grows somber as he shakes his head. "I want you, Kaiton. All of you. I don't want to just take what I can get."

I hang my head as the tears pool in my eyes and I break down the moment I speak.

"I'm sorry," I say before the tears let loose, and I cover my eyes with my hands, not wanting him to see.

He stands for a moment, only taking long-winded breaths before he pulls me in, wrapping his arm around my frame, and I feel so small against him as he tucks me into his bare chest. Birdie lays between us, right on our feet, and I wrap my arms around his waist, hugging him as the silent tears run. This is for my own good. I knew it from the start. But I'm not ready to let go of him. Not yet. I don't break my arms free, and neither does he. And the minutes pass as we stand, embracing each other tightly. But like all good things, it comes to an end.

"Let's get your car," Dutton finally says as he backs away slightly, rubbing the palms of his hands on my body before his arms drop to his sides.

I nod, wiping the tears from my eyes before I find my clothes, and as I get dressed, I try to convince myself that this is for my own good, to protect myself.

Even though it doesn't feel like it.

Not even close.

CHAPTER
THIRTY-ONE

THE HOT CERAMIC CUP warms my hands and I scrunch my knees under my sweater as the bite of the morning breeze rushes over the lake. The FaceTime tone rings, and I take a sip of my coffee as the other line picks up. She's still in her robe, Velcro rollers pinned in her hair, and she smiles the second she sees me.

"Hi, Mom."

"Hi, sweetie." She beams. "Are you okay? You look a little down this morning."

My chin starts to quiver, and I do all I can to suppress crying any further.

"I'm okay." My tone squeals only slightly and as I blink, one single tear falls.

"Kait." She sighs as the features in her face drop.

I exhale loudly as I press my eyes tight together, letting whatever was getting ready to fall, get out and done faster.

"I really like him," I whisper, defeated and exhausted with trying to block my emotions for this long.

"Oh, honey," she drags on as she clicks her tongue to her teeth. "What's wrong with that? The last time I talked to you, he made you dinner. I figured that was coming next." Her voice is gentle as she speaks, and I don't know how else to explain what I'm feeling.

"I'm...scared. I'm nervous. I'm...not good enough. I...don't know, Mom. I'm all of it. All wrapped into one. Rory was kind, believe it or not. He used to hold my hand. He used to want to take pictures with me. He said sweet words and pretty compliments and gave me kisses on the forehead. Then it became less and less, until he hated everything about me."

Hated my mouth that talked without thinking.

He used to love it for saying what was on my mind.

Hated my hair because it scratched him at night.

He used to love cuddling with me, said it kept him warm.

He used to love *me*, and then he didn't.

"I can't explain it, Mom, but I've never met anyone like Dutton. The way he makes me feel is something I've never experienced. So what if one day he wakes up and hates me? What if one day he realizes I'm not good enough for him and finds someone else, leaving me lonely and heartbroken in the process? What then? What will I do? I'll tell you one thing that could happen, I would die. And I don't mean 'oh my God, I'm gonna die if he ever leaves me.' No, Mom. I will physically die. My heart will full-on give out. Every time my heart breaks, I feel it, *I actually feel* it inside. It's a flutter, like dying petals from a rose that fall one by one. Eventually, there's going to be nothing left. Like the rose was never even there to begin with. If I continue with him...there's no turning back. My fate is sealed."

"Well, you're still getting to know each other, honey. Learning to trust is a part of the process."

"You don't understand. When I'm with him, it's just...different. We're so in sync. It's like we've known each other for years. He never makes me second guess myself. It's not just his words, either. His actions, who he is as a person, all of it, rolls into this perfect cocktail of the man of my fucking dreams, and I'm scared." The tears roll as I speak and my mom looks at me with kind eyes, her lips pressed tight as she lets me continue. "Do you know what he did this morning?" I sniffle.

"What's that?"

"He made me breakfast."

"That was sweet of him," she says with a soft smile.

"No, Mom. Listen, he doesn't cook. This man knows how to make one meal. It's spaghetti, sometimes with meatballs. That's it. But he knows how *I* feel about cooking. That it's not some daunting task for me, that it could actually be fun when you're doing it for someone you truly care about."

"And..."

"So, he makes me the most fucked up looking pancakes I've ever seen and almost burns the bacon. But he made it for me. He tried, for me. I didn't ask him to do that. He just *did*."

"That sounds very thoughtful..."

"Mom, that is the shit right there that's going to make me fall in love with him."

"Kait...honey. Now, don't get mad, but I have a question, okay?" Her voice is quiet like a mouse, almost timid as she asks. I know she can sense my hostility, so to her, it's like walking on eggshells.

"What?"

"Why do you think you won't be enough for him?"

"Because...was I ever?"

"Honey." Her eyes start to well with tears and my heart sinks the moment I see it through the screen. "Please don't think that of yourself. You think Rory's indiscretion had anything to do with you? That was all him, baby. All him. It was his insecurities, his behavior, his attitude, *his* mistake. That was nothing on you. Kaiton, you are enough. You will always be enough." The tears run faster, and I wipe my wool sleeve against my nose—disgusting behavior I know, but it's only my Mom who sees. "Why do you want to live in fear? Do you truly think you're incapable of being loved correctly?"

"I just...don't want to get hurt." The words barely push out of my tightened throat.

"Sometimes in life, we're let down. But the letdown doesn't define you, it's how you react to it. Maybe it'll take you longer to trust, but what? Are you just gonna find good men, only bring them to a certain point before you break *their* hearts? Tell them you don't want anything more? Falling in love is scary. Trusting people is scary. It's all a part of the process. It's all a part of life, Kaiton. I don't want you to miss out on finding love, and I'm not saying it's with Dutton, but my God, he seems like a great man. The way you speak so highly of him, don't think I don't notice

how your face lights up when you mention his name. I saw it when
you told me about your run-in at that festival the first week you
were there. It's the same look you still have now. Even through your
tears, I can tell. You're breaking your own heart, and it pains me to
see it."

"But I leave soon," I whisper.

"Honey, what do you have here at home? You have Dad and me,
sure, and Layla...what else?"

I pause a moment, my chin shaking as my bottom lip pouts
slightly and I let her words soak in. They were so hesitant for me
to leave, and now...they want me to stay?

"Coco." I laugh through the tears.

"And Coco." She smiles. "But what else? The way I see it, your
home and your job are right there. You're twenty-five now. You
have no children, no husband—"

"Mom, this is not making me feel better." I laugh again because
I know not a bone in her body means that negatively.

"What I'm saying is that you are free to live and work wherever
you want. You have nothing holding you back. You're going to
come back to Illinois and live with your dad and me? I love you,
baby, but we have naked taco Tuesdays and—"

"Mom!" I shout.

She laughs, snorting a little as the phone shakes with her
giggling body. "You're in charge of your life. You want to work
at the post office in Alaska? I'm happy for you. You want to
work as a receptionist in New York? Good luck, baby. You're
free, Kait. Nothing holding you back, nothing stopping you

from doing what you want to do. Life is full of heartbreaks and disappointments already. Don't let regret be one to add in with them."

My phone buzzes and Dutton's name appears at the top of the screen. I swipe down as I read the text aloud.

DUTTON BECK: Can I come over?
I don't like how things ended this morning

and I just want to talk to you, please.

Silence settles between us once I finish, and she looks at me with softened eyes and that motherly tone she uses all too well. "You had a really shitty thing happen to you, Kait. But don't let Rory's actions stop you from finding the happiness you deserve," she says.

I reply to him quietly, letting him know I'm in the back, out by the lake, and I dry my tears as my mom holds up Coco for me to see. Her small white body fits the entire frame and I grin as I coo at her, only getting a little ear twitch back.

"I saw Mrs. Ellis at the store yesterday and I think she's getting even more nuts." She laughs, trying to change the subject so I'll quit crying.

"Oh yeah? Why's that?"

Mrs. Ellis was one of my teachers back in high school and my mom was convinced she was in love with my dad. It was a whole thing, but was mostly a gag between them since my dad doesn't even *look* another female's way. He's always been all eyes for my mom ever since they met.

"Well, I don't know, she came up to me very sorrowful, like someone had just died, and said she was sorry to hear you haven't been found. I just told her you weren't missing or anything, that you had just moved for a job opportunity. It's what Dad and I have been telling everyone. She was nearly on the brink of tears, but she's always been a little cuckoo. She was spouting off about some sign she saw... I don't know, I just waved my hand at her, dismissing her because I had about eighty bags of groceries in my hands."

I giggle, watching my mom explain the story as the curlers in her hair bounce while she speaks, and we only chat a couple minutes more before I realize Dutton will be arriving soon.

"Well, thanks for the talk, Mom. I appreciate it. I've got to get ahold of Layla. I guess Rory showed up at her house looking for me a couple of days ago. She said she was going to file a protection order against him if she could, but I haven't talked to her since."

"Yeah, she called us. We gave her Allenda's information but I'm not sure what they can do."

"This is all just so...fucked."

"It's okay, baby. We'll get through it together. Now, go splash some cold water on your face. You look like you've been crying for a year straight. And make sure to tell Dutton I said hello."

"But I didn't tell you what I texted him back. How do you know I'll see him?"

"Your eyes, baby, they give everything away." She winks. "Love you."

"Love you more, Mom."

CHAPTER
THIRTY-TWO

I HEAR THE TRUCK door shut and I twist my head to the side as I wait for Dutton to come over the hill. His tall frame just peeks over before I face back forward, taking another sip of my hot coffee before I set it on the table next to me. I untuck my bare legs from my knitted sweater and as I plant them into the grass covered in morning dew, Dutton has already made his way to me.

"You don't have to get up." He grabs the other Adirondack chair, turning it to face me directly before he sits. He reaches for my hands, cupping them both as his eyes sink right into me. "I know you have this guard up, okay? I understand where you got it from. If you need time, I've got patience. I don't care how long it takes. I want to earn your trust. From the moment I met you... I don't know, Kaiton. You can tell me to fuck right off but I'm just going to be straight up as raw as I can get, okay?"

"Okay," I whisper, my quiet voice mixing with the rustling of the pines.

He swallows hard before he speaks. "From the moment I met you, my life hasn't been the same. You don't leave my mind. You're

permanently stuck there. You say you're scared? Kaiton, so am I.
I've never felt this way before. This is all brand new to me and I'm
fucking thirty years old. I think a part of me was eager to marry
Hailey because I thought, what the hell? I'm never going to settle
down anyway. I was a completely different person back then. But
even after, I kept that same mentality. I had it cemented in my
brain—it's just Birdie and I until the bitter end. Then I met you.
And I can't picture my future with just Birdie and me anymore
because you're standing there, too. I'm prepared to give you all
the time you need and if that takes years, so be it. You've got two
months left here, and then you leave, I know. I looked up all the
fun things to do in Illinois when I come visit, if that's okay with
you. And if I didn't think you felt the same, I wouldn't be spilling
all of this to you like some lunatic, but do you understand what
I'm saying? I'm saying that no matter how long it takes or how
difficult you think it may be, I will be patient. I'm going to make
you feel as safe as possible. Until you're not scared anymore."

I squeeze his hands as the words pour out of him and watch as
his chest rises and falls with every deep breath he takes.

"You would wait years just to be with me?"

"Kaiton, I would wait the rest of my life if that meant I could
still see you from time to time."

"But it's not your first choice?" I let out a small giggle.

"No, not at all." He laughs. "My first choice would be for you
to let me in, even just a little, and let me make you happy every day
you're here and every day you're not. I know you have a plan, and

I respect that. So, I'll do whatever it takes. Whatever you need me to do, to even just get a sliver of your time."

My eyes fall to our hands, still holding onto one another so tightly, and I look back at him, only using my breath to speak. "I'm scared, Dutton."

"Me too, Kaiton. But I don't want to look back on my life in five years when fear has won and be miserable that I let it."

In the depth of my soul, I know he's being true, and as I look into his eyes, it's like my heart already knows too. I feel a flutter, but not the heartbreak kind—the flutter of the pace as it picks up, the strong beats that make it feel like it's pulsing right under my skin.

That's what he does.

He makes my heart feel powerful, makes *me* feel powerful. Not the opposite. And if I had just taken a second to think, to really feel through my emotions, I would have seen that sooner.

"Where do we go from here?" I flicker my eyes as I peer through my lashes, noticing that sexy smirk spreading across his lips.

"Come here." He tugs on my hand. I stand as he pulls me in, setting me on his lap. "Wherever you want to go. You want to sleep together every night or only see me every other day? You let me know. You want me to fuck right off like I told you earlier, or do you want to marry me? I mean, you choose." He laughs so genuinely it warms over every goosebump that lines my skin from the late summer wind.

I wrap my arm around his neck, eye level with him as I lean in closer to his lips. "What I want, right in this moment, is for us to go inside and make breakfast together. Then I want to watch that movie we never got to finish with Sandra Bullock."

His dimple never fades as his pressed smile remains. "You got it, boss," he says in his usual deep tone.

With a swift pat on my ass, Dutton pushes up and follows as I lead us inside. I head to the refrigerator first, pulling out the bacon, eggs, and milk before I look for the rest to recreate his pancake breakfast from this morning. We mix, pour, and fold, and I lay the bacon on the cast iron first, frying that up before we scoop the batter onto the griddle.

"This is a lot easier with help." He chuckles and I look up at him, taking in that beautiful jawline of his, soaking up the way he looks when he's truly happy. That's the version of him that I like the best.

The bacon sizzles in the pan and I realize it's been sitting too long on one side.

"Shit!" I exclaim as I grab the tongs, flipping over each piece as the black bottoms become exposed. "Fuck, I'm sorry." My heart nearly sinks at the sight as I look at him.

"It's fine." He grins, leaning in to kiss my lips. He gives me a light tap on my ass, his palm meeting my long sweater, the tips of his fingers meeting my skin. "Give me the most burnt ones, you take the others," he says.

And in this moment, he doesn't even realize...

He's beginning to fix a heart he had no hand in breaking.

CHAPTER
THIRTY-THREE

I GRAB THE RAKE from the shelf, putting it back in its correct spot as the bells chime against the wooden frame.

"Be there in a minute!" I yell through the rows of tools lined between me and the front door.

I wipe my hands against my apron, shuffling to get to the customer, only to see Dutton's smiling face before me as I reach the open area.

"You almost done?" he asks.

"I was just cleaning up, lights were going off next."

"How did you sleep last night?" he asks as he wraps his arm around my hip, pulling me in for a kiss. I look at him after our lips unlock, eyebrows pinched while the confusion writes itself on my face. "What? I forgot to ask you this morning." He laughs.

"Great."

"I told you my mattress was better."

"I *know* your mattress is better. But I have the lake." I smile cheekily.

This past week, Dutton and I have spent every night together, bouncing between both of our places. It wasn't planned. In fact, I tried to not let myself cave in to that heated desire of being cuddled every night. But his arms...they're just so big, and his body is just so warm. I really had no choice. Today, he offered to drive me to work this morning so he could help get Ellie's done faster in time for our dinner reservation—one at the "best steakhouse in the west" or so he says. And one that *he* made, as a complete surprise to me as of last night in bed. So, while he leans against the front desk, looking as sexy as ever in a white T-shirt that clings to his body and jeans that look tailored just for him and his tall stature, I'm shutting off the lights, flipping signs, and finishing the rest of my closing duties. I lock up as Dutton stands behind me and the entire ride to Ellie's is nothing short of the affection he's shown all week. He grazes his thumb against mine while we hold hands tightly, the standard for every time I'm in the car with him, especially during our late-night drives. But even just like this, I can't help but feel so at ease, so comfortable right next to him.

"You get the food, I give the treats?" he asks as we pull in and I nod, ready to tackle taking care of Bunny and Poppy for the third time this week, now with a little bit of help.

The wind whistles and howls as we walk to the barn and the hair on the back of my neck stands. I look over my shoulder, that feeling of being watched lingering over me, and I glance at Dutton, who casually smiles. Immediately, the thought is dismissed, remembering Ellie has workers around here somewhere. I head straight for the bin that houses the grain as Dutton stays behind, doing anything but getting the treats.

"Oh, perfect!" His excited voice echoes through the barn and I turn around just in time to see him secure the cowboy hat that was left resting on a barrel.

"What do you think?" he asks as he tips the brim down slightly, giving a curt nod along with it.

"Hot." I grin and raise my eyebrows, lifting the lid from the metal bin and setting in on the ground beside it.

"What about now?" he asks, and my eyes flutter back up to him, seeing the single stalk of hay clenched between his teeth as it hangs from the corner of his mouth.

My heart rate picks up pace as I take him in. He looks like a true cowboy if I ever saw one, and a mighty fine one at that. He leans against the frame of the barn, thumb hitched in his jean pocket with that smirk that can make me fall to pieces.

"You better quit or I'm gonna have to fuck you right here." I laugh, only bantering in the slightest because I love messing with him.

He stands straight, immediately taking steps to me as he throws the stem of hay on the ground. "Say that again." He all but growls as his tall stature shades me from the setting sun behind him.

I bat my lashes, setting the bait for him to get all riled up. "I said...you better quit trying to turn me on, or I'm going to have to fuck you. Right here. Right now." I use my best low, sultry voice as I do all but whisper, looking straight into his eyes.

He shakes his head, grinning, "You asked for it," he says as he scoops me up, lifting me with one arm as his hand grabs hard at my ass.

I screech out a laugh, half shocked he can carry me with ease like this and the other because I was only fucking with him. He sets me down in a stall solely used to stack the extra bales of hay and as he closes the door, I can't contain my laughter as I speak. "Dutton, I was kidding. We can't fuck here!"

"Why not?" he asks as he hooks his finger under my chin, tilting my head up and brushing his lips against mine, teasing me with his touch.

"Because..." I lose my train of thought.

Never mind that this is Ellie's house and barn, let alone the fact that we're outside and have a perfectly nice spot to fuck—inside, *at home*.

"Why, Kaiton? Why can't you fuck me here?" His breath is hot as he keeps teasing me with only the touch of his lips against mine. I can't answer him. I have no more reasons for him. His fingers release my chin, only so he can glide them against my abdomen before they fall to the button on my jeans. "You don't want to come?" he asks as my button frees and he trails his fingers gently right against the top of my laced panties.

"I want to." My tone breaks in a whimper, but I can't help it. My breath shortens as his touch stays delicate against my skin.

"You want to what? Tell me. Remember what I said about using your words?" his husky tone groans against me as he slides his fingers on my skin, right beneath my underwear.

I suck in a breath as he goes lower, cold against my sensitive clit, his fingers circling lightly. My heart hammers through my chest.

"I want to come." The groan spills from my lips and in an instant, his mouth lands on mine.

Our tongues sweep and roll against each other, and he pushes me against the wall, rattling the pine between this stall and the next. My hands tug at my jeans, pulling the tight material over my hips further down to give him more access and he slides two fingers inside of me, shoving them deep, and I feel my body tingle with pricks of heat.

I arch my back, letting the wind gush against my bare skin that shows from my rumpled shirt and I can't contain the gasps and grunts that stem from my throat. He drills into me with such force and so much pressure, I have no choice but to scream.

But I can't.

Not here.

I try to quiet my moans, hush my whimpers, but it's almost impossible with the pressure of his fingers curling against that perfect spot. He grabs the hem of my long-sleeve shirt, pulling it up to my collarbone before tugging my bra down and wrapping his lips around my taut nipple. I can't see what he's doing—his hat blocks my view—but what I can *feel* is his cold tongue electrocuting my body, not sparing a moment to let up as he thrusts inside of me. He sucks and flicks with his tongue and lips and I push down on his hat, holding tight as I ride out my orgasm.

"Fuck," I drag out in the quietest whimper I possibly can.

"Come here," he whispers as he grabs my hip, pulling us forward to the stacked bales before stepping behind me. He places a firm hand on the small of my back and I bend forward. The pieces of hay poke through my thin shirt where my elbows rest and I hear the metal of his belt clinking as he pulls his jeans down to his knees, gripping my hip with one hand as the other fists his girth.

"Fuck," he says as he taps his cock flat against the cheek of my ass. "I don't have a condom."

My head turns back in a snap, watching as his hips barely thrust, letting his velvet cock rub against my skin. My pussy tingles at the sight of him—the way his eyes beg for me, the way his jaw drops only slightly as he looks at what's in front of him. "I'm on birth control, just do it, please," I hastily beg, not missing a beat.

I know this isn't smart. Hell, even *Layla* told me not to do it. But I've been craving this. For some goddamn reason, I've been hungry for him to fuck me like this. So close, so bare, and so fucking raw. I don't put any more thinking into it as my heart races and my chest caves from my heavy breathing.

"Fuck me," I beg, looking at him, and he grits his teeth, clenching his strong jaw tight as his eyes flicker from me to his cock.

His hips draw back, and my breathing stops when he pushes right in my center. He slides in slowly, tormenting me with every inch as he fills me. In sync, we both moan once he can't go any further, and that's when he thrusts, drilling right into me from behind as my mouth falls open. I can hear how wet I am every time he pushes in and it's so fucking hot to know that he's exposed like this inside of me, completely bare as he stretches me. He grips my hips hard, putting a foot on a single bale as he hits a different angle. The pressure pushes like he's in my stomach and my cries are becoming harder to suppress. I look behind, watching his eyes as they stare at us becoming one, and can feel myself on the verge of another orgasm as I analyze him. His shirt is clenched between his teeth with that fucking cowboy hat on and every muscle in his stomach is flexed as he leans back, driving right into me. His arms are bulked from gripping me and the veins that run along them are pushing right at their surface.

"I'm gonna fucking come," I cry softly, and his eyes flash to mine in a second. He unclenches his shirt from his teeth, bending down as his hand reaches for me, grabbing right under my chin against my throat to bring me closer to him as his mouth consumes me. My back arches even more and the muscles pull in my abdomen as our uneven kisses and rolling tongues make my mouth wet while he pounds relentlessly.

I have no choice but to explode.

I pull my head away and shut my eyes tight as I do all I can to suppress the screams that want to rip through my throat.

I finally gasp once it's finished, searching for any air to seep into my lungs, and he pulls out of me, spinning me around as he sits on the ground. He leans against the stacked bales and I get the signal and take my jeans off completely, stepping one foot over him as I lower myself. He guides his cock inside of me, and I groan as I slide down, taking all of him. His hands grip my ass, and I lean into him, kissing his soft lips as his tongue parts mine. I move up and down

MADELINE FLAGEL

as my knees dig into the pieces of straw that line the floor, and his throaty groans and moans heat me right at my core. His clipped nails drag down my back until they get to my hips again and he grips hard, pushing in the same direction as I grind while he speeds up the pace.

"Ride me, Kaiton," he breathlessly says. "Ride my fucking cock."

I keep grinding, bucking my hips while his hands stay for guidance. His hat starts to come off as his head moves against the bale and I bring my hand to it, pushing it back down to secure it on him as I ride.

He grins and uses every bit of his breath to ask, "You like that?"

"Leave it on," I whisper against his mouth.

"You got it, boss," he breathlessly says back.

I bring my lips to his neck, kissing him like he does me and his throat moves as he grunts, lifting my ass up just slightly as he drives into me from below.

"Yeah, it should be in here!" a man's voice yells.

We freeze instantly, Dutton buried deep inside of me, listening to the thumping footsteps as they enter the barn.

"You got it?" another man's voice rings.

"Yeah, it's right here, but I'll get to it when I get to it." I hear the flicker of a lighter before the smell of cigarette smoke lingers in the air.

I look back at Dutton as he brings his finger up to his lips, shushing me with a smirk, and my eyes stay wide while I try to not make a sound, even with my uneven breath.

Dutton's hips start to move slowly, dragging his cock inside of me at a steady pace, and he smiles as he pulls me in by the back of my neck, diving his tongue as far as it can go inside of my mouth. I push down on him, regaining control as I ride him while his hips stay planted on the ground. His cock throbs inside of me and I can sense he's close.

The men's conversation continues but that doesn't stop me from sitting up slightly and grabbing his shoulder for support while I fix my feet, planting them firm on the ground as I bounce with more control. My thighs start to burn but I push through as his mouth hangs open, his eyes flickering between my pussy and my eyes.

"Fuck," he grunts so quietly it would sound like a whisper from the wind to anyone else. I jolt up as he lifts me, grabbing his cock firmly as his hot cum spills onto the happy trail of hair that runs down.

I kneel back down, unable to stand from the half door of the stall, and Dutton grabs onto my cheeks and chin as he pulls me in, pressing his tender lips against mine. The thuds of the footsteps trail outside of the barn as the men's voices carry with them and I smile, pushing to my feet as I fix my jeans before pulling them on. Dutton stands, wiping his cum with the inside of his T-shirt before pulling his pants up.

"We're late for dinner," I tease.

"It was worth it," he says before grabbing my face once more, planting another heated kiss upon my lips.

CHAPTER
THIRTY-FOUR

MY FUZZY SOCKS GLIDE against Dutton's leg as I step over it, taking my seat back on the couch next to him as the half-eaten pizza slice stays locked between my teeth. I turn into him, resting my leg on top of him as I scrunch up my knee.

"Sorry we missed our reservation. I know you were looking forward to going."

"You kidding me?" He looks at me, grabbing the crust that's left in my hand as he takes a bite. He leans up quickly, tossing the rest on the plate in front of us before he sweeps me onto his lap. "This night ended up better than I imagined."

One of his hands rests gently against the side of my thigh while the other reaches out for Birdie, who's sleeping on the other end of the couch. He brushes carefully against her nose and her eyes flicker open. I take his cheeks between my hands, squishing them together as I kiss his lips.

"We didn't get to see any stars, though," I sort of whine.

It's become my favorite pastime with him. He drives, I stargaze. He sings me his favorite songs, and I sing him mine. Tonight, we stayed in—threw on pajamas the second we realized they canceled our reservation for being fifteen minutes late, and haven't left since.

I think stargazing has become Birdie's favorite pastime too. Her ears perk up once I say the word "stars" and Dutton chuckles as he looks at the both of us, his begging girls just waiting to be taken on a night ride. I stick my bottom lip out, pouting only slightly as Birdie inches closer to him, pressing her wet nose against his hand. It's like we're working as a team—not saying any words, only indicating what we both want.

"You wanna go for a ride?" he asks Birdie as she scrambles to her feet, spinning in a circle on the cushion before taking a seat closer without an inch of space between us as she paws against his arm. Her tail wags and she pants heavily with a sparkle in her eyes just like the one that's probably in mine, too.

"Get some pants on," he says with a tap of his hand to my ass, and I lean in to kiss him again, letting it linger a bit more to show my appreciation to the man who so far has done everything in his power to make me happy every time we're together, and every time we're not.

I hop off him and Birdie darts off the couch with me. My socks slide against the hardwood and tile floors as I race to the bedroom, throwing my jeans on. My smile stays glued to my face as I make my way back to the living room. Dutton stands right by the door, keys in hand with his shoes already on, and I look around as I reach him, searching for my sandals.

"I can't find my shoes."

"You don't need 'em." He takes my hand, whistling for Birdie to follow as we walk out. He bends down off the first step from the porch, letting me jump onto his back before carrying me to his truck.

I settle in the passenger seat, flipping up the center console so Birdie can sit in the middle, and as Dutton starts the ignition, the radio turns on. It's playing that same Chris Stapleton song he drunkenly sang to me at Neddy's. His eyes widen, his brows raise, and all the while he looks at me as he turns it up, reaching for my hand while he sings along to the words.

As we drive, I look up, trying to count each star, but it's impossible. There must be thousands of them tonight. It's the most I've seen since I've been here, and certainly more than last night's ride with the overcast weather.

The lull of the truck makes Birdie rest her head on my lap and as she does, Dutton brings my hand that's clasped with his up to his lips, kissing me gently just below my knuckles before I do the same. Tugging his hand over me, I place my full lips against his warm skin, returning every ounce of affection that he shows me because he deserves to feel loved just as much as I do.

I tilt my chin again, taking in the big sky as the music plays until I see a flash from the corner of my eye. Dutton fixes his rearview mirror, cursing at the driver with his high beams on behind us. I turn in my seat, wondering why they're almost at our bumper. I look at the speedometer—we're going fifty in a forty-five so there's no chance they're riding so close because we're slow.

"Jesus Christ," Dutton says as he shields his eyes from the blasting light ricocheting from his mirrors.

I keep watching as the driver stays right on us, only an inch away from hitting Dutton's tailgate before backing up, driving erratically all over the road, making sure every bit of their lights fills the inside of our truck.

"What the fuck is this guy's problem?" Dutton throws his hands up and as if the driver behind him heard, he zooms right beside us, passing us in the left lane as he flies by. Dutton relaxes in his seat, and I sit back too, wondering what the hell that was all about. He scoffs as he grips my hand a little tighter and as we come over the hill, we're met with those same bright lights staring back at us. In our lane. Dutton slows down rapidly, coming to a full stop as the other vehicle's high beams shoot straight into us. I can't make out the model. The only thing in my vision is the streaks and halos that stem from the bright light. The driver door swings open in front of us as the silhouette of a man steps out and my stomach clenches so tight it cramps. I'd know that silhouette anywhere. It's the same one that's kept me up at night and the same one that's haunted my dreams.

"It's Rory." My heart drops, my voice trembles, and the numbness sets in as he takes each step toward us.

"Wait in the truck," Dutton demands, angrily opening his door. My vison blurs as I fumble for my handle but as I go to reach, Dutton yells, "Stay here!"

Birdie's ears pop up as she lifts her head, and my eyes follow Dutton as he rounds the front of the truck. I can't steady my breath. It shakes with every exhale and my body feels weightless as the panic sets in. I hear Rory speak and his voice is like knives to my skin, setting razor-sharp goosebumps along my spine.

Dutton raises his voice, but I can't make out any words—only the muffled yells that exchange between them. Rory's manicured hair moves with the wind as he walks toward Dutton, and I become nauseated at the sight of him. His jawline is still shaven and sharp and the more I stare at him, the more of a psychopath he looks. Dutton steps closer to him as his arms move and Birdie circles in the driver's seat, wondering what the commotion is. My hands tremor and I reach for my phone, texting Henry where we're at and who we're with, but the moment I press send, my eyes flicker up to see how Rory stands inches shorter than Dutton. But none of that matters, because the blade he pulls out makes up for any size difference between them.

My body shakes at the sight of it and Dutton takes a step back, holding his hands out as he lowers his voice.

"Oh my God!" I bellow as the tears well and my hand comes to my mouth, pressing hard on it as I try to hush my cries.

Birdie comes to me, sniffing my hair as I rock back and forth and shut my eyes tight. My sobs block my air, and I can't breathe as I watch them. Rory takes a step toward him, and as if my world were shattering around me, I scream—the most blood-curdling sound that has ever expelled from me. I scream as the blade pierces through Dutton...and he falls.

Rory's glare shoots right to me and I suck in a breath to stop. I don't breathe to silence myself, but it doesn't work. He already heard. I look at Birdie as the tears stream faster from my eyes.

"Get down," I whisper to her.

She sits. And I cry harder.

"Please, get down." I snap my fingers to the floorboard.

If he sees her, he'll kill her.

I keep snapping as Rory stomps closer to my door, and when Birdie finally puts her paws to the floor, I don't think twice before swinging my door open, meeting him right outside of it.

"Look at you." Rory laughs as his hand comes up to my face. My body shudders while his fingers touch my skin, and the tears roll down my cheeks as he steps closer. "I've been looking all over for you, baby. Let's go home," he growls, gripping the back of my head, knotting a fistful of hair as he drags me away from Dutton's truck. I cry at the pull of my roots while he yanks me, and as we step beside the headlights, my throat scrapes and shatters.

"No!" I scream again when I see Dutton. He lies against the concrete, surrounded in his crimson-colored blood.

My knees give out, buckling under me, but I don't fall too far as Rory's fist pulls me up by my hair.

"Come on!" He yanks me again, pushing me across his lights to the passenger side as my legs fail me and my socks scrape against the hard pavement. My throat gives out as the raspy screams keep pushing through, and it burns as bad as the tears flooding my eyes. He shoves me into the seat, flinging the door shut with so much force it rattles, and my sobs fill the car. My feet slide against paper on the passenger floor and between the tears that block my vision, I see the red bold print on each piece, all with the same word: "missing". My hands quiver as my heart hammers through my chest, and I jump at the sound of Rory's slamming door. As the light in the car turns on again, I see the full posters. All printed with a black and white photo of *me*.

This was it.

This is how he found me.

He searched, looking for me, lying, saying I was missing. Trying to follow wherever I might have been. And he succeeded.

"Knock it off, would ya?" he screams. "You're hurting my fucking ears." His agitated tone rings through me and he throws the bloody knife down in the cup holder, bringing his fingers to his head as he grips his hair tight. He runs his hands down his face as he takes a deep exhale, shifting his body toward me as he lowers his tone. "Why are you crying like this?"

My chin trembles as I sob. I can't form any words, I can't form any thoughts. I just keep my eyes on the pavement between the cars, staring at Dutton's shoes, just praying one moves.

Rory's fist comes to my hair again, wrapping each knotted strand between his fingers and he pulls so tight, I feel he has my scalp. "You never fucking cried like this over me!" he barks. "You slept with him, didn't you?" He pushes his face closer to mine, shaking my head as his sticky breath coats my skin.

I try to keep my eyes in front, praying silently to whoever will listen that Dutton is alive, and somewhere between the hysterics and fear, I find my voice.

My rage.

"Best I've ever had, you sick fuck!"

His eyes widen. "You're a fucking whore. You know that? A real fucking whore." He slams my head against the dashboard, and the burning pain rings through my head like a wrecking ball hit it. My vision blurs further, and my cries stop as my mind becomes dazed. The fogginess washes over me but Rory's voice breaks through my ringing ears.

"Say it again. I dare you to say it again. You know what I've done to find you? How much money I spent?" he screams, and my vision homes back in. The tears fall from my eyes as realization hits at the same time the searing pain from my eyebrow does. "I told you I wasn't going to let you leave me. Who do you think you fucking are? God, baby, you're nothing without me. Don't you know that?"

I can't manage words. I can't stop shaking.

"Look at this weight you've put on. You've gotten fat. You know it as much as I do. Say it, Kaiton, that you're nothing without me. Say it!"

He yells again, spit flying from his lips as he shakes my head, and I still can't speak over my gasping breaths. My cries become deafening once again and shatter into oblivion the second I see him pull the gun from his waistband. He presses the cold metal of the muzzle against my temple. "I can't hear you, baby, say it!"

"Fuck you!" I scream as loud as my inflamed throat will let me, and in an instant, Rory's car door opens. His hand tugs on my hair before his fingers let go, and his body is pulled from his seat.

Dutton drags him out, yanking him, ripping him from the vehicle as they wrestle, and my heart wants to tear through my chest as I see him.

Alive.

They push against the car, grunting as Dutton chokes him. They tussle to the ground as their clothes scrape against the pavement. I sit up, trying to see them as they roll, but my breathing stops instantly once I hear it.

The sound of the gun firing off.

My heart falls. —

One more petal plucked from the rose.

My hands go numb as I scramble to the handle, throwing myself out of the car to run around as the sharp ringing in my ear muffles my screams. Both of them are on the ground, bloodied and still.

I freeze, unable to take any steps further. My legs don't move as the life drains from me and I only begin to take a breath the moment I see him roll over.

"Dutton." I exhale, rushing at him.

He groans and presses his hand to his side, covering the running blood that soaks his white T-shirt. I stumble as I fall to my knees beside him. I cup his face with my hands and my tears fall on him. I look beside him. Rory's lifeless body lies still, his blood painting the pavement as the wound from his chest weeps. My uneven breaths don't match my sobs. I hold Dutton's face, shaking him gently as his eyes start to roll back.

"Dutton, stay with me," I beg.

I pat his face and every time his eyes close, I scream for help.

For someone.

Anyone.

My cries start to soften as I try to gain control. I keep Dutton awake as I whisper to him, letting him know I'm here. I can't help my tears as they fall but I can do my best to calm myself for him. I hear the sirens in the distance. Far away, their sounds echo through the pines. And as I hold his head between my hands, I run my thumb against his nose, taking in the shape and the curves of it. I bring my finger down to his lips as I focus on the feel of how soft they are before I run against the shape of his jaw, trying to store exactly what he looks like.

Just so I can remember.

Every little detail.

CHAPTER
THIRTY-FIVE

Two Months Later

IN DEALING WITH LOSS, I know everyone handles it differently. There can be moments where you forget, become numb to the fact that it even happened. Then there can be moments where it rears its ugly head from the depths of the shadows and no matter how slow it creeps up on you, you can't stop it.

For me, it was neither. Even seeing Susan, I just felt...nothing. Because no matter how hard I try, I can't even begin to have an ounce of another feeling for that man. Maybe that makes me cold.

But I don't think Dutton would agree.

"Put the pan on the middle rack and the cookies should be done in about ten," I say, wiping my hands with a kitchen towel.

"You got it, boss."

I see his smirk, the one that makes my heart throb while my palms start to sweat, and I wait for him to close the oven door before wiggling my way between him and the counter. I reach my arms around his neck and he leans in, brushing the tip of his nose against mine. "I'm so lucky," he whispers against my skin.

"To be alive?" I smile wide.

"To have you," he simply states.

My body warms at his words, and I push up on my toes only to press my lips firmly against his. Out of the million and one things in the world I could want, I would choose him every time.

Tires crunch loudly against the gravel outside, and my eyes widen as I gasp. "She's here!"

I grab his hand, leading him to the porch as the chilled wind of the night slaps us in the face, and as my screen door shuts behind me, I see her—live and in person. My heart skips as she steps out of her car. "Layla!" I scream and she shrieks. I sprint toward her, leaping off my stairs and jumping, wrapping my legs around her as she nearly takes a tumble back.

"I fucking missed you." Her voice is mumbled from my vest, and I squeeze her tight, not wanting to let her go.

She lets me down slowly and I grab her hand, bringing her to the porch to see her under the lights so I can fully digest what's before me. I look at all her freckles, the ones that blurred over FaceTime that line the bridge of her nose. Her hair looks lighter, not dimmed under the shadows of her room, and my heart feels full finally being with her again.

"Layla, this is Dutton. Dutton, this is Layla," I formally introduce the two as I step to the side.

"Nice to meet you, Mr. Tall, Dark and Handsome," she says as she extends her hand.

He laughs deep and throaty as they shake. "It's really nice to meet you too, Layla."

"Come on! Come inside! We'll get my shit later." My voice rings with eagerness as I wave my hands at her, feeling frantic in the moment since I've been waiting so long for her to come.

Once things were settled in Illinois after Rory's death, Layla and my parents were able to gather the rest of my possessions from our shared home. Layla was the one to offer to bring me everything that was left, and I didn't mind at all, especially since I plan on re-signing my lease for another twelve months tomorrow.

"My God, it's even cuter in person," she says as her fingers graze against the wood of my dining chair.

Layla's been given plenty of house tours over the phone, but it's so surreal having her here right now in person. My heart is bursting at the seams, and I can only imagine what I will feel like next week, when my parents come to visit.

The kitchen timer rings and vibrates against my counter and without hesitation, Dutton rushes to the oven, pulling the cookies out before setting them on the stovetop.

"Are those snickerdoodles?" Layla asks with a questioning grin on her face.

"Just for you." I smile.

"You made those for me?" She gives me the best puppy dog eyes and pouts. I giggle at the sight.

"Actually," I say, my eyes roaming to where Dutton stands. "Dutton made them for you."

"That's so sweet!" she exclaims.

"I'm still learning," he says defensively, holding his hands out. "She's been teaching me everything." He laughs.

"So, if they suck, it's on me, is what he's basically saying." I giggle again.

"Nothing you make could ever suck," Dutton says as he comes up behind me, wrapping his arms around my midriff as he leans into the crook of my neck. "Except for that one green pasta you made, but that's just because I don't care for peas."

"Hey!" I tap his forehead playfully and he laughs.

"I'm just kidding," he whispers in my ear before placing his lips on my cheek, giving me a soft peck. "It's getting late, though. I should head out. But I'll see you both tomorrow after you're done at Ellie's."

"You're not riding with us?" Layla asks, already picking up a hot cookie from the pan, tossing it between her hands to cool it.

"I've got a couple appointments tomorrow, but I'll be done in time to meet up with you girls for lunch."

Layla smiles and nods as she bites into it and I turn to him, kissing his lips before I go to grab a cookie myself.

"Let me know what the doctor says." I beam.

"I will." He smiles. "Have a good night, girls. It's nice to finally meet you, Layla."

"You too," she mumbles with her mouth full as she tries to catch the falling crumbs that spit from her lips, and I find it hard to contain my laughter because that's just so her.

"So." She raises her brows the second the front door shuts. "You know he's ten times hotter in person, right?"

"God, I know. Shouldn't it be illegal?" I laugh as I take another bite.

"I can't imagine you two fucking. It's got to be like some sort of celestial phenomenon. Like watching Aphrodite—"

"Layla!" I shriek out in laughter. "It's probably not quite like that..." I trail off, mumbling under my breath right after, "But it is pretty close."

She pushes my arm slightly and we laugh. I catch a glimpse of the time from the oven clock, realizing it's almost eleven.

"Do you want to get your things now, or—"

"Nah, it's fine. I'll get them in the morning. Thank you for bringing all of it," I say, and we only eat one more cookie each before we call it a night. With her long day of travel and all of what I have planned for us tomorrow in The Ridge, she's going to need all the rest she can get.

As she runs back to her car to grab her suitcase, my phone buzzes against the wood on my dining table and I reach for it, not able to contain my smile as I read.

DUTTON BECK: This bed feels
extremely empty without you in it.

ME: You miss me already? Lol

DUTTON BECK: You have no idea.

I lift my eyes from the screen as my door slams shut and I race to Layla, helping her tow in the three pieces of luggage she has.

"Jesus Christ, are you signing my lease with me tomorrow?" I giggle.

"Kaiton, I had no idea what to bring. Every time I talk to you, it's different weather. I'm prepared for everything ranging from a heavy snowfall to summer."

"That's fair." I grin and shrug my shoulders before tugging at a suitcase, bringing it into my bedroom before propping it next to my dresser.

As Layla changes into her pajamas, I get the bed ready, finding extra blankets and pillows to make my rock of a mattress seem a little more desirable. But before we get snuggled in, the feeling starts to sink into my chest. This is going to be the first night I'm not sleeping next to Dutton since we became a couple. It's been months of us together, and here I am, getting ready for bed without him.

"I'm really glad to see you," her quiet voice whispers as she lays facing me, her knees touching mine under the covers.

"I'm really glad you're here," I say in the same hushed tone.

"Your eye looks really good." The tip of her finger gently brushes against the scar left from that fateful night and I only soften my eyes, not saying a word. "How's Dutton healing?" she asks as she rests her hand, tucking it under the pillow.

"Fine, I think. Physically much better now, but mentally still a little on the rocks."

"I can't imagine," she whispers, and I can tell as her eyes flutter nearly shut that she's on the edge of sleep.

I don't talk any further, letting her sink into her slumber. I wouldn't want to divulge much about Dutton's therapy anyway. Most days he's good, some days he's not. It's hard for him to grasp the concept, to wrap his head around taking another man's life. His therapist has done a great job of helping him work through it, and I'd like to think I do too, on some level. It was kill or be killed, even the judge knew that. He just has a lot to process, but I'll be here for him every step of the way.

I watch Layla's face relax, and as she drifts off, I hear my phone buzz again behind me.

DUTTON BECK: Are you up still?

ME: Yes. Wide awake.

DUTTON BECK: Can I come see you for a second? I won't take long.

ME: Of course, just text me when you're here.

I keep my phone clutched in my palm for minutes on end and I don't even wait for his text before I hear his tires crunch against my driveway. I slip out of my bed as carefully and quietly as possible, throwing on a large jacket that Dutton left here before I head outside, practically sprinting until I reach his truck. He comes around to meet me, grabbing onto my hips as he turns me gently. He pins me against his vehicle, gripping the side of his truck bed with force as his arms crowd me on either side.

"I am miserable without you," he groans softly as his dark eyes mold right into mine. "God dammit, I'm so fucking miserable without you." His breath is like fire against my cold skin as he leans into me, teasing me with his lips like he always does as he gently brushes them against mine. "Don't sign your lease tomorrow, Kaiton." His hushed tone comes out even more gravely.

"Why?" I ask as a confused smile spreads across my lips, pinching my brows together.

"Because I want you to move in with me."

His words knock against my chest and if my back wasn't leaning against his truck, I would have certainly fallen against the gravel.

"Are you sure?" I ask, feeling weightless as my stomach flutters.

"Am I sure?" he scoffs out in a laugh while his hand sweeps against the side of my cheek, his fingers intertwining with my golden locks. "Your face is the first thing I want to look at when I wake up, and the last before I fall asleep. Without you, I don't see any sense in doing either. I get that this is fast, and I respect your decision if not, but I have to at least try..." He gently brushes his thumb against my bottom lip as he pulls it down and I stare up at him through my lashes, the corners of my mouth curling up once more.

"Okay," I state, shocking even myself at my quick response.

His lips press firmly against mine, and I sink into his body, wrapping my arms around him as he does me and I know in my heart I would be a fool to have said no to him. Of course, I'm still scared, but every day it becomes less and less. Each day, he shows me how completely different he is than any other man I've ever known and all I'm doing is letting fear get in the way of everything I feel I deserve.

I've been broken, shattered into a million pieces and it was *him*... He picked them up, one by one. I don't want to be afraid anymore, I want to live. I want to love. And I want to love *him*.

I'm falling hard and fast and if that kills me, so be it.

Bury me six feet deep.

Because my fate is sealed.

EPILOGUE

Two Years Later

I PEEK AROUND THE SIDE of the barn, trying to snatch any glimpse I can of the guests starting to sit. My stomach tingles and the anticipation rises as the moment gets closer.

"Are you ready?" Ellie asks me with a smile so big and bright it *almost* washes my fears away.

I only nod, swallowing dryly as my breath rattles, and that's when I hear it— the violins.

It's almost time.

I rub my hand against the embroidery on my bodice and graze my fingers over each pearl and stitched flower, fluffing the voluminous bottom, ensuring I don't step on the lengthy dress.

I peek once more, catching another glance as each man takes their place, but I'm too far away to see the only one that matters.

My leg shakes as I bounce it and I stay hidden in my corner, hidden from everyone else while Ellie rallies up Birdie, getting her set with the small basket she's going to clench between her teeth.

Ellie gives me a wink before walking out of my line of sight and I want to look again—just so I can see Birdie and her flower crown as she trots down the aisle—but I don't have another second before I hear the firmness of my dad's tone.

"It's our time, kiddo," he says, and I whip my body around to face him.

The tears prick at the back of my eyes, and I know I'm going to be a mess before I even make it halfway, but as the violins halt, just for a moment, I relish in the silence. The rustling pines that roam around Ellie's property are the only things I focus on, and I give my dad a nod, smiling with pressed lips as I weave my arm through his.

The violins start again, playing a soft cover of "Can't Help Falling in Love" by Elvis Presley and as we make it around the corner, everyone stands from the benches.

My sight locks in with his immediately, and it doesn't take him more than a half second before his chin quivers. I've never seen him cry before, but as his eyes become glossy, so do mine.

I can't look away from him—so handsome in his black suit. But my vision gets blurred as the tears roll and I release my hand from my bouquet only to wipe them away, laughing as I do because I knew it wasn't going to take much for me to lose it.

My heels sink into the grass just a little until we get to the last benches, and I turn to my dad as he leans in, placing a gentle kiss on my cheek.

"I'm proud of you, K," he whispers with tears in his eyes and as the officiant asks who gives me away, I can't focus on any other words he speaks because all I see is *him*.

Layla stands in a pale-yellow silk dress, the same one each of my other bridesmaids have on, and once I hand her my bouquet that my mom and I picked this morning, I position myself in front of the altar. It's tall and wrapped with the same white wildflowers I just handed off. My father, Rodney, and Dutton built it last week and this is the first time I'm seeing it. They all wanted it to be a surprise. It's beautiful, more so than I ever imagined. And I have the best men to thank for it.

Dutton stands before me, looking as tall and proud as ever as he grabs my hands, bringing them up to his lips to kiss.

"You look so beautiful," he whispers as our officiant welcomes our guests and Dutton's eyes become even more glossy, fogged over as he brings his knuckle to the corner, wiping the single tear before it drops.

I try to keep from crying, but it's useless. As I look around and see our closest friends and family, all tucked together on the Boones' farm with the gray mountains and green pines surrounding us, I feel blessed. No.

Loved.

I feel loved.

And it's all because of him.

In the front row on the right side, my dad's smile is bittersweet, and my mother's is warm. The tears already flow from their eyes, but they aren't what make me weep more. It's what I see on the left side.

Dutton's side.

Three black and white photos in gold vintage frames that I found sit proudly next to each other in the front row. A photo of Dutton's dad is first, followed by his mom, and then Hailey. Her bright smile warms my skin and I wish we'd had the chance to meet.

One day.

But for now, I already made a promise to her.

A promise to love and to cherish the man we both admire so much.

The life Dutton and I have built over these two years is only getting sweeter, and in about five minutes, I get to call this fearless, talented, passionate man my husband.

A man who not once has made me second guess myself. Who has shown me love in its truest, most raw form. Never spewing any hate from his lips, only compliments. A man who took every single one of my fears and doubts and crushed them like clumps of dirt in his hand, and as they flew with the wind, he replaced them—replaced them with a sense of security. But the best part is, he doesn't make me cry.

He hasn't let any more rose petals fall.

And out of all the roads I could have taken, how lucky was I to have chosen the one that brought me here.

Right to Falton Ridge.

Acknowledgements

Wow, book number three... what a ride it's been.

Thank you to all my readers, my friends, and my family for continuing this journey with me. On one hand I would like to thank the people at fault for helping me with inspiration for this book, but I'm not going to do that. Not now. Not ever. But one great thing about being the author to my own stories is I get to kill off the villain. Which I will so happily do any day of the week. But I digress, because giving even the slightest ounce of energy to people who do not deserve it unfortunately is not in my wheelhouse anymore.

Thank you to my amazing editor, and everyone else who worked tirelessly with me on this piece. To Rachel, my cover artist- you fucking killed it again. Never in my lifetime will anyone else create the covers to my stories. To my mom, thank you for always being my biggest fan. So willing to read even the roughest draft that

I throw your way. Your opinions, critiques, and suggestions are never dismissed. Even if dad were still with us, it would be you who I would ask for feedback. (Well, let's be real. I would be physically ill if dad were alive to read what I have written. Especially All Of It, With You).

To my friends and readers who hype me up – sharing my books with the rest of the world, you guys truly mean a lot to me. How amazing is it to have people in your life that support you and your work tirelessly. There will never be enough thanks and gratitude that I could physically show you. So, I'll leave you with this; I love you. I love you. I love you.

To my kiddos. I'm going to be honest, y'all really didn't help with this book. But I still love you the same. Payton, I'm still so sorry you cannot read these, but one day (maybe – probably not) I'll let you. I do, however, love to see your face light up when I give you the synopsis of each of them. It means a lot to me that you show interest in my books and what they are about. And Vinny, my sweet boy, you're starting to read a lot more. So, I will officially have to hide all these books somewhere in the house because you out of any child will be the one nosey enough to figure out what they are really about.

Thank you to each and every one of you.

With all my love, Madeline.

About the Author

Madeline Flagel is a mom with two kids who are in every sport imaginable. So while free time is sparse, she does enjoy reading and travel. She's a beach bum, Chicago Cubs fan, and an entrepreneur, starting and selling many companies throughout her career. Madeline is an avid reader of romance novels and an even spicier writer of the genre.

MORE BOOKS BY
MADELINE:

https://rb.gy/8zueao

https://rb.gy/qu9t7l

Milton Keynes UK
Ingram Content Group UK Ltd.
UKHW012312060524
442290UK00005B/311